Dear Pat

This is my first historical novel.

Enjoy!

With love
from Linda
x

The Enchanted Glade
by
Linda Dowsett

Published
by

Thumbnail Media
Tel: 01225 345495
info@thumbnailmedia.com

Copyright © 2010 Linda Dowsett

The moral right of the author has been asserted.

All rights are reserved.
No part of this publication may be reproduced, stored in a retrieval system, or transmitted, in any form or by any means, without the prior permission in writing of the publisher, nor be otherwise circulated in any form of binding or cover other than that in which it is published and without a similar condition including this condition being imposed on the subsequent purchaser.

ISBN: 978 - 0 - 9556379 - 3 - 3

Printed and bound in Great Britain

Forward

Linda Dowsett was born in Bath but now lives with Gordon, her husband of almost forty years, in Southwick, Wiltshire. UK. They have five children, and between them and their partners they have produced 18 grand-children.

Linda has been writing poetry for many years under the name of Christine Linden and has had poetry published. She is absolutely hooked on reading romantic novels and now loves to write them herself. She cannot believe that one can become so involved with the characters and the plots of the stories. She has also fallen in love with some of her fictitious heroes and cannot believe they seem so real in one's mind. She hopes you enjoy reading about them as much as she has enjoyed writing about them.

The Enchanted Glade is the first novel in
The Greene Hollow Trilogy:

1. The Enchanted Glade
2. The House at Greene Hollow
3. Lady Annabel's Secret

Acknowledgements

For my grandmother, Florence Louise (Daisy) Tipper
whose stories of her childhood enthralled me.

Many thanks to my sons, Chris, Martyn and Ady for being
on the end of the phone each time I need advice on my
computer and also to friend, Josh for your continued
help with my artwork.

Thanks to Carolyn Bendell for her patience, constructive
criticism and ultimate excitement, whilst
proof reading for me.

Chapter 1

Spring 1806.

Clip, clop, clatter, clatter, clip, clop, clatter, clatter, the continual sound of the horses hooves on the road and the incessant turning of the wheels of the carriage woke Cissy from the deepest of sleeps. For just a moment she wondered where she was and as she looked around her she realised that they were still moving. She sat up straight and lethargically stretched her arms above her head, tilting her bonnet in the process, and she tried to stifle the gaping yawn that must have been distorting her pretty features. She was feeling a stiffness in every single part of her aching body as she stretched again and then sat upright. As the carriage swayed a little from side to side, she sighed to herself and whispered "soon be there". Although it had probably been only two or three hours since the last stop at the coaching house, it had seemed a sight longer. Sitting next to her in the carriage was her sister, Louise, who was still fast asleep, though goodness knows how, Cissy thought, with the rumbling noise and the jolting caused by the uneven surface of the road.
"Are we almost there?" she heard her brother Oliver ask their Mama, the impatience in his little voice was very evident.
"It shouldn't be too much longer, Oliver, we are on the drive to the house now, but it is a very long drive" she spoke with a sigh as she lay her head back on the headrest of the seat she occupied in the carriage and Cissy noticed that her

mother answered Oliver's question without even opening her eyes.

Their mother, Lady Annabel Templeton, now Countess of Langford was as tired as they were after the long journey from Berkshire where they had lived for as long as Cissy could remember. Cissy glanced towards her mother and thought how very pale she looked today. Poor Mama, she had worked so very hard this last month preparing for this move to their new home.

Cissy's paternal grandfather, Sir Edward Templeton, the Earl of Langford had passed away a couple of months ago and her father had inherited the title and the estate that they were now on. Her father, Sir William Templeton, was now the new landowner of Monkton Grange, which included the mansion house and estate and almost all of the surrounding farms and cottages situated in the nearby village of Monkton St James, which would now become his main source of income.

Cissy's mind wandered back now and she could vaguely remember coming here to stay when their grandmother was alive but the old man had become a recluse after his wife had passed away a few years ago and although their father had made several visits they had never been back, as a family, until now.

Her father had travelled down a week ago to prepare everything for their arrival. He had retained the skeleton staff whom his father had employed, which Cissy imagined was a great relief to most of them. Even she knew from what she'd overheard that work was scarce everywhere. In the carriage behind the one she and her family were travelling in, were the staff they were bringing with them from their old home.

Cissy had felt quite sad that their old home was now sold and they would never be going back there again.

She peered out of the window of the carriage once more and perceived that the approach to the Grange was lined with

The Enchanted Glade

large sycamore and oak trees that cast shadows across the path of the carriage as it rode on towards the house and she observed how brightly the sun was shining right now. So brightly, in fact, that she had to put her hand above her eyes to shade them as she gazed once more at these agreeable surroundings. She was pleasantly surprised to see rolling fields on either side of the drive with cattle grazing lazily against the backdrop of the lush green grass. On the left she beheld before her a sun-drenched meadow alive with the vast congregation of birds melodiously singing whilst perched high in the trees on either side of a babbling stream which was sparkling and glistening in the sunshine.

As they travelled on further up the drive a sizeable lake appeared on the left and Cissy wondered if the stream flowed into it. In the middle of the lake there was a small island which was covered with trees and shrubs, which were just beginning to sprout their new foliage and as they skirted it she could see a bridge spanning the lake, from the immense lawn to the island. She was sure that she had never seen the island before but she knew her younger brother would find it irresistible as he loved to explore.

Suddenly the impressive house came into view and she realised that it didn't seem as big as she remembered, but maybe that was because she herself was much smaller the last time they came. Taking in the vision in front of her she saw that the Palladian style facade didn't look as dilapidated as her father had recently insinuated but the house was still much larger in comparison to the home they had just left and Cissy was extremely anxious to look around. Her eyes widened as she surveyed it and she perceived that the main part of the old house looked symmetrically square with wings projecting from each side. Her mother had said there were twenty bedrooms and that the house stood four floors high but as she looked she could only see three rows of windows including those in the roof and she wondered if those were the servant's quarters.

Where will my room be, she wondered, as her eyes scanned aimlessly along the row of leaded windows on the first floor. "Mama, I thought you said there were four floors, I can only see three" the ever inquisitive Cissy enquired as she turned to face her mother.

"The kitchen and store-rooms are in the basement at the back of the house" her mother answered kindly "please be patient Cissy, everything will be revealed soon enough".

Oh! She was beginning to get so excited at the thought of exploring this fascinating old place. At first Cissy had been distressed when she'd heard that they would be moving from their old house. It was the only home she had ever known and she had grown up there, but Mama had assured her that going to live in the country would not only be healthier but also much more interesting and now Cissy was inclined to agree with her.

This seems very pleasant, thought Cissy, realising that maybe moving to a new house wasn't going to be such an ordeal after all. Suddenly her brother was frantically pulling at the sleeve of her coat and shaking her arm.

"Look over there" whispered Oliver, almost jumping off of his seat and waking Louise in the process, he was so agitated. "A castle! Cissy, a castle! How exciting is that?" Cissy followed the line of his finger pointing over towards the trees and she could see the turrets of a small castle peeping above them. Then their mother, who had obviously seen something of interest, spoke and distracted their thoughts as she pointed her finger out of the window of the carriage in the opposite direction. "Look at the beautiful fountain there, children" They all peered in the direction in which she was pointing and realised that they were now driving around the circular drive in front of the house which was surrounding a beautiful garden, and as the carriage was pulling up to stop outside the front entrance, their mother was indicating the incredible sculptured stone fountain in the centre.

The Enchanted Glade

Cissy glanced towards the house and saw that all the servants of the household were scurrying down the front steps and proceeding to line up waiting to welcome them, but although she craned her neck she realised that their father was nowhere to be seen. As Cissy climbed down from the carriage, Oliver who had alighted before her proceeded to run up the steps into the house.

"Oliver, please come back here at once!" her mother scolded "it is impolite to ignore everyone". Their mother was a stickler for etiquette and although she was always very fair the children knew she would take no nonsense.

"Now children, it's time for introductions" she immediately indicated for them to form a line and as she walked up to the first person, Cissy was sure that she and her siblings must have appeared to look like little ducks in a procession following behind her.

First of the servants to present herself was the most efficient looking housekeeper Cissy had ever seen and she introduced herself as Rose Higgins. She bobbed a slight curtsey and shook each of them by the hand and then without further ado the competent housekeeper then proceeded down the line in front of them introducing everyone else as she went. Cissy had inspected her very thoroughly and thought that she looked perfectly neat and tidy in her full length black dress with long sleeves and a high neck. Her hair was strained tightly behind her head and styled into a bun which Cissy was sure made her appear much sterner than she possibly was. She looks quite old, Cissy had reflected as she had shaken her hand, that was probably because she had been here many years or maybe it was having her hair strained back behind her ears that made her look older or perhaps it was just because everyone looked quite old to Cissy. Next was the butler, Ambrose Harvey, he looked really ancient with white hair and a slight stoop but he still nodded to her and smiled kindly and as she shook his hand it felt rather thin and bony. She thought she remembered him from her last visit but she couldn't be sure and she admired his appearance as he was very smartly dressed in livery of blue and yellow. Next was the cook, Emily Bridges, she appeared really homely in her pristine white pinafore and mob cap. Cissy was fairly sure that they hadn't met before because she knew she would have remembered such a pleasant lady and Emily's beaming smile had Cissy's attention immediately. Well at least I know I will have one friend here, she murmured under her breath as their eyes met and Cissy returned the smile. Then they carried on down to the end of the line finishing with being introduced to the gardener and handyman, Tom Phillips.

As all the servants had now been presented Cissy heard her mother say as she turned to address everyone "We are so very pleased to be here", she then proceeded to introduce herself. "You are already aware that I am Lady Templeton, so I'll introduce you to the children. This is our eldest daughter Lady Louise, who is 12 years old", her sister nodded slightly to acknowledge the statement. Louise and Cissy had always bode well together and were the best of friends. Although there was only two years between them Cissy had always looked up to her sister. Louise was quite tall and slim and had a sweet disposition. Her long rich brown hair, which she had inherited from her mother, was naturally curly and reached right down to her waist and her heart-shaped face always seemed to exude a rosy pink complexion. Lady Templeton then indicated Cissy "Lady Cecilia, who is 10"; Cissy accepted their gracious smiles and she reciprocated with one of her own. "And this" continued their mother, "is our son Lord Oliver" as she spoke she glanced towards her son and saw that he was picking his nose. "Oliver, please pay attention" she sighed with exasperation as she looked back towards the servants and said "he's 6 years old and still a little terror". Her ladyship then beamed a wide grin towards the servants and Cissy heard a few titters from them, which seemed to ease

The Enchanted Glade

the tension a little. Cissy absolutely adored her mother, she was still very elegant and beautiful and such a kind and gentle lady.

"Perhaps now we should all go inside and I will liaise with Mrs Higgins as to your individual duties. Also Cook could you please join us as we are not only very tired from the journey but rather hungry too". Annabel waved a gesture to her children to follow her and they all made their way up the steps to the front door with several of the servants milling around them and some of the other servants were moving in different directions to go back to their posts in the house and gardens.

As they entered the house Mrs Higgins indicated to some other members of staff to await instructions in the hall but beckoned to Emily to follow her into Lady Templeton's sitting room.

"Beggin' yer pardon yer Ladyship" piped up the cook "I asked 'is Lordship earlier about a meal and I 'ave a roast almost ready for you all. Just you let me know wot time you'll be wantin' it and it'll be there for you. If that be all, Milady, per'aps you'll excuse me and I can 'urry it up if you're all 'ungry".

"Certainly, Mrs Bridges, thank you".

Their cook had a very round figure and Cissy noticed it wobbled a little and as she hurried off to the kitchen which was below stairs, she smiled broadly as she passed Cissy and her siblings, who were still patiently waiting with the others in the hall.

Cissy had always been a very inquisitive child and couldn't wait to familiarise herself with the surroundings. She was also straining to hear what was going on in her mother's sitting room, where she heard the competent housekeeper saying "The dining room has been prepared, Madam" and then she suggested "Would it be convenient for everyone to freshen up and come down in half an hour".

"That would be most agreeable" Cissy heard her mother reply.
She also asked Lady Templeton if the children should be shown to their rooms immediately and went on to say that four bedrooms, one for each of the children and one for their nanny, and also a playroom-cum-schoolroom had been allocated by the Master on the first floor and that she could get the children and their nanny settled as soon as possible. Cissy was glad to hear that as she was feeling rather impatient and couldn't wait to see her new room. In their old house she and Louise had shared a bedroom so having a room of her very own here was going to be wonderful.

"Certainly" Cissy heard her mother say "and Mrs Higgins, thank you so much for organising everything in advance. It is such a relief to have competent staff. We are so grateful that you stayed on after Sir Edward passed away, it must have been a trial for you. Now if you would kindly enlighten me as to the other servants and their duties. As you know we have brought some of our own servants with us, but to hasten things along we'll just deal with the bare necessities now and finalise everything else in the morning".

They quickly ran through the list as her ladyship was as eager to get settled into her own room as the children were. When they had finished Mrs Higgins came out into the hall and allocated duties to several of the servants. Then there was pandemonium with everyone sorting out luggage and directing the children and their nanny to their rooms.

As Cissy picked up her small bag and started towards the staircase she heard her mother call to the housekeeper but she was now too far away hear the conversation and she was also very anxious to go upstairs.

Back in Lady Templeton's sitting room, Annabel enquired
"Mrs Higgins, is his Lordship here?". The housekeeper's eyes lowered slightly and a blush came to her cheeks which made her appear rather embarrassed as she answered almost inaudibly "I think he's in his study, Madam", and with that

The Enchanted Glade

she pointed to an adjoining door leading off of Lady Annabel's sitting room.

"That will be all for now, thank you, I will ring if I need you further".

Mrs Higgins bobbed a curtsey and left the room, closing the door behind her as she went.

A feeling of dread coursed right through Annabel's chest as she walked slowly towards the connecting door as she had no idea what she was going to find on the other side when she opened it.

Annabel had been a captivating beauty in her youth and was still extremely attractive and elegant now. She had been the belle of every ball when she had come-out at her season fourteen years ago. She was quite a catch, an heiress with a substantial dowry and at her come-out she could have had her choice of any of the most handsome, rich and famous men of the ton but something had drawn her to William, although no-one else could fathom what. Perhaps it was the fact that he was fifteen years older than her and at the tender age of eighteen she had felt that it would be beneficial for her to choose a more mature suitor. Also if he was a man of experience she presumed that that would also be advantageous to their union. But although the first few years had been happy she had soon realised that she had made a dreadful mistake in her choice when she had married him, but it was too late to dwell on that now.

She reached the door and as she placed her hand on the door knob and turned it slowly; her heart beat increased considerably and she felt a lump forming in her throat. As she entered the room she saw that her husband was slumped in his chair with the top half of his body sprawled across the desk. She felt an uncontrollable stray tear escape from her eye and trickle down her cheek and as she lifted her finger to wipe it away, she thought, you couldn't even stay sober long enough to welcome us to our new home, then she exuded a little sob as her heart wrenched in two. He had

Linda Dowsett

promised a new start, promised that he would make a concerted effort to stop drinking so much, but the empty bottle of brandy on the desk in front of him and the overturned goblet was all the evidence Annabel needed to know that yet another solemn promise had been broken. As she approached him she could smell the rancid stench of alcohol and could not comprehend how a man of his standing could possibly stoop to this level of degradation. She put her hand out and shook him by the shoulder in an attempt to rouse him, but feeling no response she then doubted he would come to until the morning. Well her children must be her priority now and although she had suddenly lost her own appetite she knew that they would be very hungry so she turned and left the room. As she crossed the hall and began ascending the ornate staircase to the upper floor, she gazed at all the portraits of the family ancestors as she went, wondering which of these dedicated men her husband may have taken after. Every one of the gentlemen in the pictures looked upright and honourable and each had trusting eyes but that was how her husband had appeared to her when they had first met. How deceptive appearances can be, she pondered, still feeling extremely melancholy. Then her spirits rose a little as she remembered how much she had loved this house from the very first time she had set eyes on it and had always looked forward to their visits in the past. Now that she was mistress of Monkton Grange she was determined that she would do her utmost to throw herself into the running of things and perhaps that would take her mind off of her abysmal marriage. She had reached the top of the stairs now and walked along the corridor towards her bed-chamber.

She and William had adjoining rooms at the opposite end of the house to the children. She walked through the door and saw that one of the maids she had brought with her was unpacking her trunk "Nancy, I've just come to freshen up

The Enchanted Glade

before dinner, has any hot water been sent up from the kitchen?"

"Yes, my lady, the bowl is over there on the dresser" she indicated in its direction as she placed another gown in her ladyship's closet.

Nancy had been in Annabel's employ for many years and was a trusted member of the household. She was very loyal to her mistress and Annabel valued her integrity highly.

"Could you please bring my grey dress and leave it on the bed? It will be very informal this evening as it will only be the children and myself dining".

"The children are not eating upstairs with Alice?" Nancy enquired referring to the children's nanny.

"I thought it would be a special treat for them to eat in the dining room with me this evening as it's their first night in their new home and their father won't be there". Annabel answered cheerily trying desperately to masked her disappointment; she didn't want to give the servants any more fuel to feed the fire. The one's she had brought with her already knew too much about the state of her marriage and she had decided that she couldn't bear to have another meal on her own.

Nancy knew his lordship didn't bother too much with the children and also knew that the only reason there were three children from the marriage was that the son and heir was the last to arrive. She reached into the closet and removed the grey dress, as her ladyship had requested, and as she laid it on the bed she thought how very sorry she felt for her mistress. Lady Annabel had shown her nothing but kindness ever since she had been employed at the family home in Berkshire and was the epitome of everything she imagined an exemplary employer to be. The master however was a completely different kettle of fish. It was not only the fact that the man was an arrogant, contemptuous bully but he hated the servants and treated them abominably. She was so lucky that her duties meant that she didn't come into contact with him very often and she hated the fact that he treated her mistress so unfavourably.

Annabel glanced around the room as she refreshed herself and took in the pale wedgewood blue décor and the appealing blue drapes around the four-poster bed which matched those hanging at the window and she thought how calm and soothing they looked. Although she intended to eventually renovate the whole house she thought she may retain the colour in this room as it suited her nicely.

She had now completed her toilet and Nancy helped her to dress "Thank you, Nancy, perhaps you could turn the beds down as soon as you like as none of us will be late retiring this evening as we have all had a very long day".

"Certainly, my Lady" she answered, smiling as she did so "I'll see to it immediately".

Meanwhile Cissy, whilst washing her hands and face and changing her clothes, which were rather dusty from the journey, was familiarising herself with the surroundings in her very own bed-chamber. She had been allocated a large room at the front of the house over-looking the extensive lawn and the lake, which thrilled her. What a breathtaking sight she would wake up to each morning she mused, letting out a loud contented sigh. She then gazed, wide eyed, around the room and saw that she had a large four poster bed that was so high she thought she might need a small foot stool to climb upon it. She gazed across to the other side of the bed and saw a small table on which was laid a brightly patterned wash basin and jug and on the inner wall there was a lustrous roaring fire burning in hearth. Although the winter was almost behind them now it was still a pleasing sight, and somehow made for a warmer welcome. As she looked around she realised that the entire room was a little dowdy but her mother had promised that all the rooms would be refurbished as soon as possible, which she would very much look forward to.

The Enchanted Glade

When she had finished dressing and was ready to go she made her way to her sister's bed-chamber. They had previously arranged with Alice, their nanny, to wait in Louise's room until they were all ready to go downstairs. Alice would bring Oliver when he was ready and then they could all go down to the dining room together.

"Lulu, Isn't it wonderful?" said Cissy smiling excitedly at her sister after she had knocked on the door and then entered the room. Lulu had been Oliver's pet name for Louise ever since he was a little boy as he had had a little trouble pronouncing her full name and so now Cissy called her that too "Oh, I think we are going to have an amazing time here, don't you?"

Louise had never been one to show too much emotion but she too had been delighted with her room. "Yes, and each of us having a room of our own means we can have our own secret little place to go to whenever we wish " the tone in her voice made her sound quite dreamy. Cissy knew exactly how she felt in regards to now having a room of her own although the two of them had always got on really well when they had shared one before.

Suddenly Cissy heard Oliver bounding along the corridor outside Louise's room so the two girls quickly made their way over to the door. As they were now all ready Alice brought them downstairs to the dining room and settling them into their chairs, she asked them to mind their manners and behave for their mother, who arrived shortly afterwards.

"Alice, could you please summon the butler and inform him that we are ready for dinner to be served immediately?"

"Certainly, my Lady" Alice then pulled the cord and left the room.

Ambrose Harris was waiting outside the room anticipating the request and after speaking to the nanny he relayed his mistress' message to the cook, who immediately sent for the servants to serve the meal at once.

Meanwhile Annabel seated herself at the head of the table and although children should be seen and not heard at the table, as the saying goes, they were each allowed to express what they thought of their bed-chambers.

Whilst they were discussing it there was a knock on the door and after entering, their delicious and very welcome meal was brought in by a footman and a maid whom Cissy had not seen before. Mrs Bridges, the cook had prepared succulent roast chicken with roast potatoes and fresh vegetables and a delicious apple pie for dessert with piping hot custard. Even though they had stopped for refreshments several times along the way on their long journey here they were still quite hungry and they all ate ravenously. Except for Annabel who at first picked over hers but then felt she had to finish it as she didn't want to offend the cook, who obviously excelled at her job.

When their meal was over their mother allowed Oliver to pull the cord to summon Alice to fetch them and take them upstairs to retire for the night. She was proud that all of her three children had behaved impeccably at the table, probably because they were really tired after such a laborious journey.

As they each embraced their mother and kissed her goodnight she said with a smile "Aunt Ellen will be visiting us tomorrow".

Lady Ellen Bellamy was their father's sister and was the exact opposite of him in every way. The three of them jumped for joy at the prospect of spending time with their favourite Aunt.

****

Chapter Two

One week later.

Cissy had spent the last exhilarating week with her brother and sister excitedly exploring the entire Grange inside and out. She had found that the servant's quarters were indeed on the top floor high in the roof but she and her brother and sister were forbidden by their parents from venturing up there. Also they were not allowed to stray into their mother's private sitting room or their father's study.
Cissy had also discovered that there was an enormous main sitting room situated centrally at the back of the house over-looking a beautifully landscaped garden, and as she had peered out of the window she was amazed at the extent of the panoramic view over the estate from this side of the house. Her parents had decided that this was the room they would be using to receive their visitors. The door to the left in that room led into their mother's private sitting room and the door to the right led directly into a family sitting room which they used daily. There was also a large dining room which had two doors, one from the family sitting room and another leading back to the entrance hall to enable the servant's access from the kitchen stairs just outside. The corridor outside the dining room led to a drawing room and a morning room and beyond that was the right wing that held the enormous library.

Cissy was so thrilled about the library because she absolutely loved books and Miss Hawkins; their governess had always complimented her copiously on how well she read.

The left wing on the other side of the house accommodated a large billiard room, for the men, and exploring further they had made their way beyond that room down the corridor where they had discovered what seemed to Cissy to be a gigantic ballroom but because it was locked they were unable to view it. Oliver was tall enough now to peep through the keyhole and as he described what he could see it made Cissy determined to creep back there on her own one day. When she did she was so in awe of the scene that met her gaze that she felt her jaw drop at the sight of it .The room was enormous and as she looked up she could see that there were three large twinkling crystal chandeliers that dominated the beautifully sculptured ceiling and as the afternoon sunshine touched the crystal droplets they exuded all the colours of the rainbow and Cissy thought it looked absolutely magical.

The considerably large windows which opened like doors stretched from the ceiling to the floor. She peered outside and saw that they led out onto a large patio and a fine-looking garden.

She turned around to face the room and closed her eyes where she stood spellbound and rooted to the spot as she imagined all the fascinating ladies in their splendid gowns gracefully floating around the ballroom with their handsome escorts, she could almost hear the music. Then when she opened her eyes she whirled around and around pretending to be one of the ladies who would be dancing with a handsome partner.

Cissy had always had a vivid imagination and she couldn't wait to see her mother and ask when they would be holding their first ball there. Of course she knew she wouldn't be allowed to attend as, according to her father, she was far too young.

The Enchanted Glade

A few days after they had arrived, their mother, although reluctantly, had allowed them to go below stairs to scrutinize the kitchen and to meet the servants there, but she insisted that Alice accompany them. She knew that unless she relented just this once she would get absolutely no peace from the three most inquisitive children she knew. They passed the housekeeper's room and had chattered and giggled with excitement as they entered the huge kitchen, which was the hub of all the downstairs activity in every large establishment, and Cissy was completely fascinated as she realised that it was the biggest kitchen she had ever seen. An enormous wooden table was situated in the centre with large drawers beneath its rough and uneven surface. The black-leaded polished range shone, with its fire, ovens and hotplates gleaming although they were always in use. Cissy looked up and noticed all the pots and pans hanging all around the walls. The ceilings in the house were all very high but this one here in the kitchen seemed more elevated than the rest and the windows were high up near the ceiling; probably something to do with the heat from the range. Situated off the kitchen was a scullery and a stillroom, where all the butter and preserves were made and stored and then there was also a cosy sitting room for Mrs Bridges when she wasn't too busy cooking for the household. The whole place was immaculately clean. Mrs Bridges definitely kept a tight rein in her kitchen and Cissy thought she was wonderful.

"Be you all enjoyin' your lovely new 'ome then?" The cook enquired in her broad country accent smiling from ear to ear.

"We love it, Mrs Bridges" answered Cissy, enjoying every minute of being here in the cook's domain.

Emily had really taken to Cissy, so she said quietly "Oh, you can call me Emmy if you like, deary, I don't mind". She smiled at Cissy and then turned around and said "Minnie come over 'ere girl" she called to a sweet looking scullery maid.

"This 'ere is Minnie, children, she 'elps me in the kitchen. Fetch that plate o' biscuits off the table on yer way over 'ere, Minnie". Emily stooped to whisper in Cissy's ear, "She don't read nor write mind you, she's only twelve years old but she a willin' little lass, she does as she's told, 'er does". Minnie carefully picked up the plate of warm biscuits, which Emily had earlier removed from the oven, and held them as steady as she could in her small hands as she brought them over to where the children were standing with their nanny. She then handed one each to the children and Alice. They were absolutely delicious and then Emily asked if they would all like some of the lemonade which she had made the day before. Of course they all nodded avidly.

After they had eaten the biscuits and finished the drinks they thanked Emily for the treat and deciding to explore further, so they bid Emily and Minnie farewell, and then they left the house by the kitchen door.

As they stepped outside Alice instructed "Put on your coats now and button them up. We don't want you all catching any colds, do we?" It was late March now and they were still experiencing a few chilly days. A chorus of no's echoed in reply and the children did as they were bidden. Alice then scolded Oliver for running on ahead. She knew they were excited but she still had to keep them in check.

They found lots of other very interesting places outside in the extensive grounds. The stables always aroused their enthusiasm, although the horses they had brought with them were very large carriage horses and Cissy was a little afraid of them. So when her brother and sister went in to pet them she decided to stand nearer to the door. Sam Miles, the man in charge of the horses gave them a conducted tour of the stalls and advised them that their father had mentioned that he was going to increase the stock in a few weeks. Cissy was quite relieved when they left the stables behind them as they carried on through the garden on their way towards the dairy. There they were handed a drink of fresh cow's milk

The Enchanted Glade

which was still warm. "Maybe this was one of the things that mother meant when she said we would love living in the country" she mentioned as she sampled the delicious drink.

"I think you are right, Cissy" Alice answered, finishing her own drink and handing the cup back to the overjoyed milkmaid, who normally hardly ever saw a soul and had felt very honoured that she had received some visitors today.

Next stop was the laundry which they didn't find too interesting but they met Tom Phillip's wife, Bridie, who worked there for a few hours each day, as well as looking after her husband and a family of four children at home in Monkton St James. She was a rosy cheeked, cheerful soul who was always happy. Tom had worked at the Grange all his working life and their cottage was tied to the estate.

Carrying on with their exploring they walked through some very imposing wrought iron gates and soon located the most exquisite Italian garden which, surrounded by a high wall, was protecting the most delicate array of spring flowering plants that Cissy had ever seen. There was also a charming summer house which Cissy couldn't wait to sit in so she hurried over towards it as Alice said "When the weather is fine I'll bring you all down to play in the garden as much as possible. It's good for you to come out in the fresh air and you may learn something about these plants and flowers, which wouldn't go amiss". Alice made it sound like a chore but Cissy would look forward to it very much.

After sitting in the summer house for a few minutes they decided to explore a little further and as they left the garden they came upon the most exciting discovery, especially for Oliver. They had found the old castle which he had seen that first day from the carriage. The main door was missing from its hinges and the stone steps were rather worn so Alice declined her permission to explore the place today. "It would be advisable to seek your father's permission before we venture any further" she spoke with authority in her tone.

"The structure may be dangerous and I wouldn't want to be held responsible for your safety if you entered the castle and anything befell you whilst you were under my supervision". Cissy thought that Alice was being over-cautious but whispered in her brother's ear as they made their way back to the house "Don't worry, we'll come back one day secretly on Alice's day off and when Miss Hawkins has her usual afternoon nap" Oliver loved Cissy so much she was sometimes more like a brother than a sister, she always joined in the fun.

They were taught by their governess, Miss Amelia Hawkins, whom they had brought with them from Berkshire. She was rather tall and slim and wore dresses of very dull colours which made her appear more lacklustre than she really was. Her hair was always swept up into a chignon but she had a pretty face and a charming smile and Cissy thought she was a marvellous tutor. Every day when they had finished their lessons, usually by 2 o'clock, they were allowed to play and on this particular day Cissy was descending the magnificent staircase when she heard an ominous roar.

Her father was cursing loudly "Those blasted dogs; I will not be responsible for my actions if you do not get rid of them. I have no idea what possessed my sister to bring them here in the first place" he shouted furiously.

Aunt Ellen had visited the house the week before and had brought utter delight to the three excited children with a gift of one puppy each. All the puppies were male because although Ellen loved to torment her brother and had done so ever since they were both small children, she knew three dogs were bad enough but if there was any likelihood that they would produce more puppies she knew he would gladly kill her.

Louise was given a retriever and called him Max, Oliver had a brown Labrador whom he named Bruno and Cissy was given a small white terrier who she thought looked just like a Toby jug with his pointed nose like a spout, his rounded

The Enchanted Glade

stomach and a curling tail like a handle. She decided Toby was a perfect name for him.
The dogs were temporarily being kept in a small shed at the rear of the stables because Tom, their gardener hadn't had time to build a proper kennel yet, however he was working on it. Tom was a very handy man to have there as besides doing all of the gardening he did all the odd jobs that needed doing in the house and grounds. Cissy liked Tom very much and she had spent as much time as possible outside since she had arrived here chatting to him about the plans her mother had for the garden.
The commotion continued and Cissy realised that the dogs, who were not allowed into the house, had somehow gotten in. Cissy strongly suspected that Oliver had let them in through the scullery door. The children and a footman were summoned by their father and ordered to catch them and return them to the stables. Cissy thought their father was far too strict, they were only little and she loved to play with Toby. She managed to catch him and she scooped him up in her arms.
"Come along, Toby, let's go outside and play for a while". She carried the little dog outside and without any warning he suddenly leapt from her arms and scurried off down the path at the rear of the house. She ran after him as fast as she could and then she saw him disappear down a winding earthen track towards the woods. Her heart was nearly beating out of her body as she kept on running and as she did so she could hear him barking furiously and wondered if instinct had led him this way.
Didn't dogs always love to chase rabbits, she thought suddenly. For a while she saw his white colouring appearing and then disappearing in the undergrowth and then she lost sight of him completely. She was totally exhausted by now and looking back she couldn't even see the house anymore. She could still hear Toby barking and was quite sure she

was hurrying in the right direction but then she realised that not only was she tired but she was lost as well.

She suddenly came upon a clearing in the trees; it was covered in lush green grass with a carpet of wild flowers spread out in front of her. There were primroses, daffodils and celandines, it was stunningly beautiful and it quite took her breath away. She then noticed part of a large felled tree trunk which was a very welcome sight as she was so tired. She walked towards it and sat down on the grass leaning up against the log to get her breath back. She tried to keep her eyes open but she gradually gave in and fell fast asleep.

As Alex reached the bottom of the stairs his black Hessian boots echoed on the black and white marble tiles in the foyer as he crossed towards the front door on his way out. He was an extraordinarily handsome young man with an outstanding full head of light brown hair swept back over the top of his head and curling, a tad untidily, into the back of his neck. He was blessed with very distinguished facial features and he cut a dashing figure in a pair of beige riding trousers, a white shirt with a smartly tied cravat under a darker beige waistcoat, and a forest green top coat. He carried a tall riding hat in his hand.

"Alexander, is that you?" Alex heard his mother's voice from the sanctity of her sitting room.

"Yes, Mother, it's me" he answered as he walked into the room.

"Were you going out?" she enquired.

"I'm off to town to meet a few friends; Billy is just bringing my horse around to the front door".

Billy Curtis was a trusted employee and master in charge of the stables at Amberley Hall which had been the stately home of Alex's family for generations.

His father, Lord Nicholas Kingsley, the Marquess of Wentworth was deeply embroiled in running his immense estate but he was also involved in the shipping business.

He had married the popular Lady Lavinia Makepeace some twenty years ago and it was most certainly a love match. Lavinia had come into the marriage at just nineteen years old but had taken over the running of the enormous house and had managed it competently ever since. She was an amazingly beautiful woman and still passionately in love with her handsome husband. They had three children, Alexander who was the eldest, his sister Imogen, who at sixteen years of age was two years younger than Alex and their younger brother Blake, who was only eight years old.

"We have new neighbours at Monkton Grange" his mother told him "and I thought it would be polite to welcome them, so I have invited them to visit next week. Would you be so kind as to drop the invitation off on your way to Bath, it won't be out of your way will it?"

"No, Mother, I can take the short cut through the woods and then go on from there. Was there anything you required in town?" he asked as he took the invitation and deposited it in his pocket.

His mother smiled "Thank you dear, but I can think of nothing I need at the moment. Make sure you present yourself and let me know how you fared on your return".

He bent to kiss his mothers cheek and as he did so she placed one of her hands either side of his face and looked directly at him "You are a treasure and I am so lucky to have you as my son" she looked kindly at him. Lady Lavinia knew that many eighteen year olds were much more wayward than him yet she knew Alex would never let her down. He was the immediate heir to the family seat and he took his trusted position in life very seriously.

"And I am so lucky to have you as my mother" he answered with an inimitable smile.

He bade his mother farewell, explaining that he wasn't sure what time he would return and he made his way outside. Billy was waiting with his mount Sir Galahad.

"Sorry to have kept you waiting, Billy". Alex had known Billy all his life. Billy nodded and handed him the reins.

"No trouble, my Lord". Billy had been here at Amberley ever since he was a boy as was his father before him. He had 'taken over the reins' as it were when his father had retired through ill health and he held his employer and the family in the highest regard.

In no time at all Alex was cantering down the drive towards the road. He reached the large double gates at the entrance and then crossed to the other side and proceeded to ride down what seemed to be a farm track, but this led him to his short cut through the woods to Monkton Grange. He had ridden this way many times as a young boy when he and his sister had first learned to ride.

He was half way through the woods when a sudden noise spooked Sir Galahad and he reared up, almost unseating Alex, who skilfully managed to control his mighty steed. As he pulled the horse up he heard the muffled bark of a dog. He dismounted and following the noise he suddenly realised that it came from a small hole, that of a rabbit or a fox and it was directly ahead of him. He knelt down and managed to claw back some of the soil and then he saw two back legs and a curly tail. He reached in and pulled the terrified puppy from the hole but with not so much as a thank you bark, the little imp jumped out of his arms, shook himself vigorously and took off. Alex remounted his horse and rode on, only to hear the rascal barking furiously. He once again followed the sound and riding further into the thicket, he came upon a clearing in the trees. There he spied a most delightful young girl lying on the ground. She had just awoken and was rising to a sitting position on the grass. She was rubbing her eyes and as he observed her he saw that her titian hair was flowing right down her back and was so long she was almost sitting on it. She had on a white dress which was covered with a delicate pattern of daisies. The thought

The Enchanted Glade

occurred to him that she looked just like an enchanting flower fairy.
The barking of the dog had disturbed Cissy as she had slept and she was rubbing her eyes and attempting to sit up when a large cloud blocked out the sun. Only this cloud spoke.
"Are you alright?" a concerned voice asked.
Cissy raised her hand to shield her squinting eyes as she couldn't see properly. Then she realised that it was a large man on an even larger horse and that he had just dismounted and was stood beside her. "Could you please be seated so that I may see you more clearly, I can't focus with the sun in my eyes". As he proceeded to sit down she asked
"You looked like a knight silhouetted in the sunshine, are you one?"
"Am I a knight? No, but you look like a damsel in distress to me" he was mocking her a little as he settled down beside her. "Is this your dog?" he enquired as Toby was running rings around them.
"Toby!" she called, "come here or you'll frighten the horse".
"Too late for that!" stated her visitor.
"I'm so sorry, I've only had the puppy for a week and he's not properly disciplined yet".
As she spoke she rested her elbows on her knees and cupped her chin in her hands as she was observing him intensely, taking in his fairly long light brown hair swept back over the top of his head and nuzzling into the nape of his neck. She thought he had the most handsome face she had ever seen and his smiling brown eyes shone like the sun that was beaming down on them at this very moment. His mouth curled up a little at the corner when he smiled and he really did look like that prince in her fairytale book, she was absolutely captivated by him and her heart fluttered as her eyes scrutinize his every move.
"Anyway, what's a little girl like you doing out here in the woods all alone?"

"I am not a little girl!" snapped Cissy indignantly " I am ten years and three months and two days old and I am fifty one inches in height which is four feet and three inches tall". Her face was a picture and he felt totally admonished.

"Whoa! I didn't mean to offend you" Alex was trying so hard to withhold a burst of laughter as he added "Are you lost?"

Cissy didn't really want to admit it and she felt rather embarrassed as she answered "Toby ran away and I ran after him. I have only lived here for a week so I am not altogether familiar with the surroundings yet, and yes I am lost" her lovely deep violet coloured eyes darted away from his and as she glanced downwards her expression became rather sad.

"What is your name?"

"You are very bold, Sir" Cissy looked up, admonishing him again, but she reluctantly answered. "I am Lady Cecilia Catherine Mary Templeton but my friends call me Cissy and who are you, may I ask?"

"You may ask, and I am Lord Alexander Charles Nicholas Kingsley, but my friends call me Alex". He was attempting to keep a straight expression on his face. "Can I call you Cissy?"

"But you are not one of my friends".

"But I'd like to be" he said as he was totally intrigued by this amusing yet quite stubborn little madam.

Cissy didn't know how to answer that, but replied "I will think on it".

"Look, I am on my way to your house now; I can give you a ride home".

"But how can you, you don't know where I live".

"Well you are on the Monkton Grange estate and you have only lived here for a week so am I right to presume that you are my new neighbour".

"Why are you going to my house?" she enquired innocently.

"To deliver an invitation from my mother to yours" he fancied he was dealing with a more than inquisitive little lady here.

"This is my horse, Sir Galahad" he informed her as he pointed towards his trusty steed. Then Alex stood up and offered Cissy his hand and as she took it he pulled her up to a standing position. "Have you ridden on a horse before?" She shook her head. "Step up onto this tree trunk it will be easier for you". He helped her up. "Stand there for just a moment" He then mounted his horse and steered towards her. "Come on, princess, up you come". He then held his hands out to her to lift her up and sat her in front of him on the saddle. "Let's get you home to your family they are probably worried to death about you".

"But what about Toby?" she cried anxiously.

"I'm sure he'll find his way home" and with a shout of authority Alex called the dog and Toby meekly started to follow them.

They arrived at the front of the house to be met by everyone in a state of panic and disorder. Her mother was frantic and as they approached her father came rushing out of the house and as usual he was very cross indeed. However as soon as Alex introduced himself her father's temper subsided and he was the epitome of decorum. Cissy had already deduced that her father had one face for the family and servants in private and another for visitors.

Cissy frantically tried to explain what had happened but her father wouldn't listen and with one hand he waved her explanation away. She already knew that he was furious about the dogs anyway. Then suddenly remembering in whose presence they were he politely asked her to return the dog to the stables and invited Alex into the house.

"Come along, Toby" Cissy called, as she set off towards the stables, unaware of what was afoot.

"You go ahead, my dear" William said to Annabel "I will be in shortly" and he went off in the direction Cissy had taken.

"Lord Kingsley please come this way" bid her mother, so completely relieved that Cissy was safe. "I will be forever in your debt; we truly thought she had been kidnapped. We have just relocated to this area, only a week ago" she was relating to Alex as they walked towards the house. "If you live nearby you would most likely have been acquainted with my father-in-law, the late Sir Edward Templeton, Lord Langford".

"Yes, my Lady, but after his wife died he removed himself from the social scene and we hadn't seen him for a few years" then he added "my sincere condolences on his passing".

"Thank you, you are most kind" said Annabel as she led him to the large sitting room on the ground floor and rang for the butler.

Alex then remembered the reason for his visit. He reached into his pocket and withdrew the invitation from his mother.

"I am on my way to Bath and my mother asked that I deliver this to you on the way". He handed the envelope to her.

"Thank you, my Lord" she found it a mite difficult addressing him so as he seemed so young. "However did you come to find Cecilia?"

"I was taking a short cut on my way here and I saw her in the woods, apparently she was lost. She was chasing her little dog and I believe he out-ran her" he smiled and Annabel thought what a charming young man he was.

"Well, I am very pleased to meet you" she held out her hand in welcome and Alex bowed his head as he took it "and doubly pleased that you found our daughter. I just don't know what would have happened if you hadn't come across her" there was a note of sheer relief in her voice.

"Oh, it was nothing, I expect she would have found her way back eventually"

Ambrose Harris, the butler had just arrived and Annabel asked for some refreshment and as the butler left the room she invited Alex to be seated. He would rather have continued on his journey but the last thing he would want to do was offend this lovely lady.

Cissy's father then came into the room full of apologises to Alex for any trouble that he had been put to on account of his daughter.

"It was no trouble, Sir, she is delightful" Alex replied truthfully.

Little did Alex know at that moment but Cissy's father had already severely punished her when he had followed her to the stables.

Annabel distinctly noted that her husband's breathing was extremely laboured as if he had been running. She was very concerned about his health in general as he was rather over-sized at present and the old chair creaked as he lowered himself into it. She must have a word with him later in private.

Sir William had watched his wife escort Lord Kingsley to the house and had followed Cissy as she returned Toby to the stables. He had thundered in behind her and had taken a riding crop from the wall after bellowing at all the stable hands to leave. He had then slammed the door and pushed the terrified girl over the bench, pulled up her dress and petticoats and thrashed her. "I'll teach you to defy me, you disobedient little wretch".

"No! Father please stop… please" Cissy screamed, but her cries fell on deaf ears. She was struggling to escape from his grip and the more she pleaded the more he thrashed her. She was trying so very hard to stifle the petrifying screams but had been unsuccessful and he continued to beat her until she went still, the energy to fight back had suddenly flooded out of her and she could stand it no more. When he had finished administering the punishment he caught Cissy by her hair and throwing the whip to the floor he dragged her from the stable block to the back of the house. She was still sobbing profusely and was dreadfully unsteady on her feet as Sir William held her in front of him and pushed her forward through the kitchen entrance and instructed her to use the backstairs to her room. Emily had been devastated to see Cissy so distraught and decidedly endeavoured to find out from the stable lads what had happened to cause her little friend to be in such a state of despair.

As they reached the service stairs her father threw her onto the bottom stair and ordered her to go to her room immediately where she would be confined for one week and he dared her to disobey him ever again. He left her there and then, and with an expression on his face hiding the full extent of his anger, he swiftly went off to greet his esteemed visitor.

Cissy could hardly stand, let alone walk up the stairs, so she went down on her hands and knees and started to crawl slowly upwards and it took her some time to make her way to her room. What have I done to deserve this, she cried pitifully to herself, as the tears were still rolling down her flushed cheeks. She knew her father was a bully but she had never known him as violent as this before. When she eventually reached her room she could neither sit nor lay down so she knelt beside her bed and wept into the covers.

Suddenly Emily burst into her room. "Oh, me poor little chick" she was near to tears herself "Wot 'as 'e done to you?" Emily then hurried over to the bedside to help her to her feet and Cissy fell into her arms and wept uncontrollably. Emily was so incensed she would have gladly tackled the master herself but knew in her heart that he would only sack her and then what good would that do Cissy.

She hadn't liked the new master from the first moment she had met him and at the start she thought that if there was a chance that she may be able to find other employment she would have left that first day, but she knew of no other available live-in jobs in these parts at the present time. She had been working here for almost twenty years now and had always fared well with the old master and his lovely wife and had been very happy here until now. She was infuriated by what had just happened and vowed from that moment on that she would do everything in her power to protect Cissy and her siblings from their monster of a father.

Emily guessed that her Ladyship knew nothing of this; no mother could stand the thought of her children being punished to this extent.

Alice came into the room to ask what the commotion was all about and was horrified to hear what had transpired. She was already familiar with Sir William's bad-temper from past experience and knew he could be very brutal at times. If only the master was half as amiable as his charming wife, she thought.

With Emily's help Alice undressed Cissy and they could not believe their eyes when they saw several huge wheals across the top of poor Cissy's legs and buttocks. Her bloomers were covered in blood as the skin had broken under the constant pressure of the whip. The cook hurried to the kitchen to fetch water and bandages and some salve to gently sooth the abrasions.

In the meantime Alex was bidding her parents farewell and he expressed how much his family would look forward to welcoming them to their home the following week. "Please tell Cissy I said goodbye" Alex smiled as he directed his words towards her mother.

Annabel rang for the butler "I certainly will" answered Annabel, raising her eyebrows in surprise at his use of Cissy's pet name.

Harvey tapped the door and entered when instructed "Please see Lord Kingsley to his horse, Harvey and then would you please clear the china".

"At once, Madam" he said with a slight bow.

When Alex had mounted Sir Galahad he looked around wondering if he might see Cissy. All he saw when he looked up at one of the windows was a much older woman . Well he would see her next week . What a perfectly sweet little girl she was, he thought as he rode away.

****

Chapter 3

Emily had gently soothed Cissy's wounds as best she could and with Alice's help they had put her to bed, laying her flat on her stomach as she was unable to put any pressure on her rear at all.

"Please, don't tell anyone about this, I beg you Emmy, just say that I am feeling a little poorly and I'm staying in bed" Cissy's little whispering voice pulled at the loyal cook's heartstrings .

"Sorry, my chick, but we're goin' to 'ave to call the doctor in to see you. It might fester and that would never do".

"Well just say I fell in some brambles in the woods then" she looked beseechingly at her friend and spoke with a pleading tone in her voice

"We'll see my little precious, we'll see".

Just then Cissy heard the sound of horse's hooves on the gravel drive and asked Emily to look out to see if Lord Kingsley was leaving. She saw him look up to the window after he'd mounted his horse and told Cissy that it was him riding away.

As she came back to Cissy's bedside Emily asked Alice to go downstairs to fetch the mistress as she was sure Lady Annabel would want to be informed of the incident immediately.

Alice left the room and made her way quickly along the corridor, down the staircase and across the hall to Lady

Annabel's sitting room then raising her fisted hand she knocked on the door.

"Come in" Annabel called and as Alice entered the room she glanced up and saw a very worried look on her nanny's face "What is it, Alice?" she asked with a frown.

Alice was only too relieved that the master wasn't there and as she crossed the room to where her mistress sat she spoke very quietly "Sorry to disturb you, my Lady, but would you be so kind as to come upstairs for a moment".

"Why, is something amiss?"

"Yes, my Lady, and we need to call the doctor".

Annabel's face paled considerably as she rose immediately from her chair and walked towards her children's nanny.

"Could you please come quickly, my Lady, before the master finds out that I have come to see you" urged Alice, all the time feeling as if her nerves were shredding. She didn't relish the thought of ever encountering Sir William and many of the other servants felt exactly the same.

Annabel felt desperately confused but quickly followed Alice out of her sitting room and as they made their way across the hall not a single word passed between them as they hurried up the stairs to Cissy's bed-chamber.

As they entered the room her mother could see that Emily was furious and rightly so when she heard what the cook knew of the occurrence. To say that Annabel was totally mortified when she saw Cissy's injuries was an understatement. Every conceivable emotion known to mankind flooded through her veins and if she had never dreamed of committing murder in her life before she felt like it right now. She almost collapsed herself but held herself together emotionally for the sake of her cherished little girl. How could he do this to his own flesh and blood?

"I'm here, my Darling" she whispered gently into her petrified little daughter's ear "now can you tell me exactly what happened?" Annabel was kneeling beside the bed, gently smoothing Cissy's hair.

The Enchanted Glade

"Oh, Mama" Cissy sounded pitiful "I am so sorry, I didn't mean to make father cross. I still don't know what I did to vex him" she then relayed her recollection of the events after Lord Kingsley had entered the house with her mother and she had gone to take Toby back to the stables.

Annabel rose from Cissy's bedside and her immediate concern was to ask one of the stable lads to go to fetch the doctor. Emily volunteered to go to the stable block herself to hurry it up, but as she got up to leave the room, Annabel spoke. "I'm sorry to have to ask this of you both" Annabel looked very seriously at both Emily and Alice "but please do not mention this to anyone. I will deal with it myself".

"We'll do our best, milady, but they lads at the stables was the one's wot told me abou' it" Emily answered as she turned again towards the door "I'll be going directly".

"Then please ask them to be discreet, Mrs Bridges".

"I will, milady" she said as she hurriedly left the room on her errand.

"Alice stay close to Cissy, I will be back shortly".

Annabel stormed out of Cissy's bed-chamber fury erupting inside her breast. She hurried along the corridor, down the stairs and across the hall into her husband's study trying to compose herself with every ounce of willpower that she possessed. "How dare you! How dare you just sit there and pretend that nothing has happened, are you mad?" she fumed as she opened the door and entered without knocking. He was drinking again and as he had heard her enter the room he'd glanced towards her nonchalantly and then turned away, trying to deny her presence. "I have just sent for the doctor and I will be very interested to hear your explanation of Cissy's injuries when he arrives".

Her inebriated husband looked towards her with blurred vision and slurring his words he sneered "She deserved a whipping, the defiant little chit, I told them all to put the dogs away and she runs off. Showing me up in front of

Kingsley. What sort of impression will it give the nobility around here they'll think I'm too lenient with you all, eh?"

"Brutal, that's what you are! Any normal man wouldn't beat an animal like that let alone his own daughter" she was seething "and if I only had the strength to do to you what I have a mind to, it would be you the good doctor would be coming to see or maybe even better, the undertaker would be on his way" she was almost screaming, and she was a woman who had never raised her voice to anyone in her life before.

Annabel was incensed beyond comprehension and so angry with herself for allowing the family situation to escalate to this. She saw no point in wasting her breath on him any longer as her arrogant husband wasn't taking any notice of her whatsoever, so she turned on her heels and couldn't help slamming the door behind her as she left the room. She quickly returned to Cissy's room and bade Alice go to check on the other two children. On her way up she had waylaid Harris and asked him to bring the doctor straight up to Lady Cecilia's room when he arrived.

"I do hope everything is alright with the little lady, Madam" he enquired pensively. Annabel knew that Cissy was a favourite with all the servants she always had been, at their previous residence, and now here, with the new ones.

"Just do as I ask, Harris, I daresay you'll hear soon enough, but I would appreciate some discretion amongst the staff".

Realising that what she was saying was rather difficult for his mistress Ambrose nodded and said "Your servant, my Lady". With that the butler made his way to the front entrance to await the doctor.

The doctor arrived shortly afterwards and the butler immediately escorted him upstairs to Cissy's bed-chamber. The butler knocked and waited until he was bidden then let the gentleman in and left. Only Cissy and her mother were in the room now as Emily had returned to the kitchen to

The Enchanted Glade

prepare the evening meal, although she was unsure how she would cope knowing that poor Cissy was still in agony.

The doctor held his hand out to shake hands with Annabel and as she took it he introduced himself as John Bartholomew. What a vision of loveliness, he thought as she began to speak.

"I am pleased to make your acquaintance, Doctor Bartholomew, I am Lady Templeton. We are new here at the Grange, we only arrived last week. It's my daughter, Cissy, something very unfortunate has happened to her".

The doctor moved closer to the bed and Annabel gently pulled back the covers. The doctor then proceeded to examine a very embarrassed Cissy and was appalled by what he saw. "How ever did this happen?" he asked gravely as he began to replace the more than adequate dressing that Emily had administered to Cissy's delicate skin.

Annabel knew he had guessed and she couldn't lie. She had never told a single lie in her life before. "My husband lost his temper and without my knowledge he beat our daughter with a riding crop". The embarrassing look in her eyes was glaringly evident and as her gaze lowered to the floor she had never felt so ashamed in all her life.

"You know, Madam, that I should call the constable" he sounded furious "There is discipline and there is cruelty and this goes beyond the bounds of both". The dismay in John Bartholomew's voice was palpable.

Cissy was beside herself "Please, Sir, please don't call anybody. I was really naughty and I only got what I deserved, but I won't do it again, I promise". She was almost begging because she knew that if her father discovered what the doctor had in mind he would probably make them all suffer the consequences.

The doctor knew she was just covering up for her father and he thought her a very brave little girl to be taking the blame. He advised Annabel on further treatment of the wound then gave Cissy some medicine and said he would call again the following day to see how Cissy was progressing.

Annabel rang for Harris to escort the doctor to the front entrance.

As the doctor was leaving the room he asked Annabel if he could have a word with her husband but she knew that William would probably have collapsed in a state of unconsciousness by now so she told the doctor he was unavailable. John Bartholomew looked kindly at Annabel as he said goodbye and she almost felt embarrassed at the obvious pity she detected in the man's eyes.

She heard Harris's knock at the door and after taking their leave of her ladyship he ushered the good doctor to the front door and he left.

Outside he settled into the seat of his gig and placing his bag on the seat beside him he unfettered the reins and as he rode away John Bartholomew wondered whatever had possessed that beautiful lady to marry a man who was capable of administering punishment like that.

That evening Annabel dined on her own once again, although she knew the food would stick in her throat as it had on more than one occasion lately. Instead of allowing the butler to serve the meal, Emily came herself. " I 'ope I'm not takin' liberties Milady but I came meself to enquire after Mistress Cecilia and to ask if you think she might like a bite to eat".

"That's very thoughtful of you, Mrs Bridges; I will go straight up after my meal. I think Alice is with her at the moment so perhaps you could send Minnie up to ask if they need anything".

"At once, milady" she dipped a curtsey and as she hurried from the room Annabel called her back.

"I would like to thank you so much for your help earlier".

"No mat'er, milady, anyone would 'ave done as I did" she dipped again and as she left the room, Annabel realised how

The Enchanted Glade

lucky she was to have such loyal servants. At least I have something to be thankful for, she thought.

Cissy heard the knock on the door of her room and Alice answered it and let Emily in. She crossed the room to her bedside and asked. "Feeling any bet'er, me little chick?" Cissy nodded pitifully. "'ere I've brought you a nice bowl o' soup, now you gonna be a good girl and eat it all up for Emmy?" dear Emily's smile was all that Cissy needed to cheer her up.
 "Thank you, Emmy, I am quite hungry" she said, not knowing how she was going to manage to eat anything as she couldn't even sit up straight let alone put any weight on her rear and the fact that her wounds were still very painful didn't help.
 "C'mon now, pet, just lean up on yer elbows and I'll feed you". Emmy put the tray onto the small table beside the bed and eased Cissy up until she was a little more comfortable, then she picked up the bowl and held it in front of Cissy and began to spoon feed her.
 "Oh, Emmy, I feel such a ninny, I am so very sorry to be causing you so much trouble".
 "You ain't no trouble, Miss Cissy, now c'mon and let's get this down you. You'll feel a lot bet'er once you got somefin' warm inside you".
Alice then asked to be excused whilst Emily was there because she wished to go to see the other children and re-assure them that Cissy was a little better now. After Alice had visited them earlier to tell them what had occurred they were terribly worried about their sister. Miss Hawkins had kindly stayed with them up to now but Alice didn't wish to impose on their governess' time any longer than was really necessary, so she left the room saying that she would return later and tuck Cissy up for the night.
Having devoured most of the soup and another of Emily's delicious biscuits, Cissy relaxed, face down, onto the pillow

once more. "Emmy" whispered Cissy after Alice had left "I really don't know how I am going to face my father after this".

"Don't you worry about nothin', me little chick, it's him what should be worrying about facin' people, but I daresay 'e got no conscience. Anyway I shouldn't be talkin' to you like this. Just you know you can come to Emmy anytime you need someone to talk to and you know I'll always be there for you and do me best to 'elp you". She smiled reassuringly at Cissy as she spoke.

"My father told me that I must stay in my room for the whole week and I really wanted to go to Lord Kingsley's house next Saturday. He told me he was bringing an invitation to my mother when he found me in the woods. He was so kind to me Emmy and I was so looking forward to seeing him again to thank him for his help".

"Oh you got all the time in the world to see 'im again, me little dearie, 'e don't live far and I daresay 'e'll come visitin' 'ere again afore long". Emily's optimism cheered Cissy up no end but she was beginning to feel a little drowsy. It must have been the mild dose of laudanum that Doctor Bartholomew had given her earlier to dull the pain. As Emily was chatting away she could see Cissy's eyelids wavering and soon she had drifted into her dreams.

So Emily put her hand on Cissy's head and very gently smoothed her hand over Cissy's beautiful titan locks

"That's it, my little chick, you go to sleep now and then per'aps when you wake up in the mornin' the terrible events of today will be be'ind you and I pray you will feel a lot bet'er. She stooped to kiss Cissy on her cheek and then sat back and sang a soothing lullaby until she herself was well and truly in the land of nod.

Alex arrived home later that evening and immediately crossed the large foyer towards the drawing room as he knew his mother was anxious to hear how he had fared

The Enchanted Glade

when he had called at Monkton Grange. His parents were seated opposite each other, either side of the hearth and after greeting them both he drew near to his mother and stooped to kiss her cheek.

"How did you find the Templeton's?" she enquired, anxious to find out about their new neighbours. It was typical of her to be concerned for others.

Alex relayed everything that occurred to his mother then added "Lady Annabel is a most enchanting soul and I know you will deal well with her, Mother, but Sir William is a rather strange character. I hope I am not speaking out of turn when I say that I distinctly detected a whiff of brandy on the man's breath and he appeared half in his cups when I called and that was in the middle of the afternoon."

"Maybe you were mistaken" his father said, joining in the conversation, and glancing at his son over the top of The Times newspaper as he spoke.

"I think not, Father, anyway we'll see them on Saturday" Alex said as he handed his mother the reply, which Annabel had written and asked him to kindly convey to his mother before he had left Monkton Grange. As his mother was opening the letter and reading Lady Annabel's reply Alex excused himself saying "Time will tell" and then he took his leave.

In next to no time Saturday was here and the entire Templeton family, with the exception of one, boarded the family carriage to travel the five miles to the next village of Marston Heath. This was the first time they had seen this part of the countryside and Louise and Oliver were avidly peering out of the windows of the carriage and taking in the surroundings as they made their way to the Kingsley's country house.

As they arrived and the carriage rolled through the imposing front gates of the property they could see acre upon acre of land and they knew that the Amberley Hall estate was immense.

After a run down the lengthy drive to the Hall, there was great excitement as the magnificent building came into view. It was huge and Louise and Oliver squealed with delight after confessing to never having seen a house as big as this before.

As they halted outside the front entrance two footmen and the master of the stable were there to meet them. They alighted from the carriage and were ushered through the imposing entrance into the extensive foyer, which seemed to be bigger than their largest sitting room.

Alex was there to meet them and he greeted them warmly

"Welcome to Amberley Hall". He then escorted them through the house to the large garden where a grand picnic luncheon awaited them. There they were heartily welcomed by Lord Nicholas and his fine-looking wife the Lady Lavinia and after all the introductions had been made Alex's enquired of Annabel "Where's Lady Cecilia?"

With a stutter she answered "She's not too well, so I thought it best that she stayed in bed at home today". She hated lying especially to her new neighbours, but what alternative did she have, if they found out about her husband's treatment of Cissy they would surely form a very low opinion of her. As she wrestled with her thoughts she felt herself colouring up and she realised that she couldn't possibly jeopardise her new friendship with the Kingsley's as she had met no-one else in this area to date, and this could be the opening she needed to introduce her family to other members of the aristocracy here about.

"What a shame" Lady Lavinia interjected "nothing too serious I hope".

"She'll be fit as a fiddle in a few days" was Annabel's stilted reply.

"Alex told me she was lost in the woods, the little dear likely caught a chill".

"Most probably" agreed Annabel, unable to look Lady Lavinia in the eye as she spoke.

Alex was unconvinced so he went to find Cissy's brother and drew him to one side with the pretence of pairing him in a game of quoits with his younger brother, Blake, who had just come bounding across the lawn. "Oliver, is Cissy alright?"

Oliver's answer was almost a whisper. "Father was cross with Cissy for getting lost when you came last week and he beat her and she's been abed since then. She told me she wished to come today but our father forbade it. She was proper poorly when it happened but she is a little better now".

Alex was incensed. He strode over to the assembled party and spoke quietly to his mother . "Would you please excuse me, Mother, I have a small errand to run".

His mother gazed at him quite surprised; this was not like Alex at all, wanting to leave when they had company. Then Alex whispered in her ear making some excuse and telling her he wouldn't be too long and when he smiled at her she couldn't refuse his request.

Alex quickly made his way to the stables where Billy saddled Sir Galahad as fast as he could. He skirted around the side of the house where he couldn't be seen from the garden then headed for the main gates and after crossing the main road he took the shortcut through the woods that he had taken last week and arrived at Monkton Grange in record time.

Cissy heard the horse approaching and was peering out of the window of her room when he arrived. Her excited little heart jumped in her chest when she realised who their caller was. She slowly made her way to the top of the stairs and waited patiently as Harris the butler opened the front door and allowed Alex access. "My Lord, everyone is out and it is my understanding that they are in fact visiting your own residence" relayed the ageing butler.

"But I understand, my good man, that Lady Cecilia is not at my residence and I have come to visit her here". Alex spoke in a commanding voice and the butler bowed respectfully.
He glanced behind Harris and spied Cissy as she spoke.
"Ambrose, please allow Lord Kingsley in at once" and her face broke into a heart-warming smile for the first time in a week.
It was a welcome sight for Ambrose Harris, the butler to see his favourite little Miss Cissy smiling again after what she'd endured the week before.
"I can't come down to greet you, Lord Kingsley, so perhaps you could come up".
Alice, Cissy's nanny was none to happy about this but she also knew what the darling little girl had been through.
As Alex started up the stairs Alice suggested that he may like to carry her gently down to the garden and they could all sit out in the sunshine together.
Cissy vaguely explained where she was injured so he tenderly scooped her up into his arms being very careful to avoid hurting her and they made their way outside. Cissy was so thrilled to be in Alex's arms and as she clasped her hands around his neck she rested her head on his broad chest and they made their way out to the garden at the rear of the house. Alice asked the butler to bring some tea and light refreshments. Then Cissy sat in a chair with plenty of soft cushions and made herself as comfortable as she could.
"Oh, Lord Kingsley, I am so pleased to see you again".
"Cissy, please call me Alex" he said softly and his smile sent a warm feeling throughout Cissy's whole body.
"I thought we'd agreed that we were going to be friends and friends use their given names".
"Alright Alex" she beamed as she emphasised his name.
"I'm sorry I didn't say goodbye last week. I wanted to thank you for helping me".

The Enchanted Glade

"Can you tell me exactly why you were unable to bid me farewell?" he scrutinised her face to see if he could detect any unusual expression, which he couldn't, and her tone gave him no hint.

"I was unavoidably waylaid and you'd gone before I realised".

Alex knew she was lying and trying to cover up her father's ruthlessness. "How did you hurt yourself then" he enquired, gently probing further.

She couldn't bring herself to answer but was saved any further embarrassment by the sound of a certain little creature yapping and running across the lawn. Tom, their gardener, had seen the small get-together and knowing that Cissy had been confined to the house all week he knew that she hadn't seen her precious little puppy.

"Oh, Toby....Toby" a feeling of elation coursed through her, yet still a few stray tears escaped from her eyes.

Alex caught the little blighter and hoisted him in the air then asked Cissy if she could manage to hold him.

She hadn't seen the little dog since that fateful day and she was overjoyed as Alex tenderly placed him on her lap. Alex noticed the tears but also knew that she was one tough little lady. He had all about given up on trying to prise out of her what had happened the week before.

Toby also seemed to sense that there was something not quite right with his mistress and he lay very still in her arms as she petted him.

Just then Emily came out with a tray. She placed it on the table and turning towards Alex she dipped a slight curtsey in acknowledgement "Milord"

"Lord Kingsley" Cissy said, smiling as she spoke, knowing she really shouldn't address him in any other way in front of the servants. "This is our wonderful cook, Mrs Bridges" Cissy fixed her eyes on him as she distinctly pronounced.

"So when you come to dine here in the future it will be her culinary delights of which you will be partaking " Cissy grinned widely at him.

"I'm pleased to meet you Mrs Bridges" he too smiled and continued " and I shall very much look forward to my first visit if I am to… how did you put it Cissy…partake of your culinary delights. Put like that I am sure I will be entirely unable to resist such an invitation".

"Pleased to meet you I'm sure, your Lordship" Emily dipped another slight curtsey. " 'scuse me Sir" she said as she turned to Cissy "'ow are you feeling today, me little chick, much bet'er I 'ope".

"Oh, yes Emmy, I am so much better especially as Lord Kingsley has come to visit" as she spoke Emily noticed that Cissy's beaming smile was brighter than a ray of sunshine.

"Actually I must soon be on my way, I would very much like to stay here a little longer but no-one knows where I am. Your family will think me rather rude neglecting them although I suspect they are enjoying their day. I am only sorry you missed it Cissy, perhaps you can come another day".

"Oh yes I should like that very much" her smile was infectious.

They had finished their tea and then Alex asked "Would you like me to carry you back into the house before I leave".

She nodded and called out to Tom who had gone back to the gardening. He came at once and she handed her little dog back to him and he readily assured her that he would look after Toby until she was better. Alex then picked her up as gently as he could and with Alice in tow they made their way back inside.

Alex carefully deposited Cissy at the top of the stairs and she thanked him for his kindness. He assured her that he would call in to see her again next week and as his horse had been brought to the front door he made to leave.

Cissy made her way slowly to her bed-chamber and went to the window as Alex rode away. He turned and waved to her as he went on his way and his parting smile melted her little heart.

Meanwhile back at Amberley Hall Annabel was very taken by Lady Lavinia. They were of a similar age, both had three children, and the only difference in their marriages, apart from financial, as the Kingsleys were far more affluent than the Templetons, was that Lavinia loved her husband from the bottom of her heart and her husband obviously felt the same way about her and returned the affections.

Annabel could see this in their every movement towards one another, every fleeting touch and every momentary glance. Oh, why can't my marriage be like theirs she thought as she felt a sensation of sickness emerge from the pit of her stomach?

William had been politeness itself today and she thought if only he could always be like this and stay sober maybe their marriage would stand a chance of surviving or at least be on a firmer footing. She still couldn't forgive his actions towards Cissy and it had made for an extremely strained atmosphere throughout the whole household all week. Why did people have to change so, she sighed to herself as she saw Nicholas drop a kiss on his wife's cheek as he informed her that he was going to show William his stables, of which he was tremendously proud.

Annabel thought back and remembered how attentive and loving William had been when they had first met and she sighed to herself knowing that her own marriage would never be like that again.

She glanced over at the children and saw that the younger boys were playing on the lawn and Louise and Imogen were getting along famously. They too were of a similar age and probably had a lot in common. Seeing the siblings contented her thoughts were drawn to Cissy. She knew Cissy had wanted so much to come along especially to see Alexander again to thank him for helping her the week before, but her husband had been adamant in his refusal to allow her to visit with the Kingsley's today.

Annabel then looked back to Lavinia and said "Thank you so much for inviting us today. It has been lovely. It can be quite daunting when one arrives in a new locality and doesn't know a soul. It has been extremely enjoyable for the children too. You must allow us to return the compliment and invite you to Monkton Grange next week. Did you ever visit the house before when my in-laws were in residence?" Annabel enquired.

"As a matter of fact we were rarely invited. I think they had much older friends and of course we have a social circle ourselves, which can be quite exhausting at times". Lavinia raised her eyebrows skywards but smiled all the same. She was so beautiful and even more so when she smiled.

"It's been our pleasure to receive you here today, Annabel, and I do hope we will be seeing a lot more of you all in the near future". Lavinia also thought Annabel was rather charming and was only too glad to welcome her as a new friend.

Just then Alex came through the garden and joined the two boys in their game.

"Alexander seems to get on very well with the children" Annabel commented. With everything that had been going on she hadn't noticed that he had been absent from the party for a while.

"Alexander gets on well with everyone, he is so amiable" agreed Lavinia sounding very proud of her son.

The rest of the day continued very pleasingly and after they had said their goodbyes the carriage was called to the front entrance and the Templeton's boarded, made themselves comfortable and waved avidly as the Kingsleys bade them farewell.

Oliver then promptly fell fast asleep and continued so for the entire journey home. Everyone, including Cissy, had had a very agreeable day.

****

Chapter 4

Sure enough on the afternoon of Wednesday the following week, as promised, Alex arrived to visit Cissy, but just in case her father was at home and of an unpleasant humour he rode the shortcut through the woods and made his way straight to the stable block at the rear of the house. He confidently addressed the stable lad "Good day young man and you are".

"Sam Miles, Sir" the lad answered with a nod and a finger of salute to his brow.

"I've come to see Mrs Bridges, is she on hand do you know?" Alex thought it best to proceed this way.

"I'll just check for you, Sir " answered Sam walking towards the kitchen after he had tethered the horse near the stable door. Alex ambled behind him at a slower pace.

What a dear Mrs Bridges is he thought as she came hurrying from the house towards him.

"Oh! Good afternoon, milord, 'ow very nice of you to come" Emily dipped a little curtsey. "Come to see Miss Cissy 'ave you?" she whispered quietly knowing that by now they were out of earshot of the young lad as he returned to the stable. She didn't want anyone gossiping about his lordship's visit and Emily knew Cissy would be so thrilled to see Lord Kingsley.

"Yes, Mrs Bridges, how is she today?"

"Would you care to come in this way, Sir?" Emily asked with a little uneasiness as she pointed to the kitchen door.

"It's alright, Mrs Bridges, I came to the back of the house purposely to avoid any prying eyes. I know Cissy is already in trouble with her father so I didn't want to make the matter any worse. Also I wanted to talk to you in private to ask what has been going on. Cissy very effectively evaded my questions last week".

"She's a good little soul, Sir" Emily sounded anxious "but would I be speakin' out o' turn if I tell you what 'appened?" she asked as they made their way into the kitchen.

"It is quite acceptable, Mrs Bridges, I won't be repeating what you tell me to anyone else, I just need to know for myself what happened. Oliver has already told me that her father beat her after I found her in the woods that day and I was horrified to think that she may have gotten into trouble on my account".

"Oh! No Milord it ain't nothin' to do with you, I don't think. I shouldn't say it, Sir, but the master can be a bully at times, 'e is very cruel with words and actions to the servants. I'm afraid I've only known 'im for abou' four weeks and I am not fond of 'im at all. Would you like a cup of tea, Milord?"

"That would be very agreeable, thank you, Mrs Bridges" he had Emily hooked with that breathtaking smile of his.

Emily asked Alex to be seated at the small table in her little parlour and she brought them both a drink and home-made biscuits and they sat like old friends talking about previous events. Emily thought what a wonderful young man he was. After they had conversed for quite a while Emily requested that if he wouldn't mind staying where he was for a minute she would slip up the back stairs to locate Cissy whom she found in the school room with her siblings.

After knocking and entering the room, Cissy frowned as Emily whispered in her ear "Would you like to come downstairs with me, Miss Cissy, I have a surprise for you" and then she winked at her. Then quite loudly Emily declared "I've made another batch o' them biscuits you all like so if you'd like to come wi' me, Miss Cissy, I'll send a plate up for you all to enjoy". The others certainly sounded as if they were pleased about that and although she was mystified

Cissy went with Emily anyway. On the back stairs she couldn't wait to ask what this was all about but Emily just put her finger up to her lips and then crooked her index finger gesturing Cissy to follow her.

Cissy was overjoyed as she walked into Emily's parlour and saw Alex and he was delighted to see that she was much better.

They conversed for a half hour and then Alex said he must be off but he told her that he had been invited with his parents to dine with her parents, this coming Saturday.

Cissy knew she wouldn't be able to see him then, as the children were never allowed downstairs when there were visitors to the house, unless it was Aunt Ellen, of course.

As he left, Alex took both of Cissy's little hands in his and looking affectionately into her eyes he said "You will take care of yourself, won't you? If you ever need my help you only have to send word and I'll come at once".

Although a mite befuddled by his remarks she smiled profusely and thanked him, not knowing of the serious talk he had had with Emily.

She watched him from the kitchen door and as he strode towards the stables he turned and raised his hand in a wave and she did the same in return. His gesture made her heart skip a beat and she felt a warm glow flooding over her. She felt so fortunate to have found such a good friend in Alex. As he went out of sight she turned around and went back into the kitchen to see Emily hurriedly putting some home-made biscuits on a plate for her to take back up to the playroom.

"Thank you so much, my dear Emmy" she beamed a bright grin at her friend and then she gave Emily a warm embrace. Emily knew it had made the little girl's day to have seen his lordship so unexpectedly

"T'was my pleasure, Miss Cissy" Emily answered with a smile and an affectionate glance.

The Enchanted Glade

Saturday soon dawned and as the Kingsleys had been invited to dine at Monkton Grange that day the ever curious Cissy went to the kitchen quite early to see Emily and to ask her what extraordinary and wonderful 'culinary delights' she would be serving for Alex and his family.

"I 'ope you ain't goin' to get in trouble for bein' 'ere with me, me chick". Emily sounded very concerned.

"No-one knows I'm here. I told Alice I was going to lie down in my room and I crept down the back stairs when no-one was looking. Oh, please don't worry Emmy, and do tell me what you'll be serving this evening" she asked earnestly.

Emily raised her eyebrows in resignation and grinned as she said "They'll be 'aving me special recipe Roast beef wiv 'orseradish sauce and Yorkshire puddin', and vegetables from the garden. In fact, Miss Cissy, per'aps you would like to come wiv' me to see Tom and then you can 'elp me choose 'em. We must 'ave 'em fresh for your Lord Kingsley mustn't we?" Emily smiled to herself knowing Cissy had a soft spot for the young Lord.

Cissy was thrilled to be involved with the planning of the meal and there was a spring in her step as she followed the cook into the garden. She was almost back to her normal self now but still felt the odd twinge in her legs so she made her way carefully to the vegetable patch.

When they returned to the kitchen Cissy enquired as to what the dessert would be .

"I thought me scrumptious apple crumble would be first-class, Miss Cissy".

"What is apple crumble?" asked Cissy "I've heard of apple pie but not apple crumble".

"Well it 'as apple at the bot'om and then I put flour, fat and sugar in a bowl and rub it together until it looks like crumbs and then I puts that on the top".

"Well why can't you put pastry on the bottom like in the apple pie. Then place the apple on top of the pastry and put the crumble mix on the top of the apple. Then we could call it Apple Crumble Pie".

"Well, my word, Miss Cissy, you are a one. What a fine notion you 'ave. I might try that yet".

"Oh, please do Emmy and perhaps you could sprinkle sugar on the top to make it crunchy like your biscuits".

Emily then scolded Cissy lightly "You 'ad bet'er run along now or you'll be getting' in trouble if anyone finds you 'ere wiv me". As Cissy bid her farewell and left the kitchen Emily forever marvelled at Cissy and the things she came out with.

The children always ate upstairs with Alice when the household were expecting guests so Cissy was not allowed downstairs this evening which made her feel rather upset.

As the adults usually ate at around 8 o'clock in the evening she had finished her meal and had withdrawn to her bedchamber as the carriage from Amberley Hall drew up at the front of the house and she peered out of her window to see if Alex had come. He had, and although it was quite dark, as he alighted from the carriage he glanced up to see Cissy peeping out of the window. He waved discreetly as he walked with his parents to the front door, where Harris was waiting to escort them in. That was all she saw of him that evening which disappointed her greatly.

Dinner was always the main meal in any household and it was customary to dress for the occasion. The ladies, who tonight included Lady Annabel, Lady Lavinia and Sir William's sister, Lady Ellen, all wore full length evening gowns and looked absolutely stunning. Lady Annabel chose to wear a peach gown in a taffeta material which complimented her striking auburn locks. This was adorned with pearls at the neck making her appearance exquisite. Lady Lavinia's blonde tresses complimented her emerald green ensemble which was accompanied by dazzling jewellery and Lady Ellen, who was a few years older than the other two, wore an eye-catching gown of blue silk. The gentlemen also looked very debonair in their white cravats, waistcoats, evening pantaloons and silk stockings.

Sir William sat at the head of the table with Lady Lavinia at his right hand and Lord Kingsley on his left. Annabel was seated beside Nicholas whilst Alex sat beside Lady Lavinia directly opposite his mother and the delightfully charming Lady Ellen was seated on his other side.

The meal that Emily had cooked tonight was very well received. There was cold consommé to start followed by a delicious beef roast with all the trimmings. Then for dessert Russian Charlotte with seasonal fruit and, of course, Cissy's new creation smothered in fresh cream.

Minnie came up to Cissy's room with a message from Emily to say how much everyone had enjoyed the new

'Apple Crumble Pie' for dessert and was assured that the cook had made it known to the mistress that it had been Cissy's idea. There was much hilarity in the dining room when Annabel mentioned it and Alex smiled to himself as he sampled Mrs Bridges 'culinary delights' and at the thought of Cissy taking so much interest in the cooking of everything.

"Talking of Cissy" he said, directing his words at her father "would you mind if I taught her to ride. She says she has never ridden and I think it might be something she would enjoy".

"When did she mention that?" snapped her father.

"I asked her when we first met " answered Alex rather surprised at the man's gruff tone.

Annabel, looking across the table at her husband, was worried he'd imbibed too much wine and that it was having an undesired effect on him. "What an excellent idea, my lord", she interrupted quickly "and how kind of you to be willing to give up your time to help Cissy" though as she spoke she doubted whether her daughter would be able to sit on a horse comfortably yet after the episode with her father.

"We have an ideal mount for her" Nicholas chipped in "a little mare called Velvet. I'm sure your daughter will be able to handle her especially with Alexander's guidance. He's noted for his work with horses and is an excellent judge of character ".

Annabel cringed inside; she was hoping it was just horses that Alexander was a good judge of. If it was people how long would it take for him to discover the sort of man her husband was. Never, she hoped or maybe her new friendship with Lavinia would be in jeopardy and she couldn't stand that.

"As it is Sunday tomorrow and you'll all be at church in the morning maybe I could fetch Cissy and Oliver in the afternoon and bring them to Amberley and introduce Cissy to Velvet. Does Oliver ride yet?"

"Not yet" William informed them " but the boy's a fast learner. The only horses we have here at present are the one's we use for the carriages. I haven't had the time to sort out all my affairs what with only just re-locating".

You haven't had time thought Annabel because you've been too busy getting drunk. Well she wasn't going to spoil the evening dwelling on his misdemeanours so she settled that the next afternoon would be fine and added that she knew her two youngest children would be overjoyed to be going to Amberley, particularly Cissy who hadn't seen it yet.

Alex felt he had gained an enormous victory in persuading her parents to allow them some time away from the Grange. He felt that the children, especially Cissy, would benefit from being allowed a little extra freedom as they hadn't seemed to have had much of it in the past.

The meal was now over, so the ladies decided to withdraw to the main sitting room leaving the three men alone to enjoy their port or brandy and cigars. Although Alex abstained from the latter he still enjoyed the accompanying conversation immensely.

Lady Ellen was avidly relating to the other two women of an invitation she had received from a friend to take afternoon tea with her and some companions the following Wednesday just as the gentlemen emerged from the dining room .

"Afternoon tea?" enquired Nicholas, frowning as he did so. Ellen went on to explain "It has recently become fashionable to invite the ladies in the area to an afternoon get-together and partake of tea and cakes. I have asked that Annabel be invited also, as being new to the district I am very eager to help her integrate with the local gentry".

Ellen absolutely adored her sister-in-law and was very keen to help her in any way that she could.

Annabel was delighted to accept and then Lavinia suggested it might be satisfactory for Annabel to have an afternoon tea gathering of her own. "I'm sure it will help immensely in you becoming recognized as a society hostess yourself, perhaps I'll have one myself, Nicholas" she smiled fondly at her husband "it will afford you a good excuse to extricate yourself from the house and spend a much loved afternoon fishing".

"You fish, Kingsley" William enquired.

"Yes, do you?".

"Haven't done for years" admitted William.

"Maybe we could spend a few hours together next week, I have plenty of rods. I have an appointment with my accountants and bankers in Bristol on Monday and Tuesday and I will also call in at my shipping office, but I'm free for the rest of the week" Nicholas replied.

"You are in trade?" William asked, sounding astonished.

"Not really" then Nicholas explained that he was a shareholder in the shipping company that belonged to an old friend. He had been asked for his help when the company, which his friend had founded, was in financial trouble and

being the compassionate man he was, Nicholas couldn't let his old friend down, so he had invested heavily and the now thriving business had been saved. The company was situated at the port of Bristol some ten miles away, but now-a-days he only visited once in a while to check that things were continuously being kept in order.
"Well, shall we say Wednesday for the fishing?"
"That will be fine" as he replied William actually smiled.
Annabel was relieved that the two men were notably sociable and she was so looking forward to her afternoon out with Ellen, whom she had never been able to believe was sired by the same parents as William as she was so completely different from her brother. Please God don't let anyone find out about William's secret addiction, she prayed, as she couldn't bear to be classed as a pariah when she felt she had only just begun to feel accepted here.
The rest of the evening proceeded well and when the Kingsley's had thanked them for a thoroughly pleasurable evening and taken their leave, her husband retired to his bed-chamber and she remained in the sitting room with Ellen for a while. Ellen was staying over for a few days. She lived alone in a large Georgian house in the prestigious Royal Crescent in the nearby town of Bath. Her second husband, Lord Francis Bellamy, had passed away only a year ago and had left her copiously affluent, but lonely and she appreciated Annabel's company immensely, in fact she was thrilled that Annabel now lived almost on her doorstep. Ellen had a son, Miles, from her first marriage to Lord Barnaby Ellwood, who had died after contacting typhoid on one of his many trips abroad. Miles was twenty four years old now and lived mostly in London where he conducted his business. He had inherited substantially from his father when he had attained his 21st birthday and Ellen's second husband, his step-father, had also left him wealthy. He didn't need to work at all but he had supposed that he would go mad with boredom if he didn't do something. So as he

was an enthusiastic artist himself he had purchased some premises and was now the proud owner of a renowned art gallery, which was extremely popular in the capital at this time.

"What happened to Cissy last week?" Ellen enquired directly, having picked up on some rumblings from conversations overheard when Cissy's injuries had been the topic of discussion amongst the servants.

Annabel was a little loathed to speak of it but she knew Ellen was well aware of her brother's failings. She explained, but didn't go into too much detail and Ellen was distressed to discover that it was her gift to Cissy that had sparked the occurrence in the first place. Annabel readily reassured her that Cissy was smitten with the little puppy and was recovering well from her ordeal.

" Perhaps when I go home next week Cissy can visit with me for a few days " the suggestion was welcomed by Annabel as Cissy had been avoiding her father ever since the dreadful incident and the tension in the house was palpable at the best of times of late.

"That would be a marvellous idea, I'll talk to her about it tomorrow" said Annabel knowing that Ellen would do anything for herself and her children.

They carried on conversing in general especially about the new fashions and discussing what they would be wearing out to tea on Wednesday and then they decided to retire for the night.

Annabel went quietly to her bed-chamber, not taking the trouble to wish her husband goodnight. Her maid was waiting to help her undress and after seeing to her mistress' needs Nancy left so she settled down hoping for a restful night. It was to no avail as her obnoxious husband had apparently heard her retire and came through the adjoining door and Annabel cursed herself for forgetting to lock it. Having imbibed too much wine earlier he stumbled towards her obviously expecting to have his way with her and she cringed at the thought. He launched himself onto her bed and although she protested he ignored her pleas and proceeded to violate her in a most brutal way.

Oh! how she hated this man and trying to put her mind to something other than what was happening she just laid in her bed and stared up towards the ceiling and prayed for an end to this misery as quickly as possible.

The next afternoon Alex came to call for Cissy and Oliver, who were ready and waiting for their outing. As it was a fine April day and the sun was shining he had brought an open carriage driven by Ned, one of the grooms from the Hall. He, himself, had ridden Sir Galahad and on arriving at the Grange he had suggested that Annabel might like to join them on the trip as his mother had mentioned that if Lady Annabel was available, could he give her a message.

"My mother has made a list of possible persons to whom you could extend an invitation should you decide to have a little gathering of your own for afternoon tea" Alex informed her "she also thought you might welcome some company as would Imogen should Louise decide to accompany us" His sister had enquired as to whether Louise would be coming as well.

Annabel was delighted to accept and grateful for the diversion but was concerned that Ellen would be left on her own. Ellen however was more than happy to potter in the extensive gardens as she had only a small cobbled yard at the rear of her own house so she encouraged her sister-in-law to go "You go off and enjoy the afternoon and I'll see you when you return".

Annabel then sent for Louise who was overjoyed at the prospect of spending time with her new friend Imogen again. Alex helped the ladies into the carriage and Oliver clambered up by himself and soon they were on their way.

They soon arrived at the Hall and Fenton the butler was there to welcome them.

The Enchanted Glade

"Let's go to see mother first" Alex suggested as he instructed the groom to make ready the two horses that they had discussed earlier for the children to ride.

They then entered the house and Lavinia was in the drawing room waiting with Imogen. "I'm so glad you could come" she beamed as she saw Annabel and Louise. "what a wonderful afternoon we'll have".

"Mother, may Louise and I go into the garden" Imogen asked.

"Certainly, my dear, it's such a lovely day maybe Annabel and I will sit out on the terrace also".

"That would be very pleasant" Annabel smiled. She always felt so welcome whenever she visited Lavinia and even more comfortable because William wasn't here.

Alex gestured to Cissy and Oliver, bade his mother farewell for the moment and took the two excited youngsters to the extensive stables in the grounds of the Hall.

Cissy was so eager to meet Velvet and as soon as she saw the splendid little horse she knew that they would be the best of friends.

"Hello, girl, how beautiful you are" the little horse snorted just as if she knew what Cissy was saying to her " I have been so looking forward to meeting you" Cissy whispered as she smoothed the little horse's deep brown coat which felt just like velvet. When she mentioned this to Alex he informed her that that was how the little mare had acquired her name in the first instance. Oliver's pony was called Oscar and he was grey and white. This particular pony was smaller than Velvet and had been chosen for the little lad because of it's agreeable disposition.

Billy Curtis the stable manager handed them some carrots to feed to the horses .

"I'm very nervous" said Cissy, grimacing and she glanced towards Alex for some support.

"Just hold your hand completely flat and she won't hurt you" Alex said as he held her hand out flat to demonstrate the way to feed carrots to horses.

Both children were a mite anxious but very soon their confidence increased.

"Right, now it's time for your first lesson". Alex saw that Cissy winced a little.

"It's perfectly natural to be apprehensive" Alex observed with a smile "look here Cissy, Billy has put a very soft saddle on for you". It was lined with sheepskin and she was very grateful. Billy placed some wooden steps along side Velvet and she carefully climbed up and then mounted "Are you comfortable, my Lady" Billy enquired, aware of his station.

"Yes, thank you very much, Billy. May I call you Billy?".

"That's alright by me, my lady" he grinned.

Cissy sat side-saddle at first because it felt more comfortable and the stable master then helped Oliver onto his horse. After about an hour gently leading and then allowing them to take the reins and ride slowly around the field, Alex suggested that they go back to the house for some refreshment so they cautiously rode back to the stables and as they were dismounting Billy asked them if they had enjoyed themselves.

"Oh! Billy, it was breathtaking" exclaimed Cissy "May we do it again soon, my Lord" She looked at Alex as she spoke. She didn't want to call him by his first name in front of his servant.

"If you're really enthusiastic about it and I'm not too busy, maybe we could make it a regular thing".

"Oh, could we Alex, could we please?" she was so excited that she'd forgotten herself and called him by his given name but Billy didn't seem to notice and if he did he was very discreet about it.

After saying goodbye to the horses and Billy they made their way back to the house and ecstatically told their mother

The Enchanted Glade

about their exciting adventure and also that his lordship had said they could come again.

"I trust they haven't been too much of a bother, my Lord" Annabel asked Alex.

"They have been a delight to spend time with and very easy to teach and Cissy especially took to handling Velvet with consummate ease. And please, Lady Annabel would you call me Alex. I really do prefer it".

"As you wish, my Lord, sorry, Alex" she answered with a beaming smile. She herself had had a wonderfully pleasing visit with Lavinia and as they waited for tea to be served they arranged for Alex to call the following Saturday to bring the children to the Hall for more instruction.

After tea Alex called for the carriage to take them back and although exhausted they had enjoyed a very pleasurable afternoon.

The next week passed quite speedily for Cissy, as on the Monday she went back to stay with Aunt Ellen for a few days and didn't return home until the Friday afternoon. She had had a wonderful time.

When Saturday did arrive Alex, riding Sir Galahad, came as promised and again brought the carriage driven by Ned, the groom.

"Ready" he asked an excited Cissy and looking around as he dismounted he enquired "where's young Oliver?"

They suddenly realised that Oliver had disappeared and Cissy remembered he had wandered over to the lake as they waited impatiently for Alex to arrive. She was hurrying across the lawn and over the bridge to call her brother when a sudden gust of wind took her bonnet and it flew from her head and lodged on the parapet of the bridge. She leaned over to reach it but went too far and although Alex had been watching her it wasn't until she screamed as she over-balanced and fell into the water that he speedily re-mounted Sir Galahad and galloped to her aid.

Cissy couldn't swim and was terrified as the murky water engulfed her. She was screaming his name as he reached the lake and leapt off his horse and tearing his jacket from his body, he plunged into the water. He swam for all he was worth to reach her. She had almost disappeared when he caught her arm and pulled her almost lifeless body towards him. Then holding her head well above the surface of the water as he swam, he made for the bank. "Please God let Cissy live" he prayed, he wasn't sure if she was breathing or not and then he heard a slight murmur and he felt elated. As he carried her out of the water they were both gasping for breath and water was pouring from Cissy's mouth as she coughed. He laid her onto the grass, face down at first and then he cradled her in his arms and as she began to recover he looked into her beautiful, although very wet and bedraggled, little face and smiled with relief "Are you all right, my little princess, I thought I'd lost you then".

She was coughing and spluttering as she spoke and looking directly into his eyes she whispered "I'll always be alright as long as I'm with you, Alex". Knowing she was safe in his arms she slowly closed her eyes and felt herself drift off into unconsciousness.

Her mother was beside herself as she ran towards them. She had sent Louise to get help although Alex's groom had followed her as she sped across the lawn towards the lake as fast as she could. "Oh, my baby, please dear Lord let her be safe". She saw that Alex was holding Cissy as they lay on the grass both breathing heavily and she realised that her daughter was alive."Oh, Thank God, is she unharmed".

"Don't worry, my Lady, I think she's just feeling very weak after her ordeal and I think she has just fainted. Let's get her back to the house as quickly as possible. I think our riding lesson will have to be postponed for today".

Just then Oliver came bounding back over the bridge wondering what all the commotion was about and was quite

The Enchanted Glade

astonished to see what had transpired whilst he had been exploring.

The groom assisted with carrying the invalid back to the house and was then sent back to Amberley Hall with a message for Lady Lavinia telling her not to worry and explaining the reason for the delay. Alex stayed until he was sure his little friend was fully recovered and Harris the butler attended him in removing his wet clothes and finding some alternative attire which belonged to the master. Although they were rather large for Alex at least they were dry.

Before he was due to leave he asked the butler if he could see Cissy's mother.

Harris went to Lady Annabel's sitting room and knocked. She bade him enter and he enquired if she was available to see Lord Kingsley.

"Of course, Ambrose, show his Lordship in immediately".

Alex entered and nodded his head in a slight bow. When she saw him dressed in her husband's clothes, she put her hand to her mouth but failed miserably to suppress the giggle that emerged.

Alex also smiled but he was more concerned with Cissy

"Lady Annabel, is Cissy improved?"

"I think she's going to be fine. She is so disappointed that she won't be going to Amberley today. Alex, how can I ever thank you for saving her".

"You don't need to thank me, it was down to me that she was out there in the first place. Could I please see her before I go?"

"Certainly, we'll go up together".

Cissy was safely tucked up in bed after Alice had given her a soothing hot bath and she had changed into her dry night-shift. Her mother had sent for Doctor Bartholomew just to convince herself that her daughter was recovering satisfactorily.

The doctor had just arrived as Annabel and Alex emerged from her sitting room and the three of them ascended the stairs together to see how Cissy was feeling.

After a short examination the doctor spoke to Annabel "I would advise that you keep her in bed for the rest of today, my Lady, she should be well by the morning. I have given her something to relieve the feeling of sickness. Poor little child she's had a rough few weeks of it hasn't she?" the doctor noticed the veritably painful look on her mother's face as he spoke.

Annabel looked uneasily towards Alex hoping he hadn't heard what the doctor had said. Just then Emily knocked the door, she had brought some piping hot soup for Cissy and she stopped abruptly as she entered . "Oh! Beggin' your pardon, Milady, I thought Miss Cissy would like somethin' warm inside 'er".

Annabel was glad of the distraction "Please come in Mrs Bridges, I'm sure she would love some". Annabel rang for the butler and the doctor bid them all farewell and as he was leaving he asked to have a few quiet words with her.

"Are you well, my lady, you look extremely pale and you appear rather tired. Is there anything I can do for you?" he sounded very sympathetic.

Annabel held back a tear, she had only met the good doctor twice and he was more concerned about her than her own husband. "I am well thank you, Doctor, I think it was the move and the shock of what has happened to Cissy these last few weeks".

The doctor gently patted her arm and said "I understand, but please know that I am here any time you need me".

"I'll remember that" she said as she looked deeply into his soft brown eyes for the first time and noticed how kindly he observed her.

"Now, I must be off " he spoke abruptly "I have many more patients to see today. You were lucky to catch me and I'm sure your daughter will be fine".

The Enchanted Glade

"Thank you once again" she said, with a smile, as Harris came to escort the doctor to the door . John Bartholomew then nodded in response and left the room.

Cissy was so pleased to see Alex and as he came to sit beside her she thanked him for saving her "That's the second time you've rescued me".

He quietly whispered "Well don't make a habit of it. I got soaking wet and now look at me" he indicated the outsized attire and laughed as he did so.

"I'm so sorry to be such an annoyance to you, Alex, and I was so looking forward to coming to Amberley with you today and seeing Velvet again" Cissy appeared quite serious.

"Don't worry we can make it next weekend if your parents are agreeable" and he tweaked her cheek as he shot her a comforting smile.

"Excuse me, Lord Kingsley, could Cissy 'ave this while it's still 'ot?" it was Emily, still standing patiently on the other side of the bed, with the soup. She moved forward and placed the tray on Cissy's lap and whilst Cissy ate it, Emily turned to speak to Alex. "I don't know what I would 'ave done if anything 'ad 'appened to little Miss Cissy, Sir" she was so relieved that her little friend was feeling better.

"Well please don't worry, Mrs Bridges, she's all right now". As Cissy was finishing her soup she gazed lovingly at Alex and Emmy and as they conversed the thought occurred to her that, apart from her mother, these two people in front of her were the most important in her life at present and the ones that she felt most comfortable with.

****

Chapter 5

Five years later, April 1811

As Louise is almost eighteen years old she is to have her come-out ball in July. The invitations had been prepared and sent and all of the other preparations are well underway. According to her father, Cissy, at fifteen and a half isn't old enough to attend so her mother has insisted that she be allowed to help with the arrangements. The ball will be held at Monkton Grange and no expense will be spared.

It is Easter now and a few weeks ago Annabel had been informed by Rose, the housekeeper that every Bank Holiday Monday the family and staff used to arrange a picnic to Greene Hollow, a local beauty spot. It was a yearly treat and the whole household usually participated. But the old master had stopped it after his wife had died and the staff would be so grateful if the tradition could be reinstated. Emily always cooked all the food on the Sunday, Rose said, and the staff went ahead to the picnic spot and prepared everything. They would take tables and chairs, tablecloths, crockery and cutlery and they'd always had a wonderful day out.
Annabel had always taken care of her servants and she wouldn't deprive them of this treat although she couldn't imagine what her husband would say about it as he absolutely hated the servants and wanted no dealings with any of them whatsoever.

The Enchanted Glade

The Bank Holiday morning arrived and all was prepared. Annabel was rather dubious due to the fact that her husband had not returned from his club the night before, so just as she thought, he obviously would not be coming to the picnic. They set off, everyone in a jovial mood and it wasn't until they had arrived that Cissy asked Emily where Minnie was.

"She's gone to visit 'er sister, as 'er mother wasn't well an' so I baked a few things for 'er to take wiv 'er. She's a good little soul, a mite backward but she 'as a good 'eart, and she always does as I tells 'er".

Cissy asked Emily if she could help with the food but Emily wouldn't allow it "You must remember that you are growin' up now an' you're a lady. You're goin' to 'ave to start actin' like one. You can't 'elp wiv the food that just ain't done, you just go an' enjoy yourself, me chick". Emily gave Cissy a little squeeze on her arm and looked kindly into her eyes. "I'm goin' to ave' to start callin' you milady soon, but old 'abits die 'ard as they say and I know I'm not goin' to find that very easy. I think of you as me own, Cissy". Cissy looked back at her faithful friend and said with the utmost sincerity "I love you, my darling Emmy, as if you were my own mother. I will never forget what you have done for me since I came to Monkton Grange and I won't mind if you call Cissy forever" a stray tear trickled down her cheek.

"Now don't you go startin' me off wiv them tears or I won't be fit for nuthin'" Emily smiled "Go on, off you go then an' I'll be seein' you presently".

Emily watched as Cissy walked over to the others and the tears started rolling down her cheeks and just wouldn't stop. She had so wanted a family of her own but fate had not been kind to her and she had never had any children. Her mind then wandered back to the time when as a young girl she was full of expectations. She remembered when she was first married and she and her new husband had moved into a tied cottage on the farm where he was employed. Less than one year after they had married he had died in an accident during the harvest and she had lost the cottage to the family of his successor. The owners of the farm had been very sympathetic but she had to survive so she had been forced to take any job she could as long as it was a live-in position. She had felt very lucky when she had successfully acquired the job she still held at the Grange and had been there for about twenty years now. Although she didn't care for the master she loved Lady Annabel and the children. Cissy was her favourite and they had been the best of friends since that first day. "Pull yourself together, Emily Bridges" she chided herself as she retrieved a handkerchief from her pocket to wipe her eyes, it was almost time to serve luncheon.

Everyone relished the cold ham and beef, cheese and salad, cold new potatoes, meat patties in delicious pastry and freshly made bread with newly churned butter. Then they all enjoyed jelly and blancmange and an abundance of fancy cakes that Emily had made the day before.

After the meal several of the servants joined in the playing of games whilst others looked on with jollity. Then whilst the servants were packing up the family took a walk to the top of the hill to take in the panoramic view which was recognized locally as legendary.

Cissy and Oliver forged on ahead and their mother called after them to take care and not tire themselves too much.

"I'll race you to the top, Cissy" Oliver teased and although she ran as fast as she could she couldn't keep up with him and he won the challenge.

When she reached the summit she could see rolling hills sweeping down to a lush green valley with a quaint little stream meandering through it. "It really is so beautiful up here. I think I can see further than I ever have before"

To the left were fertile meadows and suddenly she spotted some movement "Oliver, look a herd of wild deer. Have you ever seen as many as that at any one time before?"

"Never" answered her brother "I wish we were nearer then we would be able to observe them at closer proximity. Do you think Father will allow us to come to see them one day".

"I doubt that very much" Cissy sounded quite sure on that point.

"Then perhaps Alex could bring us when we go out riding with him again" uttered Oliver hopefully

"We could ask him" she answered and glancing over to the right she spied an old house which looked uninhabited as the grounds were very overgrown and the gate looked as if it hadn't been opened for years. "I wonder who lived over there".

"The Greene family" their mother's voice came from behind them. She had caught up with them and had overheard their conversation. "Rose told me all about them earlier. They were renowned in this area for their affluence and then their son invested highly in some new business enterprise which failed and then there were several family scandals which eventually led to their downfall. So let that be a lesson to you Oliver! When you grow up you must only take advise from people you trust or you may end up like the Greene family" her voice sounded very cynical. The two children just looked at one another and Cissy stifled a chuckle.

They spent some time taking in the view and then their mother indicated that as they had quite a long journey ahead of them they had better make their way back to the carriages. When they got back the servants had finished loading so they boarded the carriage and made themselves as comfortable as possible and then set off for home. As Cissy closed her eyes she thought back and decided it had been a very exhausting, but exciting day.

Meanwhile earlier that same afternoon Minnie had returned to the house sooner than she had expected. She let herself in by the scullery door, removed her hat and coat and hung them up on the peg behind it. She was preparing something to eat for herself when she heard the sound of the service bell to the master's study. She ignored it because she knew everyone was out and she presumed the master had gone with the others on the outing, also it was not her job as scullery maid to answer the bell calls. She was on her way up to her room about fifteen minutes later when she encountered a very irate Sir William. He bellowed "Where the blazes is everybody?"

Minnie faced him but her eyes were lowered to the floor, she knew he hated the servants and she was terrified of him.

"Beggin' yer pardon, Sir , but they be all gone out" she dipped a curtsey, turned and hurried away up the servants staircase.

"Don't you walk away from me before you've been dismissed, you insolent little chit" he hollered and with that he proceeded to chase after her up the stairs. He reached her room and she tried to hold the door closed but he was too strong for her and he barged in, causing her to fall backwards onto the floor.

She screamed as he pulled her up and he caught her by the throat to silence her "Shut up you little guttersnipe or I'll strangle you" He let go of her neck but as she struggled to free herself he ripped her dress and then tore the rest of her clothes from her body. He threw her, naked, onto her bed and removed most of his lower clothing .

Little did she know that Sir William had spent the night before at his club and the appealing courtesan he had taken there had been well worth the guinea he'd paid for her services but she had whetted his appetite for more and the unfortunate little scullery maid was now his victim.

She was cowering on the bed and she knew he was drunk because she had smelt the stench of alcohol on his breath as soon as he had confronted her in the corridor but she was very naïve and although she was now seventeen years old she still had no notion as to what her master's vile intentions were. As he crawled onto her bed and began groping her she screamed again so he put his hand over her mouth to silence her. She tried to struggle but it was futile, his weight was almost crushing her and she couldn't breathe. With his other hand he forced her legs apart and he then proceeded to thrust his enormous manhood into the innocent little virgin. As the house was empty, there was no-one there to hear her bloodcurdling screams as Sir William brutally raped the defenceless little maid. The more she screamed the more pleasure he took. After he had satisfied his rampant lust he left the distraught young girl sobbing uncontrollably in a pool of blood.

And that was how Cissy found her. After everyone had returned from Greene Hollow she had decided to go straight upstairs. She always used the back stairs because it was the quickest way to her room and as she reached the bottom of the stairs to the servant's quarters she heard someone crying hysterically. She rushed up to investigate and as she went into Minnie's room she almost collapsed herself. If Minnie hadn't been sobbing Cissy would have thought she was dead there was so much blood.

"Minnie, what happened?" asked Cissy earnestly but Minnie seemed as if she was struck dumb. "I'll get some help".

Cissy ran down the stairs and happened upon her mother who was making her way to her own room. "Mama, quickly we must get some help for Minnie, she's naked in her bed and I think she's dying".

"Whatever are you talking about, Cissy?" there was a distinct look of confusion on Annabel's face.

"Please, Mama, please hurry, there's lots of blood" Cissy gasped, her voice full of panic.

"Go quickly and fetch Mrs Bridges and ask her to come at once and bring some towels and bandages. I'll go on up"

Cissy ran as fast as her legs would carry her to the kitchen.

"Emmy, Emmy you must come at once, its Minnie, she's hurt. My mother asks that you bring some bandages, oh and towels".

"Minnie?" said Emily puzzled as she went to the housekeeper's store cupboard "I didn't know she was back". Emily beckoned to Cissy to hold out her hands and she handed her lint, bandages and towels "will you 'elp me carry this up, me chick" Emily had no hot water ready so she filled a basin with cold.

"Please hurry, Emmy, I'm really frightened for her".

Lady Annabel suspected what had transpired as soon as she entered the room and saw the scene of carnage. "What happened, Minnie?"

Minnie couldn't speak and just looked so pathetic that Annabel felt extremely sorry for her.

"Poor, poor girl" Annabel whispered trying herself to hold back the furious feelings inside as she covered the little maid's naked body with a sheet. "Minnie, I need to talk to you. Please don't tell anyone what has happened until I get back. Mrs Bridges is coming to help you".

At that moment Emily and Cissy arrived on the scene.

"Cissy, Mrs Bridges and I will deal with this, will you please ring for Ambrose at once and ask him to call the doctor"

"Mama, is Minnie going to be alright?" By now Cissy was immensely worried.

"Quickly, Cissy, do as I have asked you, now!" her mother ordered "The quicker we get the doctor here the sooner we shall know". Cissy hurried away to do as her mother had requested.

"Mrs Bridges?"

Emily was totally shocked and stood rooted to the spot with her mouth open "Milady?" she said as if in a daze, and then she hastily went to Minnie to comfort her.

"I know what this looks like but we mustn't jump to conclusions" Annabel pleaded.

The Enchanted Glade

"Beggin' your pardon, milady, but I think we'd be bet'er seein' to the little maid than talkin'" Emily had also guessed what had happened.

Annabel asked Emily to excuse her for a moment and she quickly made her way down the stairs and along the first floor corridor to her husband's bed chamber. She was absolutely sickened by the incident and was determined to get to the bottom of it. If her husband had played a part in the defilement of the little maid, and she half suspected that he had, she couldn't afford a scandal. She entered without knocking but he wouldn't have heard even if she had knocked because he was laid on the bed unconscious. He had no trousers on and the rest of his attire was dishevelled and she saw all she needed to, to know that he was obviously responsible for what had happened to Minnie. The immense sadness she felt tore at her heartstrings. She knew it had been her own choice but what had she done in her life to merit being saddled with a man like William. She knew about the courtesans and the light skirts but this was too close to home and she was totally distraught. She rang for his valet, Horace Brett, and when he arrived she asked him to deal with the situation and keep a tight lip about it. She then left the room, broken-hearted, and returned along the corridor and back up the stairs to Minnie's room.

By the time the doctor had arrived downstairs Emily had washed the terrified girl and Annabel had asked the cook to arrange with Rose, the housekeeper, to get the bed linen changed.

"Don't you think the good Doctor will be wantin' to see 'er as she is, Milady?"

"Please ask Mrs Higgins to change the linen as soon as possible, Mrs Bridges, I'm sure Minnie will be more comfortable however we will keep soiled linen here for the moment".

Emily left the room to fetch Rose and the clean linen which gave Annabel the opportunity to talk in private to the scullery maid.

"How are you feeling, Minnie" Annabel asked sympathetically "Can you tell me what happened?"

Minnie fought back the tears as she managed to whisper

"T'wer the master M'um and 'e were very cruel to me. I dunno what 'e done but 'e 'urt me bad" she began sobbing again.

"Minnie, listen very carefully to what I am saying" and with that Annabel proceeded with her plan to offer her money to keep quiet. Just as Annabel was saying "But don't forget Minnie, we only have an agreement if you keep your part of the bargain" Minnie was nodding, "so not a word to anyone" there was a knock at the door. "Come" she directed and as she caught Minnie's eye she put her index finger up to her mouth and said "Shh" and with that the little maid acknowledged her mistress' actions with a nod.

"Your Ladyship, Doctor Bartholomew is here" the butler spoke as he ushered the doctor into the room, followed by Emily, and then he left.

"What happened?" The doctor enquired, looking directly at Annabel.

"I think she has been raped" Annabel's voice wavered.

John Bartholomew only had to look at Annabel's painful expression to know she knew more than she was saying but he set about helping his patient directly.

After a careful examination and re-assurance that Minnie was a little more comfortable the doctor asked to speak to Annabel alone so they left Minnie with Emily and proceeded down to Annabel's private sitting room.

As he followed her down the stairs he noticed how upright she held herself as she walked in front of him, almost as if this nightmare had not happened. He had moved in the same social circles as Annabel for the last five years and they were now very well acquainted. He knew exactly what she had endured at the hands of her cruel husband. But if her husband was ostracized then so would she be and he was sure that would kill her. She was well respected in her own right in the community, she was appointed to many well connected committees, and she carried out a great deal of charity work and was welcomed in the most prestigious circles. No way was he going to jeopardise her standing in the pinnacles of society as he sincerely felt that she had already suffered enough. Everyone knew that indiscretions often occurred within the confines of large households but vicious rape was a completely different matter.

When he had closed the door behind them he approached her and she recognized the fury in his expression. "It is blatantly obvious to me that you are fully aware of exactly what has transpired, Annabel"

"Please, John" she pleaded "I cannot take much more" she faltered and almost keeled over. He rushed to her side and helped her to the chair as she continued "This can't get out, it will ruin us".

"Is he worth saving?" John Bartholomew was furious

"Where the hell is he? I want to kill him myself but he isn't worth my going to the gallows".

She told him that her husband was in his bed-chamber and also mentioned the state in which she had found him. She stood up and walked towards the window. "You know my life with him is hell" she threw the comment over her shoulder "I thought it couldn't get much worse but now this! I have spoken to the maid and she is to be compensated for her discretion" she turned around to face him wringing her hands as she was talking.

He had walked towards her and as he reached her he could see the pain in her eyes. He put his hands out and held her shoulders and looked at her so tenderly "You know that it is only my respect for you that stops me taking this further".

"I know and thank you" she whispered, tears forming in the back of her eyes as they lowered to the floor. " I feel so ashamed".

"What have you to be ashamed of?" he exclaimed.

"The servants are my responsibility" she retorted sharply "and if I cannot protect them from events such as this then I am a very poor employer" she glanced at him as she spoke and he noticed that her normally beautiful eyes were now full of misery and sadness.

"But you cannot be held responsible for what he did when you weren't even here in the house when it happened. Annabel, please don't blame yourself" he had left her side now and was pacing up and down as if thinking as he talked.

"You will make yourself ill and that won't help matters at all" he came back to face her "I cannot bear to see you so terribly distressed".

If anything it was the pity she saw in his eyes at that moment that distressed her as he continued. "I so admire your immense courage, being married to a heartless beast in a loveless marriage yet you still hold yourself with dignity and exist in a state of affairs that anyone with the strongest of resolve could not endure".

"You have never been married, John?" she enquired, raising one eyebrow as she spoke.

"No" he looked towards her dubiously.

"Then how can you possibly comment on it". She sounded rather aloof "You live in that big house on your own" then gazing directly at him she asked " Is there any reason why you have never married?"

"The only person I have ever loved, Annabel, was not free to marry me". He sounded so miserable that at that moment she actually pitied him. "and as there is no-one else in my life I have resigned myself to the fact that I will probably die a bachelor with only my old housekeeper for company" he was smiling faintly to lighten the tension in the air.

As he spoke in the past tense she presumed that this 'love' did not feature in his life anymore. Little did she know.

"I'm sorry" she said sympathetically, then trying to change the subject she added "Could we please try to forget that this terrible occurrence has happened for the time being. I am so very worried that if any of this gets out it may cause a scandal and have a devastating effect on Louise's coming out and that would be inconceivable. I know her party is not for another three months but I can only pray that all this has died down by then. You've received your invitation?" she skilfully changed the subject.

"Yes, thank you kindly, although I will probably feel rather out of place amongst all the young bucks" he tried to smile and she noticed he had kindly eyes that crinkled at the edges each time he did so.

" Please come, you may find somebody who takes your eye there. I hate the thought of you living alone in that big house of yours when there may be someone somewhere who could give you the love you deserve"

His eyes darkened as they looked deeply into hers. "You may be right, Annabel, we'll have to wait and see" he said with a heavy heart. "Well, I really must take my leave of you now as I have several more patients to visit today. Promise me you'll take care and let me know at once if I can be of assistance to you in any way".

"I will, and John thank you so much for your constant understanding".

"I'll call in to see Minnie again tomorrow" and with a swift bow he saw himself out .

Annabel was actually quite relieved when he had left as the feeling of unease in the room had become substantially intense. Although she welcomed his support, as she was unable to unburden her misery on anyone else, she felt that sometimes the good doctor took too personal an interest in her life. Then she thought no matter what was wrong in her life she was so lucky to have him as a friend.

Later that day Cissy knocked on the door of her mother's sitting room . "Come" her mother called not knowing who was there.
Cissy was surprised to see that her mother had been crying "Mama, are you unwell?"
"Oh it's you Cissy, no, I am alright" she put her handkerchief to her nose and sniffed a little "Just a slight cold, I think, it should be gone by tomorrow".
"I was wondering how Minnie was"
"Doctor Bartholomew will be here again in the morning to see her. I think she'll be confined to her bed for a few days and then we'll know a little more. I think it will be best if she doesn't have any visitors just yet".
Cissy thought her mother didn't seem very concerned about it, maybe she was wrong.
"Now Cissy we must carry on with the arrangements for Louise's come-out" Annabel was becoming increasingly proficient in changing the subject when it suited her and was trying to think of anything to distract Cissy from talking about Minnie. "I'll ring for Ambrose and ask him if we had any more replies whilst we were out today and then we can update the guest list"
"Very well, Mother".
To Annabel's relief it seemed to do the trick.

For the next couple of months Cissy went to see Minnie almost every day and the little maid seemed to be growing stronger. She was back doing menial tasks in the kitchen and appeared to have almost gotten over her ordeal.
When she went to Minnie's room one particular day she was surprised to see her packing a small trunk so she asked her why.
"I be leavin' to go an' stay wiv' me sister for a while 'cause the doctor says I'm goin' to 'ave a babby an' 'er ladyship says I can't stay 'ere no more".

The Enchanted Glade

"Oh, Minnie, this is all the fault of the person who hurt you, can you please tell me who it was?"

"No, Miss Cissy, I can't say, 'er ladyship says if I tells anyone I won't be gettin' any money from 'er an' I needs it for me an' the babby, you see"

"What money?" Cissy enquired.

"I'm to 'ave five pounds now and two pounds every year to 'elp wiv' food an' clothes for us both". For a scullery maid who earned one shilling and sixpence a week this was a fortune.

"I'll miss you, Minnie. You will let me know how you go along won't you?"

"Oh, I will, Miss Cissy. Mrs Bridges will come to visit me, she promised".

"Well maybe I could visit with her one day".

"I'd like that", Milady".

Cissy embraced Minnie and then left the room.

Poor Minnie, she thought, although she was seventeen she was very young and childish for her age and now she was going to have a baby. Cissy's heart went out to the little maid. She made her way to her mother's sitting room and tapped the door.

"Come" said her mother.

"Mama, Minnie has just told me she is leaving"

"Yes, I think it's for the best" Annabel couldn't look her daughter in the eye.

"But why? She's told me about the baby" Cissy was old enough to know the basic facts of life and she wasn't a fool.

"Then you've answered your own question Cissy, we can't have servants with babies here"

"But why is she to be paid money to go?"

"She told you about the money?" her mother sounded astonished.

"Yes but she won't tell me who gave her the baby, she says it has to be kept a secret".

"Cissy, please leave it be, it really is of no concern of yours".

"It may not concern me, Mama, but that does not stop me being concerned about it. I am not brainless and even though I am young it's not hard to put two and two together and fathom out what happened to Minnie".

"Please, Cissy, please don't say any more" her mother was almost pleading.

"It was father wasn't it? That's why you were crying that day I came to see you and asked about Minnie. Oh Mama, I am so very sorry"

"Cissy this cannot get out or we will be ruined, we must keep it a closely guarded secret. I know I can rely on your discretion for all our sakes. When Minnie leaves we will have to forget all about her"

"But the baby will be related to us, surely you can't ignore that".

"I know you're growing up now, Cissy, but there are things you still don't understand just yet. You will do when you are a little older but now we must be sensible about this. Think of Louise. We must concentrate on giving her a successful come-out and we can't do that unless we give it our wholehearted attention. The party is in a little over two weeks which doesn't give us much time to finalise everything. You know that Louise and I have an appointment with the modiste this coming week for the final fitting for our gowns".

"Yes, Mama, I understand what you are saying" and with that Cissy, feeling completely down-hearted, left the room and went for a long walk in the garden.

On her way back she came through the kitchen.

"How are you today?" Emily tried to sound bright and breezy. "Oh my, you look like you lost a sixpence and found a penny, me little chick". She smiled but that did nothing to raise Cissy's spirits.

"Oh, Emmy, why do we sometimes have to keep secrets, especially other peoples"

"We all 'ave secrets, me chick, some are of others and some are personal which we keep 'idden deep inside our very

The Enchanted Glade

souls but sometimes tis bet'er for everyone if we keep silent about 'em even if we don't think tis right" Emily knew exactly what Cissy was referring to.

Cissy knew Emily was right in what she said and realised that this was all part of the hard lesson of growing up.

****

Chapter 6

The house was the centre of expeditious activity during the next two weeks and at last the day of Louise's come-out ball had arrived. The ballroom was decked out with an abundance of flowers and colourful garlands and the servants had worked so very hard cleaning the whole room from top to bottom. The floor was polished and, after a thorough clean, the sparkle from the crystal droplets on the chandelier almost lit it up without the candles. Emily had supervised the preparing of all the food and Cissy, well, she felt like the proverbial bad penny. She was not allowed to go to the party and as the day wore on she began to feel very morose. She tried to cheer up for Louise's sake and when the time came for her sister to get dressed she asked if she could help. However Louise's maid, Polly, was there to prepare her for probably the most important day of her life so far. So Cissy just watched and marvelled at the transformation of her sister into a beautiful debutante.

Louise did not appear to be the least bit excited which baffled Cissy somewhat. "You look wonderful, Lulu" Cissy said referring to the pet name which Oliver had called their sister ever since he was a small boy. "I wish it was my come-out party".

"I wish it was yours too, Cissy" her sister answered quite curtly.

"Are you not looking forward to it?". Cissy asked frowning.

"Not really, all this to-do just to hopefully marry me off to someone I neither know nor will ever love" Louise sounded very downhearted.

The Enchanted Glade

"But Lulu, you may meet someone whom you will come to love" said her sister, optimistic as ever.

"I very much doubt it".

Now Cissy thought Louise sounded really negative. Poor Lulu, she mused, wondering whatever had prompted this look of sadness that was so evident in her sister's face.

At that moment their mother entered the room looking absolutely stunning herself.

"Oh, Mama, you look beautiful".

"Thank you, Cissy. Louise are you almost ready? Everyone has arrived and your father has sent me to fetch you. He will be at the top of the stairs in five minutes to escort you down to the ballroom".

"I don't feel well, Mother" Louise was almost in tears as she took a cotton handkerchief from the drawer and blew her nose.

"Oh, you are just feeling a little nervous as you've never done this before. Now we don't want to keep your father waiting do we? Please don't cry or you will smudge your rouge. Polly could you quickly put some more carmine on her lips, I'm sure you've just wiped it half off and try to stop fretting dearest".

"I'll try, Mother" Louise mumbled, and composing herself as best she could she rose to her feet, turned and walked towards the door looking like a lamb going into a lion's den, as she made her way to the top of the stairs.

Cissy watched from the doorway as her sister in a stunningly attractive taffeta gown in shimmering lilac walked towards their father. The flowing train, dropping from her trim waist, brushed the floor as she went. Her diamond jewellery sparkled at her neck, ears and wrist and her feathered headdress, glittering with diamantes, shone in the candlelight as she took her father's arm and they started down the staircase, closely followed by their mother. Cissy couldn't stand the disappointment of not going and went sullenly to her room and laid flat on her back in bed staring up at the drapes. She closed her eyes and tried to imagine the awe-inspiring scene.

After a little while she heard the music and decided to creep along the upstairs corridor to peep through the door of the balcony overlooking the ballroom. There were two balconies upstairs in the ballroom, one at either end. The small orchestra was at one end and Cissy quietly opened the door of the opposite one, let herself in and silently closing the door behind her she laid down on the floor. She was leaning on her elbows with her hands under her chin looking through the railings. She marvelled at the spectacle and watched as the couples danced merrily together and then she saw Alex. He was dancing with a very pretty lady and Cissy unexpectedly felt a slight wrench in her breast which she didn't really understand. As he swirled his partner around the room Cissy was wishing that it was herself in his arms, so she closed her eyes for a moment imagining his strong arm around her own waist and his other hand clasping hers. Suddenly Alex glanced up and Cissy caught her breath as their eyes met. He smiled and her heart almost melted. She adored his smile, it never failed to touch her heart.

When Alex had heard that she was not allowed to attend her sister's party he had felt so sorry for her, so as he saw her irresistible twinkling eyes peeping through the railings, he was so glad that she had stolen a few moments to enjoy the festivities.

Cissy was terribly upset that she had been discovered observing the merriment, so she immediately rose to her feet and crept out of the balcony door because if Alex had seen her then her father could so easily have and she didn't think she could stand his wrath if he had found her there.

She returned to her room and prepared herself for bed but then decided to sit in her armchair and read a book to take her mind off of the proceedings. After a few hours curled up in the chair she realised that several of the coaches drawing up to the front door were assembling to take the guests home. She knew Alex and his family were staying the night, as was Aunt Ellen, and she was looking forward to seeing them all at breakfast in the morning. Very soon the evening would be over so she decided to go to bed.

The excitement of everything that had occurred in the house that night was still on her mind as she tried so hard to get to sleep. She was restless and began tossing and turning in her bed. As it was a very hot and clammy night she had left the window open slightly and had not yet drawn the curtains. She knew she was not going to settle down so she got up and walked towards the window. The rolling hills in the distance were basking in the moonlight which was especially bright tonight and as she gazed up out into the darkness she saw thousands of stars sparkling like a blanket of diamonds in the sky. What an amazing sight she thought, as she put on her slippers and turned towards the door. She then opened the door of her room very gently and closed it as silently as she could behind her, then she crept quietly along the passage and down the stairs. It was well after midnight and as some of the servants were still cleaning the ballroom after the party she took the corridor to the left wing and tiptoed through the library. She let herself out of one of the French windows taking great care to see that she left it unlocked so that she could get back in when she returned later.

A cloud suddenly covered the light from the moon so she quickly crossed the lawn to the lake side. It was such a beautiful night .

Alex was undressing near the window in one of the guest rooms above the library. His room was at the end of the corridor so it directly overlooked the lawn and the lake. He suddenly glimpsed a flash of white reflected in the light as the moon emerged from behind a cloud. He strained to look and thought he was seeing things. Cissy? Surely it couldn't be. He looked again. Whatever was she up to now!

He quickly and quietly went downstairs and once outside he crossed the lawn. As he came to the lake he saw Cissy lost in her own little dream world dancing with an imaginary partner. He wondered if there was a limit to Cissy's unpredictability.

He didn't mean to startle her but as he called her name she jumped out of her dreamlike state.

"Whatever are you thinking of, Cissy, coming out here in the middle of the night in your night clothes".

"Oh, Alex, thank goodness it's you" she sighed dreamily.

"I was just dancing with the moon and the stars. Just look up at the sky, Alex, it's all so dazzling and I feel so free out here on my own" she then looked at him "oh, how I loved watching all of those stunningly beautiful ladies in their finery tonight and how lucky they were to be dancing with you, Alex".

Alex's knew how disappointed Cissy had been to miss the ball and his eyes softened into a smile as he said tenderly

"Come here, Cissy". He held both of his hands out to her. As she walked towards him he couldn't tear his eyes away from her and he noticed that the light from the moon was picking out the golden streaks in her beautiful titian hair. Suddenly he realised that Cissy was not a dreamy eyed little girl anymore. Cissy was growing up, he thought. Then he whispered quite seductively "Shall we dance, Lady Templeton".

"Why it would be my pleasure, Lord Kingsley" she replied and he noticed that her smile was magical and her eyes were sparkling like the stars above.

She took his hands and he pulled her towards him and as she hummed the tune of the waltz she'd heard earlier he held her intimately close to his chest as they moved to and fro on the grass beside the lake.

Cissy was in seventh heaven and was dizzy with excitement, her darling Alex was holding her at last, and closely at that. When he had swept her into his arms he had placed his hand in the centre of her back and she felt a tingling sensation every time his hand moved slightly up and down as they

The Enchanted Glade

danced. She inhaled the scent of him as her face and hair brushed his chest. He was wearing a white silk shirt with the buttons half undone and she could almost imagine what it would be like to run her fingers over his naked chest. Oh, he was so tall, so handsome and so adorable.

And at this very moment Alex was in some kind of dream of his own. As he was swirling her around under the stars he was inhaling the perfume of her beautiful hair, an aroma of lavender and rosemary, he thought. Holding her so close had made him realise what a lovely young woman Cissy was becoming. She was certainly blooming before her time but she was still very young and he mustn't forget that. She had on only a thin nightshift and he could feel her breasts and stomach pressing against him. Then it hit him and he stopped abruptly. "Whatever are we doing, Cissy, if anyone saw us we'd be in terrible trouble" he almost shouted.

She looked up into his eyes, the previously smiling eyes now seemingly so dejected. The light from the moon glistened onto an isolated tear that was trickling down her cheek "Please don't be cross with me, Alex".

"I'm not cross with you, Princess" he whispered softly as with his thumb he wiped the tear away. A small wisp of hair had escaped and was straying over her eye so Alex gently swept the curl aside and the feel of his finger sweeping the hair across her skin was the depth of tenderness and the most intimate sensation she had ever felt in her entire life. Then cupping the sides of her face in his hands, he drew her towards him and placed a feather-like kiss on her forehead. She closed her eyes drinking in the moment, the warmth of his lips rippling through her and then he spoilt the moment by declaring as he pulled away "We must be getting back to the house now".

"Let's just stay a few minutes more" she pleaded not wanting this wonderful rendezvous to end.

It was mid July and the night was still quite warm so Cissy lay down on her back on the grass. As he lay down beside her he couldn't believe he was actually doing the same. After a few moments of silence Cissy said " Alex look up at all of those radiant stars. My sister says that each one has a wish to grant. What would you wish for?"

Alex levered himself up to lean on one elbow and look at Cissy, his dark eyes caressing her form in the moonlight. She lay with her eyes closed, her hair feathered out around her face and he suddenly felt a stirring in his loins that he hadn't felt for a long time. He noticed that the shift she was wearing was hugging the contours of her body and leaving nothing to the imagination. His eyes then scanned the fabric moulding her pert breasts, his gaze lowered further to her rounded stomach and then down to her shapely legs. Had this been anyone other than Cissy he would have taken her now. God, Kingsley, take a hold of yourself, he thought, this is Cissy... Cissy, for God's sake, whom he loved like a sister....didn't he? He was unable to answer her question truthfully so he quickly changed the subject as he lay back down and looked up into the night sky. He was always rescuing Cissy from precarious situations and now he felt as if he was placing her in one.

Alex who was almost twenty-four now was about to embark on a military career and as they both lay looking up at the stars he revealed "Cissy, I'm going away to Spain very soon".

"Why?" she enquired

"I'm going into the army, I have a commission and I'm to join the Duke of Wellington in two weeks time"

"But they are fighting a war over there, you might get hurt" her eyes widened and she sounded petrified.

"I'll be alright, Cissy"

"You can't be sure of that . Oh please, Alex, please don't go" she was completely beside herself with anxiety, she then turned over onto her stomach and propped herself up on her elbows and looked dolefully at him. "You are my very best friend and I couldn't bear it if anything bad happened to you"

He looked directly into her eyes and said softly "I will always be your best friend, Cissy, no matter what happens, never ever forget that".

As he spoke her heart was melting in her chest. Was he not aware of how grown up she was, of the devastating effect he had on her heart and had always had….no, of course not? All he saw was a child. Didn't he realise how much she loved him, had always loved him from the first day they had met, and now he was going away and she may never see him again.

Alex rose to his feet "Come on we really must be getting back now" he held his hand out to her.

As she took his hand, she pleaded "But will I see you again before you go away?" she sounded totally depressed and miserable.

"I'll make sure I call to say goodbye" he promised.

"How long will you be gone" her heart was breaking as she spoke.

"I'm not sure, it could be months or years, however long the war lasts, I suppose".

Oh, thought Cissy, how can I possibly endure maybe years of not seeing him. "Are you allowed any correspondence whilst you're there? I'd like to write to you"

"Of course, but etiquette demands that it is conducted through a third party. Perhaps you could leave anything for me with my mother and she could send it on". Cissy nodded

"I'll let her know before I go"

Luckily the clouds had gathered over the moon and it was darker now. Hopefully everyone would be asleep so no-one would see them as they returned to the house.

They had been outside for quite a while now and she earnestly hoped that one of the servants hadn't checked the library doors and locked them. She had no idea what they would do if that happened.

They crossed the lawn and then walked very close to the walls of the house and Alex felt like a burglar. He quietly told her to walk on ahead so that if anyone should be looking out they wouldn't be seen together. So she went on alone and waited inside the library until he came. He quietly closed the door and locked it then he turned around and told her he would see her in the morning. He then bade her go straight back to her room. He was worried for Cissy's sake more than his own.

He waited for another ten minutes perusing the books even though it was hard to see anything in the dark. He then stealthily returned to the guest room upstairs that he was occupying for the rest of the night but at the same time he was wondering if he would be able to sleep after realising his true feelings for Cissy. Seeing Cissy's perfectly formed body beneath her shift tonight had awakened sensations within him that he hadn't even realised he possessed. He must bury those feelings deep inside himself as he wouldn't want to put Cissy in a compromising position. Although she was now blossoming she was still too young and he must try to put thoughts of her far from his mind, although he didn't know how. As he removed his clothes and retired to bed he knew he would be unable to sleep. Perhaps it was fortuitous that he was going away for a while, maybe if Cissy was 'out of sight' she would be 'out of mind' but he doubted it.

Meanwhile Cissy was peering out of the window of her bed-chamber and as she looked up into the sky, she mouthed "Thank you" to the moon, the stars and the heavens above. She was so elated that Alex had held her and danced with her and kissed her, even if it was only an innocent tender kiss on her forehead. His lips had seared her skin with a warmth that she had never known before and that she would probably never experience again. He was going away and the feeling of despair was etched deeply in her heart. She muttered a silent prayer that her beloved Alex would survive the war and come back to her unscathed. With this thought on her mind she climbed into her bed hopefully to sleep and dream of the man she thought the most desirable in the entire world.

Two weeks later Alex had been to say goodbye and her heart was almost breaking. She had secretly given him a miniature silver photo frame with a small painting of herself to take with him hoping it may be of some comfort to him whilst he was so far away. Her mother had recently commissioned portraits of them all and their cousin, Aunt Ellen's son, Miles had been the artist. Alex had been overwhelmed and as they had strolled unseen in the garden, he had embraced her lightly and said he would treasure it always and now he was gone.

Now, almost two months had passed and this morning, feeling rather melancholy, she decided to walk to the church in the village and when she arrived she let herself in. She went to the front pew and knelt in prayer. "Please, dear Lord, will you keep my darling Alex safe and bring him back to me unharmed", the tears were rolling down her little face and she could hardly see through them. Then she stood and moved to the rack of candles. She lit a candle for her love and vowed to come each week and light another until he returned. On the way back she decided to visit the little stream, which was her solace ever since Alex had departed for the war. She went there as often as she could just to sit in silence except for the noises of nature surrounding her and today as she looked around she marvelled at the beauty of this place. It was now the end of September and the autumn countryside glowed with the deep shades of brown and orange, and the red and gold of the leaves that spread before her were like a carpet of flames. She found a comfy spot to sit on the grass at the edge of the water and leaned back against the tree behind her. She then closed her eyes as the tinkling music of the water passing by almost sent her into a slumber. Here she could sit and peacefully dream of her beloved Alex whom she missed so much. No-one knew how she felt and she really had no-one else to confide in except Emmy. She felt so sorry for herself at this moment, and so alone. She had a good cry, felt a little better and then decided to make her way home.

When she reached the house she went to the kitchen to see Emily. "Hello me chick, wot's troublin' you today"

"Oh, Emmy I'm just feeling so sad".

"Missin' your little friend, are you, deary?" Emily knew only too well that Cissy and Alex had been on easy terms with one another ever since they had first met.

"I'm just so worried about him, Emmy, what if he gets injured or even worse…killed . I won't be there to help him. I can't sleep at night thinking about him".

"That won't do nobody no good , you worryin' like that". Emily walked over to the pantry "'ere I've made some o' them biscuits that you love and I'll make you a drink and we'll talk about somethin' else, shall we?"

Cissy lowered her head a little and Emily could see that her eyes were watery so she put the plate she was holding in her hand down onto the table and walked across the kitchen towards her. As Cissy turned to face her Emily could see the tears rolling down her cheeks like an overflowing river so she held her arms out and the little lass ran into her embrace, held onto her tightly and sobbed uncontrollably.

Two days later Cissy had just finished writing her first letter to Alex hoping he would be interested in keeping up to date with all the latest news from home. She knew that it would have taken some time for him to travel first to London and then go to Dover to board a ship to sail to Spain and she wasn't sure how long this journey would take so she had waited until now to write. She descended the stairs and with a spring in her step she skipped across the hall to her mother's sitting room and knocked before entering.

"Mother is anyone going to Amberley Hall today".

The Enchanted Glade

Her mother asked why and Cissy explained in detail that Alex had advised her that whilst he was in Spain it would be proper to send any correspondence to him through his mother.

"I will be visiting Amberley to see Lady Lavinia myself tomorrow, I could take the letter then".

"Thank you so much" they exchanged smiles as Cissy handed her mother the letter which Annabel then placed in her bureau "Would it be all right for me to take a walk down by the old stream I'm feeling a little lethargic this morning and would very much like to go outside for some fresh air" all she wanted was to be by herself as she was still missing Alex's company so much.

Her mother agreed. Annabel thought that she had looked a little pale recently and that perhaps a walk across the meadow would do her good. Recently she hadn't had a lot of exercise. Although she still visited Amberley to ride Velvet once in a while she didn't go as often as she did when Alex was home.

Cissy started out across the field which was the quickest way on foot to the little stream and as she ambled along she thought back to when she had first noticed it as they were riding up the drive on that first day here. So much had happened since that day but she never ever regretted their move here. She often went just to sit undisturbed in the peaceful surroundings there to contemplate the events in her life and inhale the undeniably sweet fresh fragrance of the meadow.

She was ambling aimlessly on her way through the small copse when she heard voices so she hid behind a nearby bush and went down on her haunches. As she peered between the leaves she was shocked to see her sister Louise in the arms of a very tall yet roughly dressed young man. He appeared to have a shock of gorgeous black curly hair and a very handsome face and strong muscular arms as he lifted Louise in the air and whirled her around before gently planting her feet firmly on the ground then he lowered his lips to place a ravenous kiss on hers.

Cissy quickly looked away and she gasped as the action had almost taken her breath away. This was a bolt out of the blue and it had put Cissy in quite a dither. What was Louise doing out here in the trees all alone with this man. She seemed captivated by him and quite honestly Cissy had never seen her sister looking so happy. Just then they lay down in the grass and Cissy was reminded of herself and Alex on the night of Louise's party.

It was no wonder that her sister wasn't keen on having her come-out if she was already involved with another and Cissy knew by his appearance that her mother and father would never approve of him as a fitting suitor for her sister. As she watched, the man enveloped her sister in his arms and they began to kiss again, but frantically this time, so Cissy decided to leave the scene as she wouldn't like her sister to find out that she had been spying on her. The two lovers were so engrossed in their activities that they didn't hear Cissy creep away.

All the way to the stream Cissy couldn't take her mind off of what she had just witnessed. Should she confront her sister or just say nothing, she would think on it and decide presently.

****

Chapter 7

A few weeks later pandemonium engulfed the whole household as it was revealed that Louise had eloped with her lover. She had asked her mother if she could go to stay with one of her friends who had attended her come-out. She had packed a trunk and unbeknownst to others she had also secretly packed all of her precious jewellery that she had been given over the last two or three years as gifts, plus the exquisitely expensive pieces that her parents had presented to her to wear at her come-out ball. She very carefully placed all the valuable items in a velvet pouch which she had then hidden in a concealed pocket of the trunk. She also took all of her trinket boxes and any items which would prove valuable that she could take to the pawn-broker to pay for the trip, the wedding and somewhere to live.

Her mother, not realising what was afoot, had arranged for a carriage to take her to Bath to her friend's home but her friend was in on the conspiracy and had aided the lovers in their bid to marry. She and her paramour, one Sydney Burton, had left as soon as possible on a trip to Gretna Green. Although the journey was many hundreds of miles, they had had a good start as no-one had suspected that anything was amiss. They knew their union would be vehemently opposed by her parents so Gretna Green seemed the only solution.

Traditionally in Scotland a couple over the age of sixteen could be married just by declaring themselves husband and wife in front of witnesses but in England such marriages were prohibited.

It seemed very appropriate that they should marry over the anvil with the "Blacksmith Priest" officiating as Sydney was a blacksmith's son and worked with his father at the Smithy in the nearby village of Inglesbrook. It was when he had visited Monkton Grange to attend to the horses months before that he and Louise had first met and begun their affair. The Templeton's only discovered the dilemma after Louise was married and to add to the anguish it transpired that she was now pregnant.

Sir William was furious, especially after spending a fortune on her come-out. He immediately disowned her and said he would cut her off from the family without a penny and Annabel was beside herself with grief when her husband ordered her never to contact her wayward daughter again. She dearly loved all of her children and couldn't even contemplate life without Louise. She had dreamed of someday having grand-children and enjoying them, not suffering in this way, knowing she was to have a grandchild and never being able to see he or she.

Annabel rang for Ambrose and asked that he request that Sam or one of the stable lads ready a carriage as she has decided to pay an impromptu visit to see Lavinia. Although John Bartholomew was her complete confidant she thought she should discuss this with Lavinia first and ask her advice.

Lavinia was alone in her private sitting room having tea when Fenton their butler knocked on the door. She answered the knock and the butler announced that the Countess of Langford was in the foyer.

"Do show her ladyship in immediately, Fenton, and could you please arrange for another tea cup and saucer and some more cakes".

"Certainly, My Lady" said Fenton and he ushered Annabel into the room without delay.

The Enchanted Glade

Lavinia was always delighted to welcome Annabel. She was however dismayed to see her dearest companion almost in tears. Immediately placing her own cup and saucer down upon the small table beside her chair, she rose and walked towards her distraught friend. "Whatever is the matter, my dear? Do come and sit down" and as she spoke she placed a comforting arm around Annabel's shoulder and guided her towards the armchair next to her own.

Annabel couldn't hold her emotions in any longer and she burst into tears.

She relayed to Lavinia the scant details of the elopement and wondered if Louise had confided in Imogen as they were such good friends.

When the maid brought the tea Lavinia asked " Please, Ellie, could you ask Lady Imogen to come to see me directly".

Ellie nodded "I'll go at once, my Lady".

After a few minutes Imogen knocked on the door and when bidden, she entered the room and was as surprised as her mother to hear that Louise had eloped although she did admit to knowing about Sydney Burton.

"All I want, Imogen, is to find Louise; I am extremely worried about her. Did she tell you where he lives or anything that may help?" Annabel was desperate for the slightest fragment of information.

"All I know is that he works at the Blacksmith's in Inglesbrook and Louise met him when he came to your stables to attend to the horses. She told me she liked him very much but I thought they were just friends and that he was a passing fancy. I really can't remember anything else".

"Thank you so much for telling me, it gives me a little hope that I may find her soon. If anything further comes to mind perhaps you could let me know"

"Of course I will" Imogen looked very sympathetically towards Annabel.

Lavinia asked Imogen to excuse them so she left the room.

Fenton had poured Annabel some tea before he had left the room but she apologised to Lavinia for leaving it as she felt so nauseous she couldn't face it.

"Please don't apologise I totally understand the stress you must be feeling. Now let me see. If only you could get a message to her" mused Lavinia, pacing up and down, her hand on her chin, deep in thought "perhaps you could leave a letter for her at the blacksmiths and with luck she may get in touch".

"William is furious with her and has said he will cut her off. But he has also ordered that I have no further contact with her at all, but that is completely unthinkable. I cannot go to Inglesbrook myself and I am unsure who I can take into my confidence" she thought for just a moment and then it suddenly dawned on her, "John Bartholomew, of course! I am almost sure he will help. He must have patients in that village. Perhaps he could call at the smithy whilst he's on his rounds".

"What a superb idea, perhaps you could write a letter now and leave it here with me. I can summon John to call here to dispel any suspicion anyone may have if he called at The Grange unsummoned. I could then ask John if he would be so kind as to deliver the communication and to report back to me as soon as is humanly possible and then I can keep you informed".

"Oh, Lavinia, how fortunate I am to have a friend in you" Annabel was welling up. She knew if her husband found out he would be enraged but she was willing to take the chance. Even if she didn't get to see Louise she just needed to know her daughter was safe and being taken care of.

"We had better keep this between ourselves for the present and I will inform John when I see him that only the three of us are aware of the state of affairs". Lavinia was already walking over to her bureau to fetch some writing materials. She sat down and removed some parchment, beckoned to

The Enchanted Glade

Annabel to come to sit beside her, handed her the pen and paper, and then the two women set about putting their plan into action.

Two days later Annabel unexpectedly had to summon the doctor to call on Oliver as he was unwell. Alice reported that he had woken with a slight fever and although Annabel was sorry about her son's condition she was glad of the opportunity to see John to discover if he had any news about Louise.

Lavinia had sent a boy with a note the day before to inform her that everything was going to plan. The lad was told to hand it only to the Lady Annabel or to return with it intact.

Annabel thanked the boy and handed him a coin for his trouble but she was almost too afraid to open it in case she got her hopes up and was then disappointed.

Ambrose announced that the doctor had arrived so she ask that he be shown into her sitting room at once. She had already checked that her husband was not in his study to ensure that he was unable to overhear any conversation that she may be having with the doctor. The first thing John noticed was the expectation in her eyes and he hoped he wasn't going to disappoint her.

The butler left and as soon as they were alone she asked if he had any news. He explained that he had called at the smithy and had met Louise's husband. He had found Sydney Burton to be a very pleasant young man who worked very hard. He had delivered the letter and ask Sydney to give it to Louise as soon as possible and was assured that he would do so.

"Did he say that Louise was alright? Oh! John, whatever am I going to do, you do know that she's pregnant!" Annabel was becoming overwrought.

He held both her hands trying to re-assure her "No I didn't realise".

"Please will you take care of her until she has the baby?" Annabel pleaded and as he nodded she continued "We will have to be discreet about it. Her father must never find out that I am communicating with her in any way"

John squeezed her hands gently and said "You know you can rely on me, Annabel and yes, I will gladly take care of her if that is what you wish".

At that moment their eyes met and she so wanted him to hold her in his arms to calm her at this very traumatic time. She had tolerated so many incidents and dramas over the past few years and she knew she was close to breaking down. She had no support at all from her erring husband and at times like this even she needed some help to maintain her sanity. John Bartholomew was her dearest friend and if he couldn't afford her some comfort her then no-one could.

John seemed to sense what she was feeling but wouldn't dream of acting with such impropriety, although he would willingly appease her, he thought it wrong to venture down that path.

He broke eye contact with her as he said "I had better go up to see Master Oliver" his comment cut through the air and ended the palpable tension which had suddenly filled the room.

"Of course, how thoughtless of me" she said with an audible sigh.

"No, Annabel" he said, looking tenderly into her eyes once more "you are never thoughtless, never that" and she felt a most warm feeling penetrate her soul at the look of kindness afforded to her from his handsome face.

They turned together to leave the room and to make their way up to Oliver's bed-chamber where the invalid was happily playing with his toy soldiers and seemed to be not the least bit poorly. The doctor had a look at him anyway just to justify his call if nothing else.

Annabel didn't mind, she now knew that her daughter would have received her secret correspondence and would

The Enchanted Glade

hopefully get in touch. The letter had asked that should Louise reply to her mother's letter perhaps her husband would kindly take it to his workplace and the doctor would call at the smithy during his rounds, in the next day or two, to collect it.

A few weeks had passed and Annabel discovered that her husband had to go to London on business. He would be in the capital for at least a week. She was overjoyed and after he had left she confided in Cissy that she had been corresponding with Louise this last month. But she was so terrified that someone would find out, she swore her second daughter to secrecy. Cissy crossed her heart and promised that she would never betray her mother's confidence as she was so glad to see her mother smiling again. She told Cissy that she had a plan and asked Cissy to accompany her to town the following day on the pretence of a shopping spree. Next morning they boarded the carriage she had sent for at the front entrance and set off on their way. Annabel had instructed her groom to make his way to Oak Street, a small road off the main Bristol Road into Bath. She and Cissy then alighted and Annabel asked Sam to wait where he was and they would return shortly as they were visiting a friend.

"Is this where Louise lives?" Cissy whispered to her mother as soon as they were out of earshot of the carriage driver.

"No." her mother whispered back "but it's not far".

They walked up to the dead end and then Cissy noticed some steps leading up to another road high above this one.

When they reached the top Cissy was breathless "Where are we now?" she enquired of her mother.

"This is the road leading to Wells and Louise lives over there." She pointed to the other side of the road to a very steep cobbled hill which was named Paradise Street. They crossed to the opposite side of the road and began to climb until they reached No 10.

Annabel cautiously knocked and they both held their breath as they heard footsteps along the passage beyond coming towards the front door.

Louise opened the door and the look on her face was priceless. She quickly ushered them both in and as soon as the door closed behind them she was in her mother's arms and sobbing like a baby.

Annabel was crying, and of course, that made Cissy well up, so Louise hugged her too.

After the greetings Louise invited them into her parlour and she went through to her little kitchen to put the kettle on.

"Will you stay for some tea, Mother, I have so much to tell you".

Cissy's eyes scanned the room and she observed that Louise kept a very neat and tidy little home.

"We can't stay long". Annabel called to her daughter " We have left Sam Miles with the carriage in Oak street. How clever of you to suggest the diversion. I hope no-one suspects anything".

Just at that moment Louise returned to the room and put the tea tray with a china teapot, sugar basin and cream jug and a small plate of what looked like homemade biscuits onto the small dining table. Annabel held her hand out to take Louise's hand "Are you well my Darling? I've been so very worried about you".

"Mother, you will never know how sorry I am to have caused you all this anxiety, but I adore Sydney and there was no way I could marry someone of Father's choosing whom I did not love. This was the only course open for me and then there's the babe to think of."

"Of course, I understand, has Doctor Bartholomew been to see you?"

"Yes, Mother, he has been wonderful and I'm so grateful to you for the care". As they were talking she poured the tea and handed a cup to her mother and then to Cissy .

The Enchanted Glade

It seemed very strange to both Annabel and Cissy that Louise was waiting on them like a servant but Louise appeared very content in her new role.

Annabel took a small pouch from her pocket and handed it to her daughter "Here's something to help with the things you need for yourself and the baby"

"Thank you, Mother but there's no need, I do have some money. I'm so sorry about the jewellery but I had to sell it. It meant Sydney and I could buy this house and although he didn't want me to use my money for the things he felt he should be providing, it was a great help and I talked him around in the end. Just because he's poor it doesn't mean he has no pride."

"I know, Darling, but I want you to have this, for the baby".

"Thank you, Mother, I'll put it aside for him….or her" she added smiling broadly.

"You know that your father has cut you out of his will and he never wants to see you again and has forbidden any contact with any of the family members".

"Quite honestly, Mother, I really don't care if I ever see Father again as long as I live and the money means nothing to me. Sydney loves me very much and I am more than happy to spend the rest of my life in this tiny little house, if I have to, as long as I can be with him. We are so looking forward to having a family and I hope one day you'll be able to meet Sydney and judge for yourself what a good, kind and hard-working man he is". Louise sounded very emotional as she added " I am however very concerned that I will not see enough of you, Cissy and Oliver but perhaps we can work something out".

"Please, my darling, don't upset yourself too much. It isn't wise in your condition". Annabel rose from her chair and went to her daughter and embraced her. "I'm sure Sydney is very worthy. As you know Doctor Bartholomew has met him and has conveyed his opinion, which was very favourable, may I add, but your father has disowned you and I am so distraught. I have no idea when or even if I may visit you again for some time. We could only get away now because your father has been called to London on business."

"And I am so very grateful that you came….. Mother…" she sounded very serious "can you ever forgive me for leaving so suddenly?"

"Of course, Darling, there's nothing to forgive. No matter what your father says or does I will never desert you. We may still communicate surreptitiously through the doctor but we must be so very careful. Only Lady Lavinia, the doctor and the three of us here, oh and your husband know anything of it. It really must stay a closely guarded secret ". Louise nodded in agreement and was also thrilled that her mother had referred to 'her husband'.

"We must be going now or we will raise suspicion. I know Sam is loyal to me but he must never find out the purpose of our visit. We must bid you farewell and hope that it is not too long before I can see you again. Don't forget that you can contact me at any time through Doctor Bartholomew" she put her arms out to Louise, drew her close and held her tightly.

Louise then turned to Cissy " I miss you so much, Cissy" she said as she hugged her sister.

"Me too Lulu. I will light a candle in church on Sunday for you and your family when I light one for Alex". Cissy had tears in her eyes.

"Oh, how is Alex, have you heard from him?" Louise asked as they walked along the passage to the front door.

"Not yet, but it sometimes takes months for a letter to get through and they have to go to his parent's home first. I just hope he's alright. I pray for him every night so I'll say one for you as well ".

"Thank you, dearest" she said as she kissed her mother and sister goodbye and then waved when they reached the bottom of the street.

The Enchanted Glade

As they made their way back down the steps to Oak Street Cissy was so pleased to see the contented look on her mother's face and she knew that they would both feel so much better about Louise now, thankful that she was so well and happy. Annabel felt a huge weight had been lifted from her knowing that John would be keeping her informed of her daughter's progress throughout her pregnancy.

That night Cissy lay in bed thinking back on the day. How cosy, warm and snug Louise's little home was. Such a neat parlour and very well kept by her sister. She imagined what sort of home she would have with Alex if she was married to him. It would be a dream, she thought, then back to reality she realised that's all it could ever be …..a dream.

The months passed by and Annabel was unable to get away to visit Louise's house again which prayed on her mind daily. She felt she was lacking in her role as a mother in effectively abandoning her daughter although she knew that John was taking good care of her. When he made his visits during those last few months he would make sure he reported back to her through Lavinia. She hoped so desperately that Louise would understand the situation that her mother found herself in.

Eventually Louise and Sydney were the proud parents of twins. A fine-looking boy called Fredrick Sydney and a beautiful little girl called Mary Louise.

Annabel had asked John to see that a hamper of fresh produce and groceries was delivered to Louise's house each week, which she hoped would be helpful. John had brought a note from Louise, which he had left with Lavinia, thanking her mother profusely for her generosity and begging her mother to call if she could but Annabel knew that that would be impossible at the present time.

John kindly offered Louise his assistance in this matter and with Lavinia's help Annabel and Cissy were invited to Amberley Hall for tea one afternoon. Lavinia sent

Annabel's carriage away saying she would arrange the transport back to Monkton Grange. Then Annabel, Cissy, Lavinia and Imogen boarded another carriage and although she was very puzzled by the events Annabel refrained from asking where they were going.

John had arranged for a carriage to fetch Louise and her family to come to his house in Monkton-St-James and they were already in the house when Lavinia's carriage arrived.

The satisfaction he felt seeing the delight on the faces of all concerned as Annabel entered the room and saw her daughter and her family sat waiting to see her. The gratifying look as Annabel held her new grand-children was all the reward he needed to know that he had made the right decision. There was nothing that he would not do for Annabel in his quest to bring her a little happiness.

Imogen and Cissy were enchanted by the little babes and suddenly Cissy realised she was now an Aunt herself and she felt she couldn't wait until she was able to have children of her own .

Annabel met her son-in-law for the first time and was most impressed with Louise's choice of husband.

John's housekeeper brought refreshments and everyone enjoyed the occasion immensely.

When it was time to leave, Annabel was heart-broken but she took John to one side and thanked him from the bottom of her heart for arranging the get-together.

"I will never be able to repay your kindness during this difficult time, how can I ever thank you for this today?".

"The fact that you have enjoyed it so much is thanks enough" he said, with a devastating smile.

He escorted them all to the door and witnessed the love and compassion as they said farewell outside the house and after the two carriages had departed he sat alone in his study, elbows on the desk, fingers steepled in front of his face as he reflected on the afternoon and wishing so much that he had a loving family of his own.

****

Chapter 8

Summer 1813.

Cissy was going to attain her eighteenth birthday in December and it was time to formally launch her into society. Her mother thought that it would be advantageous for her to stay with Aunt Ellen for her first and hopefully her last season. Although they only lived approximately 7 miles apart her aunt had earlier suggested that as it was Cissy's come-out year it would be best if she was at the hub of all the festivities in the town. Ellen's house, in the illustrious Royal Crescent in Bath, was definitely very impressive and would help in Cissy's quest to find a match. Bath was positively the most fashionable place to be at present and Ellen had booked the awe-inspiring Assembly Rooms in Bennett Street, just off The Circus, for Cissy's Come-out Ball.
They had already been invited to, and attended, many soirees and several balls but Cissy had met no-one who compared to Alex and she despaired of ever finding a husband who would measure up to him in any way.
Aunt Ellen had bought her a complete new wardrobe including two very smart riding habits, one in royal blue and another in emerald green, which meticulously suited her colouring and she felt extremely smart in both of them. She also had many walking out and day dresses and the evening gowns which had been designed exclusively for her, were dazzlingly beautiful. When the modiste had first brought them to the house and she had tried them on she had whirled

The Enchanted Glade

around in front of the mirror feeling like the proverbial princess. Alex had always called her his princess and as she span around he was uppermost in her thoughts. She just closed her eyes and imagined herself in the ballroom being held by her beloved. Of course disappointment engulfed her when she'd opened her eyes and realised that she was once again only day-dreaming.

One sunny morning Cissy came down for breakfast and was informed by Aunt Ellen that they would be riding down to the town that day to visit the popular Sydney Gardens.

"It will enable you to become further acquainted with several more members of the ton, my dear, so put on one of your more fetching walking out dresses and please wear that lovely rose decorated bonnet, it is my favourite and you look charming in it. We will depart directly as soon as you are organized ". Ellen's eyes were radiating admiration as she spoke. She adored all of her brother's children but somehow Cissy was special, and Ellen, who did not have a daughter of her own, loved her very much.

"I would like that, Aunt Ellen". Cissy smiled at her dearest Aunt and added "Thank you so much for all you have done to assist me".

"It is my pleasure, darling girl, after all I am having as much fun as you are. You know, Cissy, it reminds me of my come-out and I have such fond memories of that special time in my life. Now no more reminiscing, let us make haste or we will miss those most worthy of note".

Cissy readied herself and in no time at all they were in the carriage that her Aunt had summoned earlier and were on their way. When they arrived at the park they set down in front of the large gates and began their stroll through the beautiful gardens. As it was June the floral displays were a delight to behold and they seemed even more enthralling in the sparkling sunshine.

They met several persons who were well known to her Aunt and Cissy was duly introduced. One such young couple were presented as Miss Camilla Marlin and Sir Guy Hamilton. The lady was strikingly attractive in a very pretty outfit with a matching hat that sat atop dark curls which were tumbling down onto her shoulders. Cissy noticed that the gentleman had fair hair and his side whiskers grew down his face to a small goatie beard on his chin. When introduced he raised his hat in one hand and took Cissy's hand with the other. He then bent to kiss it but at the same time he never took his hypnotic eyes from hers. "How do you do, Lady Templeton, it's a pleasure to meet you. I'm sure".

She suddenly felt that her cheeks were in a flush and she just nodded in response, as he had rendered her absolutely speechless. Cissy noticed that his eyes were small and beady and she promptly looked away. But as he was staring at her, against her inner wishes, she felt her gaze being drawn back to his, and then just as quickly she came to her senses and attempting to retrieve her hand from his, she quickly averted her eyes to look at her aunt. She also felt an uncomfortable frisson sear through her body at his touch and was quite relieved when he'd relinquished his hold on her.

After they had walked on a little way, Cissy asked her Aunt about the man and was informed that he was a distant relation, "A second cousin, I think" reflected her Aunt "of Lady Emma Hamilton, who was the mistress of Admiral Horatio Nelson, before he died at Waterloo in 1805. Lady Hamilton has now moved with her daughter, Horatia, to France but I am not sure how Sir Guy is occupying himself at the moment, but I could find out".

"Oh, please don't trouble yourself on my account, Aunt; I really have no wish to know what he is about".

"I know he is unmarried, and that the lady on his arm is a friend of his sister but I am unaware as to her status in the marriage stakes at present".

Cissy was not the least bit interested in either of them and as they walked on over the ornate iron bridge which

The Enchanted Glade

spanned the canal they changed the subject to the soiree they would be attending that evening at Lady Kendrow's.

"I'm sure you'll enjoy this evening, my dear" Ellen's glance was directed towards her niece "Lady Kendrow is such a spirited character, so full of life and an inimitable hostess. Perhaps there will be several eligible bachelors attending who may take a shine to you" she smiled as she mentioned the men.

"Aunt Ellen, I won't just marry anybody. I cannot possibly contemplate a loveless marriage" Cissy sounded quite exasperated, which was quite out of character for her "I would rather live an uncomplicated life as a bluestocking than marry a man I do not love".

"Oh dear! what brought that on, I was only joshing".

At that moment another couple wished them 'Good Morning' and Ellen introduced her niece, they exchanged niceties and then moved on once more.

Cissy could not get the leering look of that terrible man out of her mind. It had her in an absolute quandary and she felt very touchy and uncomfortable as they continued their walk. After several more introductions and the fact that they had achieved a complete circuit of the park Ellen summoned the carriage and they proceeded to board the landau for the journey back to her Aunt's house in the Royal Crescent.

"A thoroughly exhilarating morning" her Aunt commented as they alighted from the carriage and made their way towards the front door.

I wouldn't say that, thought Cissy, as she duly followed her aunt into the house and her thoughts strayed back to that nauseating encounter with Sir Guy Hamilton.

That evening they had a very light dinner much earlier than usual and then went to their respective bed-chambers to ready themselves for the forthcoming occasion. By seven o'clock they were prepared and ready to depart. Each were attired in the most beautiful of gowns. Ellen, who looked much younger than her fifty years, was clad in a delicate, yet shimmering shade of gold which made her radiant features even more apparent, and Cissy who, in a deep peach coloured gown, with her titian hair swept up on top of her head, looked the epitome of a goddess. They both wore similar wraps, just in case the evening turned cold on the way home later.

As they settled into the carriage facing one another Ellen couldn't help but mention Cissy's appearance. "Cissy, dearest, you look so very beautiful tonight. I am reminded of the time of your mother's come-out which was the first time I met her. She radiated warmth and was most gracious and you look so like her. She was the darling of the social circuit in her season and there was no-one to equal her at the time. I quite expect you to have the same effect at your own come-out next week".

"Oh, Aunt Ellen, I can hardly believe that it is only next week. I am nervous to distraction, I do hope I will not disappoint you after all the time and effort you have so kindly put in to help me to find a husband. But I do feel so very apprehensive about whether I could settle on a match with someone I do not love immediately". Cissy sighed sounding almost as if she was about to burst into tears.

"Do not fret, dearest, I felt exactly the same way as you on my come-out and I had a very pleasing result. You are already taking the ton by storm……oh, I see we have arrived at Lady Kendrow's" she commented as the carriage came to a halt. As they prepared to alight from the carriage her Aunt was quick to re-assure her that she had nothing to worry about and that the evening would surely be a resounding success.

They alighted from the carriage and walked up the steps to the front door to be greeted by a footman who took their wraps and directed them to the music room where everyone was assembled and seated ready for the concert that Lady Kendrow had arranged.

The Enchanted Glade

At the door their hostess welcomed them and complimented them both on their stylish appearance " How wonderful to meet you at last, Cecilia" she raised her hand to shake Cissy's, who reciprocated and bobbed a little curtsey in response. "Your Aunt has told me so much about you, my dear, and you look absolutely stunning and I sincerely hope that you enjoy yourself this evening, especially the entertainment" she expressed.

After assuring their hostess that they expected the evening to be superb they took their seats and relaxed awaiting the start of the concert.

The concert commenced and as Cissy sat enjoying the music she experienced the most unusual sensation, as if someone was watching her intensely. She stealthily glanced around hoping that no-one would notice as they were all listening attentively to the music. To her dismay she spied the gentleman whom she had met in the park that very morning. He was sat between two very fine-looking women, neither of whom were the lady he'd had on his arm in the park, but he was staring directly at her and she felt most uncomfortable. She quickly averted her gaze back to the pianist who was enthralling the whole audience with his rendition of one of the classics. Inside she was feeling quite sick and at that moment she wished she could get up from her chair and flee the room but she knew that was impossible. Thoughts of how she could avoid him for the rest of the evening were flooding her mind.

Just then the concert ended and after much applause Lady Kendrow announced that, before the dancing commenced in the ballroom, the buffet supper would be served in the adjacent room.

Cissy was feeling decidedly unwell and when asked by Aunt Ellen to accompany her to the buffet Cissy excused herself, and informed her that she would join her in a while and made her way to the ladies powder room. When she got there she glanced at her reflection in the mirror as she passed and was dismayed to see that her complexion seemed very pale, so after refreshing herself she pinched her cheeks to redden them a little which enhanced her appearance immensely.

She was on her way back to her aunt when Sir Guy Hamilton suddenly appeared from behind a pillar.

"We meet again, my lady, how very fortunate"

Not for me, thought Cissy "Please excuse me, Sir" she bobbed a slight curtsey "my aunt is waiting for me" she couldn't think of anything else to say on the spur of the moment.

"Perhaps we could dance later?" he enquired and his leering smile gave Cissy the shivers.

"I really must be getting back to my aunt" she turned to walk away but he caught hold of her wrist as she went. He was gripping it very tightly and as she tried to pull away she exclaimed "Please unhand me, Sir, I hardly know you" a feeling of panic completely engulfed her.

"Well I certainly hope we can resolve that situation very shortly, my dear" his voice sounded extremely repulsive.

Cissy was incensed, how dare he call her 'my dear'! She snatched her hand away from him and hurried as fast as she could back to the room where the buffet was being served. Her eyes scanned the faces within as she searched frantically for Aunt Ellen.

"Oh, there you are, Cissy, dearest" her Aunt had found her and seeing the distraught expression on her niece's face she added "whatever is the matter? You look flushed my dear, is everything alright?"

"Aunt Ellen, could we possibly go home now, I'm feeling a little unwell". Cissy whispered, suffering an anxiety in her chest that she had never experienced in her whole life before.

"Well this is all very sudden, dearest, you seemed perfectly fine a few moments ago. I'm very sorry you are feeling out of sorts but it would be so rude of us to leave now. I wouldn't like to offend our hostess as she has always been so courteous and welcoming. Can I get you a glass of water, yes that will make you feel a little better" Ellen beckoned to her niece "Come along we'll go and sit down in a quiet corner of the ballroom and see how you progress". Ellen immediately called a footman over to fetch the drink and as a very reluctant Cissy followed her Aunt she was glancing over her shoulder at every turn to make sure that that appalling man was nowhere to be seen.

When the orchestra commenced playing several young gentlemen approached her and asked to dance but she proclaimed that her card was full.

"Cissy, dearest, this is not like you at all, something is the matter, I'm sure" whispered her Aunt "will you please tell me what is troubling you".

"It's that man we met in the park this morning, Hamilton, I met him on my way back from the powder room and his behaviour was inappropriate"

"Oh, my dear, he did not compromise you in any way did he?" Ellen sounded rather shocked.

"No, Aunt Ellen, but he made me feel very uneasy and I really don't want to see him again tonight, yet I don't see how I can avoid it if we stay".

"I will not leave your side whilst we are sat here nor will I let you out of my sight when you are dancing, dearest".

" But I really don't feel like dancing now".

"Please Cissy we must keep up appearances, think of your Come-out. For my sake will you please try?"

"Of course, I'm so sorry to be an annoyance to you, Aunt, will you please forgive me?" Cissy had been brought up to abide by the rules of etiquette and although this was her first experience of social life she knew that she must buckle under and give way to the strict protocol of society whether she liked it or not.

"Think no more of it, my dear, you'll feel better in a few moments" Ellen did sound very sympathetic.

Just then a very handsome young man approached and bowed before he introduced himself and asked Cissy to join him in the next dance, so just to please her Aunt she accepted. He took her hand and guided her onto the dance floor and as they danced he must have thought that Cissy was besotted with him as she never took her eyes from his for the entire time. But it was only because she was afraid to look around in case Hamilton caught her eye as they danced.

She managed to suffer the rest of the evening without encountering the man again and was very relieved when it was time to leave.

They thanked their hostess for a most enjoyable evening and Aunt Ellen enquired as to whether she would be attending the theatre two days hence. Lady Kendrow assured them that she would be and invited them both to join her in her box. Ellen thanked her kindly and said they would very much look forward to seeing her again. Cissy bobbed a polite curtsey to Lady Kendrow as the footman brought their wraps and informed them that their carriage was waiting.

In the carriage on the way home Ellen asked how she was feeling now.

"I am feeling much better now, thank you, Aunt" she half smiled as she spoke.

"Well we have no appointments tomorrow so maybe it will help if you stay in bed during the morning and then you will feel refreshed and we can relax for the rest of the day. I must say I am looking forward to our trip to the theatre on Friday, it will be most pleasurable".

"So am I" Cissy assured her as she settled down in her seat to make the most of the ride back to the house. Cissy had never been to the theatre before so it was going to be a completely new experience for her.

They arrived back at the house and were met by Ellen's butler, Carson, and as he took their wraps Cissy asked her Aunt to excuse her as she was a little tired and had a

The Enchanted Glade

headache. Ellen was most understanding, especially after what had happened earlier so she arranged for some laudenum be sent up with a warm drink and assured Cissy that it would help her sleep. She thanked her Aunt and made her way straight to her bed-chamber.

She still had trouble going to sleep that night as her mind was constantly wandering back to the encounter with Hamilton and she was wondering how she was going to steer clear of him in the near future. Then her mind shifted to Alex and she wished so hard that he could be here to protect her as he always had done in the past, before he had left for Spain. "I'll write to Alex tomorrow" she said to herself as she turned over to make herself a little more comfortable and immediately with him on her mind, and probably with the help of the laudenum, she had no difficulty in drifting into sleep and as she descended into her fantasy she hugged a spare pillow imagining it was Alex she was holding there beside her.

Next day after a morning in bed Cissy rose feeling a lot better. She completed her toilette, dressed and then after having breakfast with her Aunt she had returned to her bed-chamber and decided to sit down and write to Alex. Not a day had passed since he had left for Spain when she didn't think about him, worrying whether he was looking after himself and also very anxious as to whether he may have gotten hurt. But the worst thing, was knowing that even if he was hurt, she could do absolutely nothing about it as he was so far away. Every night she said a prayer for him and whenever she was able she lit a candle in the village church on her occasional visits back home during this very important time in her life.

She mentioned in the letter all the things that were happening at present, the events she had attended and the plans for her Come-out, which she told him she wasn't really looking forward to. She up-dated him on Louise and her little family, telling him that since she had been staying with her Aunt she had been fortunate enough to visit her sister several times and was delighted to see the progress of her niece and nephew who were now almost sixteen months old. She finished the letter saying she would so look forward to his reply whenever he could manage to find time to write back to her.

"My Darling Alex, I miss you so very much" she was thinking aloud as she sealed the envelope. "How will I ever fare without you in my life to help me and I am so unhappy at this moment, why, oh, why does life have to be so hard. I love you so very much and the ironic thing about that is that you will never know and if anything terrible happens to you I will never forgive myself for not having told you before you left." She uttered a huge sigh and stood up, walked over to the window and she looked longingly up into the sunny sky above knowing that the same sun was shining down on her beloved. She held the letter over her heart and kissed it as she walked towards the door and prepared to take it downstairs to call a messenger to deliver it to Amberley Hall.

Friday arrived and even though they were going to the theatre tonight Ellen insisted that they take a bracing walk in the Sydney Gardens this morning. The carriage dropped them at the gate and they commenced their walk.

"Have you ever visited the wonderful Pump Rooms since you came to live in the area, Dearest".

"No Aunt, we've been to several places but not there yet".

"I was going to take you there today but I've been informed that they are redecorating the main lounge and that it is closed to the public at present, so I thought that a stroll in the park would compensate"

Aunt Ellen stopped every now and then to converse with other walkers out enjoying the morning sunshine. She had spoken to quite a few acquaintances this morning and from

The Enchanted Glade

several of the conversations Cissy had gleaned that Lady Kendrow's nephew was to join them in the theatre box tonight. This made Cissy even more nervous about the trip as she was sure her Aunt would play matchmaker with absolutely any eligible bachelor they may encounter.

Cissy hadn't mention it to her aunt this morning but she was beside herself, worrying that Hamilton would be out walking too, but as luck would have it they were not to encounter him here today. So a reprieved Cissy sighed with relief as they returned to the carriage by the gate after once again walking a full circuit of the park.

She boarded and relaxed back into her seat in the carriage and closed her eyes for a second and she let her thoughts wander back to Alex, imagining what a trip to the park or the theatre would feel like were she to be on his arm. Then she heaved a contented sigh as she knew that where-ever she went with Alex it would be wonderful.

"You sound very relaxed, Cissy, what are you thinking about, dearest?"

"Oh nothing really, I'm just enjoying the sunshine and I also enjoyed our walk today thank you Aunt" she was actually insinuating that not seeing Guy Hamilton today after fretting about it earlier had made their outing much more pleasant.

They arrived back at the house, alighted from the carriage and made their way to the front door to be greeted by the butler, who bowed to Ellen and informed her that she had a visitor awaiting audience in the drawing room.

"Whoever is calling so early, Carson, you know I don't usually receive callers until after 2 o'clock. Didn't you tell them to go away and return later" Ellen sounded quite irate.

"It is Sir Guy Hamilton, my Lady, and although I advise him of the same he insisted upon awaiting your return" the butler was very apologetic.

Cissy froze on the spot and her insides immediately flew into panic, oh my God, what is he doing here, she suddenly felt very sick "Please would you be so kind as to excuse me for a moment Aunt, I need to go to my room directly".

Ellen, remembering the incident which Cissy had related to her at Lady Kendrow's, nodded in agreement and advised Cissy that she would see her later at luncheon.

So without further hesitation Cissy hastily made her way up to her bed-chamber and locked the door. She realised she may appear to be making too much of the situation but she really couldn't bear the thought of seeing that repulsive man again.

Perhaps if she relaxed on her bed for a while she might feel a little better, so she removed her coat and laid on top of the covers. Within minutes of laying her head on the pillow she promptly fell asleep, to be woken two hours later by Kitty knocking on the door to be allowed access. She was surprised herself that she had slept so long considering her state of mind when she had returned to her room.

She got up and quickly crossed the room to unlock the door for Kitty.

Kitty was her personal lady's maid whom she had brought with her from Monkton Grange. "Are you unwell, my Lady, I was very worried about you".

"I'm alright Kitty, just a little tired, that's all. What time is it?"

"Lady Ellen has sent me to fetch you for your luncheon, it's almost one o'clock and she is waiting for you"

" Could you please inform my aunt that I will be down directly"

"Certainly, my Lady" Kitty curtsied and vacated the room. When her maid had left Cissy began to wonder what had transpired in the drawing room earlier. Daresay her aunt would advise her when she went downstairs, so after refreshing herself she made her way down to the dining room.

"I'm so sorry to have kept you waiting Aunt. I really can't imagine why I should have felt so weary earlier".

The Enchanted Glade

"No matter, my dear, come and sit beside me" Ellen beckoned to the maid to serve her niece and then dismissed her from the room so that she could talk to Cissy in private.

"Do you want to know why Sir Guy Hamilton was here?"

"I don't want to sound rude, Aunt, but if it's anything to do with me, no".

"Well it does concern you, so I think you should be informed that he wished to be invited to your come-out next week".

"Oh Aunt Ellen, please tell me you refused him" Cissy was close to tears.

"Please don't worry, dearest, I apologised profusely to him and informed him that the venue was full to capacity and that we couldn't possibly afford an invitation to another soul. He also asked to call upon you but I told him he would have to approach your father on that matter as I was only your official chaperon until your come-out ball. Don't fret dearest, hopefully he will tire of trying before he gets to meet your father. Now keep your chin up and don't think anymore about the man for the moment. Don't forget we are off to the theatre tonight so lets concentrate on that" Ellen was trying so hard to sound positive and pull Cissy out of the doldrums that she had so sadly fallen into of late.

"Thank you so much, Aunt, but I have a peculiar feeling that I haven't heard the last of Sir Guy Hamilton" Cissy sounded as if she was resigning herself to a fate that she certainly wasn't very happy about.

****

Chapter 9

That evening Cissy was in her bed-chamber excitedly dressing for their trip to the theatre. Kitty was carefully arranging her hair into a chignon and adding a small diamante and feathered head-dress as her Aunt knocked on the door and then entered her room.

"I am so looking forward to going out this evening, are you almost ready?" she said as she crossed the room to the dressing table. Then catching sight of Cissy's reflection in the mirror she gasped. "Oh! Cissy, you look splendid, dearest. Oh, how proud I shall be of you tonight".

Cissy was wearing a full length red gown with a closely fitted bodice which revealed the full splendour of her breasts. The bodice dropped slenderly to her waist and had small puffed sleeves that were worn off the shoulder. The full skirt was frilled at the bottom and small diamantes were scattered all over it. Cissy was very curvaceous and every gown and outfit that her Aunt had so kindly purchased for her not only revealed her shapely figure but made Cissy look and feel like a princess. "Thank you, Aunt Ellen" Cissy answered with such a sweet smile "you are too kind and I wouldn't be looking like this if it wasn't for you".

"Oh, piffle! Cissy, you look absolutely divine and it's you making the clothes look wonderful not the other way around".

"There, my Lady, all finished" said Kitty as she stood back to behold her beautiful mistress.

"Thank you, Kitty, would you please fetch my wrap, the little diamante bag and the red feathered fan from the dressing room" and then turning to her Aunt she murmured with a smile "and then I'll be ready, Aunt".

"Oh my fan, Cissy, I had completely forgotten about it, thank goodness you reminded me. It gets so hot in the theatre at this time of year. I'll just summon Violet and ask her to bring one down to the hall. Carson is already there with my wrap. I don't think we'll need them now but it may be a little chilly later when we leave the theatre. I have asked him to summon the carriage without delay so it should be here by now, come along, my dear, let's go down together". As they were about to leave the room Cissy turned and said to her maid "Kitty, don't wait up, I'm not sure what time we are returning" she was always very thoughtful.

"Please don't fret, my Lady, I hope you have a wonderful evening" Kitty then added quietly " I'll be thrilled to hear all about it when you get back".

"We may be invited back to Lady Kendrow's after the play or perhaps as this is the last night of the current production we may even be asked back-stage to the after show party" added her Aunt. "Lady Kendrow's husband is a benefactor, you see and the theatre was only completed in 1805 and he apparently put up a great deal of the money, but it appears that it was a sound investment. Anyway shall we go I don't want to be late, I absolutely cannot tolerate tardiness myself". They exchanged smiles and Ellen and Cissy made their way to the stairs and descended as Carson announced that their transport was indeed waiting.

Carson handed his mistress her wrap and hurried ahead of them both to open the front door and then he escorted them to the carriage and assisted them in boarding. When they were settled in comfortably Ellen thanked him and he closed the door of the carriage and instructed the coachman to be on his way.

All the way to the theatre Cissy was trying to visualise what the interior would look like and that was what was on her mind as she alighted from the carriage. She was certainly not concentrating and unexpectedly she caught the heel of her shoe in between two flagstones. She felt very unsteady and realised that she was actually falling. As she braced herself thinking she was about to hit the pavement she felt a pair of very strong arms around her and was very relieved as her rescuer brought her steadily back onto her feet.

"Cissy, dearest, are you hurt" she heard her Aunt's frantic tone.

"I am fine thank you Aunt Ellen, thanks to this gentleman" and as Cissy turned her head towards him she was confronted by Guy Hamilton and she felt shock and horror course right through her. Although she was grateful to him for saving her from injury he was the last person in the world that she would want to be rescued by.

He stood there beside her, looking very debonair in his evening attire but she still couldn't bring herself to feel any kindness towards this man. In fact she was still speechless as her Aunt gushed "Oh my dear Sir Guy, we are indebted to you, you have probably saved my niece from a serious injury. How can I ever thank you?"

"The fact that your niece is unhurt is consolation enough, my Lady. Now shall we all proceed into the theatre or we may be late for the start of the performance".

He sounded the epitome of the perfect gentleman but Cissy was unconvinced. Had she been mistaken in her first impressions of this man, was he a man of honour and integrity, at this moment she was still unsure. She hadn't forgotten their last two encounters. The frisson of fear she had felt as he had kissed her hand in the park and the fact that he had gripped her wrist with such force at Lady Kendrow's. No, she wasn't going to be drawn into a false sense of security just because he happened to be there when she fell. Little did Cissy realise then but Hamilton had delighted in the encounter and had enjoyed every moment ogling her cleavage which was exposed a little as her wrap became dislodged during her fall.

"After you, my ladies" he indicated with a slight bow and the smooth tone of his voice seared right through Cissy as they all proceeded towards the auditorium. Ellen thanked him again as they went their separate ways inside and she and Cissy took their allotted seats in Lady Kendrow's box. The other members of their party had already arrived and they were duly introduced to the Kendrow's nephew who seemed to be a very polite and pleasant young man. His name was Edwin Lichfield. " I'm so very honoured to make your acquaintance, Lady Templeton, my Aunt has told me so much about you" he revealed as he bestowed upon her a decidedly agreeable gaze .

Oh no, not another match-maker, thought Cissy, referring to Lady Kendrow. He sounded just like all the others she had been introduced to over the past few weeks. But she was determined to appear polite so she smiled sweetly as he took her hand and brought it to his lips "I hope that everything your Aunt has told you about me was flattering" she smiled again and he looked smitten as he replied

"Most certainly, my Lady, and she did not exaggerate when she described your beauty" he whispered quietly as he raised his head from kissing her hand.

"You are most kind, Sir" she blushed a little as she spoke, thanked him and then turning to settle down into her seat beside him she reflected that on first impression she actually liked this man.

He was very tall and his dark brown hair was swept across his head from a side parting. He had pleasing facial features but she was unable to determine the colour of his eyes in the subdued lighting in the theatre. He had a small pencil thin moustache but still his characteristics portrayed him as being a kind and considerate gentleman. She was incapable of fathoming how old he might be but she guessed he looked in his mid-twenties.

As Cissy made herself more comfortable and just before the production was about to start she looked up and was dismayed to see that Guy Hamilton's party was in the box directly opposite their own and even though she opened her fan quickly and held it up to her face she knew that his eyes were constantly upon her and it made for a very uncomfortable feeling.

Between acts and throughout breaks in the first half of the performance Cissy made a point of gaily chatting to Edwin so that every time Guy Hamilton just happened to look their way she appeared to be very happily engrossed in conversation with her companion.

In the intermission she excused herself to go to the ladies powder room and was feeling quite pleased with herself when she realised that she was actually enjoying Edwin's company and thought that after tonight she may even look forward to seeing him again if he so wished.

She was so completely engrossed in her thoughts as she was returning along a corridor towards the box that she didn't notice that she was being followed. Suddenly someone caught hold of her arm and opening a door to her right pushed her into a darkened room. At first she was taken so much by surprise that she hadn't realised what had become so apparent, then as she attempted to free herself she let out a shriek and immediately a hand came over her mouth. Her assailant quickly pivoted her until she was clasped tightly in his arms and as she was struggling for breath he quietly murmured "What lengths one has to go to get your attention, my dear" and as he took his hands from her mouth she started to scream again so he promptly replaced his hands with his lips and the intensity of it almost made her swoon. She had never been kissed on the lips before, let alone so thoroughly. Then she suddenly felt the beard and she realised who this intruder was. She forcefully pulled herself away and gasped "How dare you touch me like this,

The Enchanted Glade

Hamilton, you scoundrel" she turned to try to locate the door but in the darkness it was impossible to see clearly.

"Let me out of here now before I scream again".

"And alert the ushers. Then, my lady, your reputation will be in tatters and I will have to offer for you."

"Why are you doing this to me" she was actually becoming quite frightened after his last comment. What she didn't realise at this moment was that he had no wish to offer for anyone, he just wanted her body and then he would cast her aside whilst he moved onto another young unsuspecting virgin. Virgins, how he loved to deflower them.

"You continually avoid me and I do not like to be ignored" he snarled.

"You are mistaken, Sir. I have never sought to purposely avoid you. Until tonight when you so kindly assisted me I have not seen you since I first met you in the park". Her heart was pounding inside her chest and she was trying to humour him, but he snapped back.

"At Lady Kendrow's you deliberately avoided me after I asked you to dance".

"Oh, I had forgotten that occasion, I'm sorry but you startled me and I was unwell" she was trying so hard to appease the situation but she was becoming progressively more anxious.

"You also shunned me when I called at your Aunt's house this morning" he sounded increasingly agitated " I saw you from the window when you returned in the carriage with your Aunt".

"I'm sorry but her butler said you were calling upon her. I would never presume the circumstances of your visit. Please may I return to my Aunt now, the longer I am gone the more she will be worried about me ".

" I will let you go back to your Aunt on one condition and that is that you agree to an audience when I call on you in the morning"

She knew she would agree to any request at this moment to get out of this situation as quickly as possible. "I agree, but you know full well that I cannot see you alone, that I will have to have a chaperon".

He ignored her comment and walked passed her to open the door "I will see you tomorrow, my Lady". He then had the nerve to afford her a bow as she rushed passed him and swiftly returned to the box where her Aunt was beside herself with worry. "Where-ever have you been, Cissy, we sent an usher to look for you but you were nowhere to be found".

"I am so very sorry Aunt I encountered an old friend of Louise's" she lied "and I completely forgot the time" no-one commented on the fact that Cissy looked rather flushed and dishevelled

"You seem a little out of breath, dearest, are you ailing"

"No, Aunt I just hurried back when I realised how long I had been away, please forgive me".

"Certainly, my dear, think no more of it, now let us settle down and enjoy the remainder of the evening. I am just thankful you have returned in time for the rest of the performance" her Aunt then took her own seat and Edwin held Cissy's chair whilst she too sat down.

Cissy was almost too frightened to glance over to the opposite box to see if Guy Hamilton was watching her, but when she did summon up enough courage she saw that his seat was empty and remained so for the rest of the performance.

Next day she woke from a dreamless sleep as the early morning sun was dancing across the room and it's rays were shimmering brightly through the window. Cissy suddenly remembered what had transpired the previous evening and she froze in revulsion, dreading the thought of what might occur when Guy Hamilton came to call this morning. Then she realised there was absolutely nothing she could possibly do about it now so stretching her arms above her head she yawned as she got out of bed. She walked over to the dresser, to the wash basin of water that had been brought earlier whilst she was still asleep and she proceeded to remove her night shift to commence her toilette. Her mind then wandered back once again to the night before.

From the theatre they had proceeded to an after show-party and although Edwin was very attentive she could not draw her mind away from Guy Hamilton and the events in the interval.

They had arrived back after midnight and Cissy had excused herself immediately and had made her way to her bedchamber where Kitty was waiting to hear how the evening had progressed. As she had helped her mistress to undress Cissy told her how she had met Edwin Lichfield whom she had taken to immediately and she also told Kitty that he had spent the whole evening paying special attention to her, but she mentioned nothing about Guy Hamilton. Kitty was getting quite excited at the thought of her mistress actually meeting someone she liked.

Duties over, Kitty had then retired to her own room and although Cissy had gone straight to bed she could not sleep, no matter how much she tried. She couldn't stop thinking about Guy Hamilton and the audience later this morning and she faced the proceedings to come with distasteful trepidation. All she could do was wonder what this despicable man wanted with her. She ran the incident over and over in her mind again and again and she still couldn't fathom why he had acted the way he had. She had eventually succumbed to sleep in the early hours of the morning.

Last night she had requested that Kitty bring her breakfast in bed today and as she finished dressing she heard her maid outside the door. Kitty entered wishing her mistress a very cheerful "Good Morning, my Lady" she then added "I've brought you some eggs, bacon, bread and butter and a pot of tea. Shall I pour it directly" then she crossed the room and laid a small table near the window.

"Thank you, Kitty, that would be lovely" she said walking over to sit down. Cissy's bed-chamber was at the front of the house and over-looked a grassed area which resembled a small park that was frequently used by the residents to either walk out with their children or their dogs. She attempted to eat her breakfast but because she was feeling very sick deep inside her stomach she wasn't having much success. As she peered out to watch the events of the day unfolding she could see that there were nannies outside pushing basinets, an older gentleman out walking with a cane to assist him, and as she regarded others she noticed several delivery persons walking along the cobbles with their wares.

A carriage turned the corner at the edge of the Crescent and her heart leapt in her chest at the thought of the encounter she was about to endure. But as she watched, feeling a large lump forming in her throat, the carriage passed her Aunt's house and stopped further along the thoroughfare. Several other carriages came and went and she was so cross with herself for acting so impulsively in imagining that every carriage that came into view belonged to Guy Hamilton. She felt she was becoming obsessed with the man and her nerves were in pieces by the time she had finished eating.

Kitty came to retrieve the tray and asked Cissy if she needed her at all before this evening as she would very much like to go to visit her mother who lived across town on the other side of the river.

"You go and enjoy your day and I will see you this evening" Cissy smiled "Give my regards to your mother".

After thanking her mistress Kitty left the room and that left Cissy with her thoughts which weren't very encouraging.

The morning seemed to drag and she was on edge the whole time. She couldn't stop peering out of the window if she heard the slightest noise from below. She decided she would have to do something to drag her mind away from Guy Hamilton so she sat down to write a letter to her mother. She

The Enchanted Glade

told her that she was having a wonderful time with Aunt Ellen and she relayed news of the visits they had made that week and all the enjoyable things that had occurred at the theatre. She also said she was keeping very well although she was apprehensive about her come-out ball next week. She told her mother that she was missing her and was very much looking forward to seeing her on Friday, which was the day that her parents were arriving to stay at her Aunt's house for the weekend. She finished by asking that should there be any correspondence for her perhaps her mother would kindly bring it with her. She then put the letter in an envelope, sealed it and placed it on the dresser to take downstairs later.

By midday she was beside herself so she rang for the butler and when he arrived she asked him if her Aunt was at home.

"Her Ladyship is out visiting her modiste, my Lady, I'm not sure when she expects to return" he bowed his head slightly as he spoke.

"Would you kindly bring me some tea in the small parlour"

"Certainly, My Lady" he turned to walk towards the door.

"Oh, and Carson" she called out as an afterthought.

He turned back to face her "Yes, my Lady".

"Were their any callers this morning?"

"No, my Lady. Lady Bellamy only takes callers in the afternoon".

"Thank you" she murmured seemingly disappointed.

"I'll fetch your tea directly" and off he went in the direction of the kitchen.

As she made her way to the small parlour she reflected that she had hoped Guy Hamilton had called and that she had somehow missed him. If he had no intention of calling why had he caused the incident the night before. He had given the impression that he was adamant in his pursuit of her but she was actually relieved to think that he may have given up the chase. He appeared to be totally unpredictable so maybe she had nothing to worry about.

Just then there was a knock at the door and her heart leapt in her chest. Oh! no he has arrived she thought, as a terrified feeling gripped her at the concept of encountering him again.

"Yes" she called meekly

"I have brought your tea, my Lady"

"Oh it's you, Carson" relief raced through her veins as she sighed and bade him come in.

He laid the tray on a small table beside her and asked if she would like him to pour it for her. Unable to stop shaking she nodded assent and thanked him as he left the room.

She was deep in thought as she relaxed back into the chair a little with her eyes closed and the teacup in her hand. She had almost finished drinking her tea when the door suddenly opened again and Aunt Ellen entered.

"Oh there you are, dearest, I'm sorry I didn't inform you of my visit to town this morning but I was of the opinion that you were still asleep when I left. I have purchased some really beautiful and very unusual accessories to match my outfit for your come-out next week and I am so pleased with them, they will be delivered this afternoon. How did your morning go?".

Cissy almost choked on her tea. She couldn't possibly convey to her Aunt what had or had not transpired in her confused mind so she just mumbled "I had breakfast in my room and then wrote a letter to my mother" she then added

"Are you expecting any callers this afternoon?"

"Yes, Lady Kendrow and her nephew are calling at 2 o'clock"

Cissy's spirits were suddenly elated but as her Aunt continued she felt more than a little distressed.

"Also Guy Hamilton sent his man around with a card this morning but I had Carson send him back with a message to say I was not at home, so he has arranged to call later this afternoon. I have no idea what he wants. If he is pursuing you again I shall tell him what I told him before that he will have to approach your father".

The Enchanted Glade

Cissy cringed, she thought she had succeeded in avoiding him but it seemed that it was not the case. She would reluctantly face him as she had agreed last night even if she detested the very idea of it. " If he insists I shall receive him, Aunt, but you must promise not to leave the room".

"You do surprise me, Cissy dear, what is this, a change of heart on your part?".

"Well he was very gallant at the theatre when I stumbled last evening; perhaps he is just calling to ensure that I am none the worst for it". She could think of nothing else to say to throw her aunt off the scent of the real reason he may be calling.

"As you wish, my dear, I shall call you when he arrives. Now we had better not delay our luncheon any longer if we are to be ready to receive our visitors by 2 o'clock" and with that Ellen rang for Carson to serve luncheon immediately.

Knowing she would be unable to eat anything due to the likely events to come Cissy rose from her chair and obediently followed her Aunt to the dining room with the heaviest of hearts. How she was going to endure the events of the afternoon she did not know but she resolved to try to tolerate it for the sake of her dear Aunt.

Lady Kendrow and Edwin arrived on time at 2 o'clock and stayed for an hour. They enjoyed light conversation and refreshments and Lady Kendrow, obviously intent on pushing the young couple together, invited them to a picnic the next afternoon. Ellen was delighted and accepted immediately on behalf of them both.

"Why don't you both walk in the garden" Aunt Ellen suggested to Cissy and Edwin, with a broad smile.

There was a large open French window leading to the outside from the room in which they were seated and Cissy was amazed that her Aunt had suggested that they 'walk in the garden' because she didn't really have a garden. It was just an enclosed paved area with two garden seats and edged with a few large Grecian urn styled plant pots filled with the most exquisite flowering shrubs that appeared to have been imported from abroad. Aunt Ellen's husband, Barnaby, had travelled abroad numerous times before he had died and probably her aunt was still in contact with some of their old acquaintances.

The two of them rose from their seats and walked towards the window and Edwin very chivalrously half bowed and swept his arm across in front of him saying "After you my Lady".

"Thank you" replied Cissy, smiling sweetly, as they made their way outside "but please call me Cissy". They sat together on one of the garden seats and, although they were not out of earshot of the other two women, they gaily talked about the trip to the theatre the night before.

Cissy found that talking to Edwin was very enlightening and as they continued their conversation she discovered that he was training to be a doctor at The Mineral Water Hospital. She was interested in many subjects including medicine and had read some books about it. Edwin , of course, was very impressed by this.

"Eventually, I would like to become a surgeon" he said, now Cissy was impressed with Edwin.

Soon it was time for their respected guests to depart but before they left Ellen arranged the time of the picnic with Lady Kendrow and expressed their delight at being asked to attend, then they said their goodbyes and left.

Cissy was immediately on tender hooks as the thought loomed in her mind that their next visitor was most probably for her and when the door knocker sounded very loudly she felt quite faint. She knew she would have to face him sometime, because she would never go back on her word, so she steeled herself for the encounter in question.

Carson came to the morning room and tapped the door.

"Come in" Ellen instructed at the same time keeping an eye on Cissy's reaction.

The Enchanted Glade

"Sir Guy Hamilton is here, My Lady, will you receive him?". Ellen looked at Cissy once more and detected a slight panic but as her niece had earlier indicated that she was prepared to see the man Ellen instructed Carson to admit him.

Carson showed Hamilton in and after welcoming him Ellen asked Carson to fetch some refreshment.

"Please won't you sit down, Sir Guy" Ellen invited, so he seated himself in a winged chair next to Cissy who nodded an insignificant welcome.

"It is very agreeable that you should visit us today, did you enjoy the play last night?". Ellen was being very diplomatic indeed.

"I most certainly enjoyed the events at the theatre last evening, my Lady" he responded and as he glanced at Cissy, she knew he was not referring to the performance, as he had missed half of it, but to his temporary abduction of herself.

"I would like to thank you for saving me from falling when I alighted from the carriage, Sir Guy. It was very perceptive of you to anticipate what was about to happen". Cissy's insides were twisting in knots.

"That was the reason for my visit today to see how you are feeling, my lady" he sounded so very sincere but she knew he was lying.

"Because of your swift action, Sir, I was unhurt but I would like to thank you for taking the trouble to call anyway" she was being as polite as she possibly could without appearing to overdo it.

"I also came to ask your Aunt" he then directed his gaze towards Ellen "if you would both accompany me, as my guests, to the gala-night at the Sydney Gardens on Tuesday evening next week. There will be music, singing, cascades, fire-works and superb illuminations. I thought you may both enjoy an excursion such as this, especially as the evenings are still quite light and comparatively warm at this time of year. What do you say, Lady Ellen?"

"Well as you are aware my niece is having her Come-out ball on Saturday so I really don't know if she can cope with many more outings in the coming week. How do you feel about it, dearest?".

Hamilton interjected "If you recall, my Lady" he was addressing Ellen "I was very keen to attend the festivities on Saturday evening but you informed me that the venue was full so maybe this will sufficiently compensate me for my disappointment".

Knowing that the man wouldn't give up until she had decided in his favour Cissy indicated agreement "That's very thoughtful of you, we'd be pleased to accompany you" inside she was very unsettled about the whole situation but she thought to get it over and done with as soon as possible and then perhaps he'd leave her alone in future.

Soon after partaking of the tea Hamilton expressed his thanks and Ellen called for Carson to see him out. Hamilton stood up and bowed to both ladies saying he would collect them in his carriage on Tuesday evening at 7 o'clock and he then took his leave.

Cissy was totally unsure as to whether she had made the right decision but only time would tell.

The picnic on Sunday was most enjoyable and much to the delight of the two older ladies Cissy and Edwin spent a very pleasurable afternoon together. They sat on the grass and talked mostly about their families. Edwin revealing that his parents lived near Plymouth as his father was in the shipping business. He was staying with his Aunt until he had achieved his medical appraisal, but he was undecided whether to go back to live in Plymouth and work at the hospital there.

"Have you ever been to Plymouth, my Lady" he enquired.

"No, Edwin, I haven't and as I said earlier, please call me Cissy, that's what all of my friends call me" a smile teased across her lips as she spoke.

The Enchanted Glade

"Thank you Cissy, it is comforting that you consider me one of your friends. Maybe you would like to visit Plymouth one day, my parents home is very near the beach. Do you like the beach?".

"I do, Edwin, and I may take you up on your offer sometime. I have taken so much pleasure in our time together and have so enjoyed our conversations and of course I hope you will be attending my Come-out ball on Saturday".

"With pleasure" he replied with a twinkle in his eye "I wouldn't miss it".

"I will look forward to seeing you and also reserving a dance or two for you" At last Cissy seemed to have changed her mind about her come-out and for the first time since it was booked she felt herself warming to the idea of it.

The remainder of the afternoon went swimmingly and when they returned home Cissy and her Aunt reflected that they had really enjoyed the day.

On Tuesday morning Cissy was so traumatised thinking about the evening ahead she even thought of feigning a head cold but thought better of it as she didn't want any further repercussions reflecting on her Aunt. After all her aunt had done for her she would never embarrass her in any way whatsoever. Under normal circumstances she would have looked forward immensely to an evening such as this but because it was in the company of Guy Hamilton it was a different story.

She stayed in her room all morning and as Ellen was worried about her she sent for Kitty to ascertain how her niece was feeling. Ellen fully understood that Cissy may feel a little apprehensive but what she definitely could not understand was why Cissy had agreed to go so readily in the first place. Not surprisingly she actually hadn't grasped the situation that Cissy had found herself in.

The afternoon passed too quickly for Cissy, she was hoping that it would drag out as she was dreading the evening drawing closer. But inevitably it arrived and Kitty came to her room to help her ready herself for the evening ahead. She had no heart in what she wore tonight and she certainly wasn't going out of her way to dress-up for him so she requested quite a plain yet classically styled blue gown with a scooped neckline. Her cleavage wasn't so evident in this gown which was why she felt more at ease with it. Kitty still thought her mistress looked very elegant in whatever she wore. She and her Aunt had both decided to take brocade shawls as the event was outdoors and it may turn chilly a little later on in the evening.

Sir Guy arrived exactly on time in his carriage and was politeness itself as he called at the door, he was admitted by the butler and as they were ready to leave he then escorted the two ladies back to the carriage to commence their excursion to the impressive event at the gardens.

The journey took quite a while as it seemed as if the whole of the ton was converging on the gardens for the festivities this evening. They had not engaged in much conversation on the way as Cissy didn't feel she had anything to say to Guy Hamilton and she also felt that she had agreed to this meeting under duress. They alighted from the carriage after he had chivalrously handed both women down and he offered each one an arm as they walked up the gradual ascent of the principal walk that they had visited on Friday morning, although it appeared completely different under this lighting. The lamps at each side of the walk that illuminated their way gave a very captivating appearance and her aunt remarked to her that it rendered these gardens very similar to the Vauxhall Gardens in London at the height of the season. At the top of the park they saw the half-circle stone pavilion, supported by several pillars which they had been seated in last week and as they passed Cissy noticed that Lady Kendrow and Edwin were now seated there with friends. Edwin must have sensed something as he looked up and acknowledged her party with a nod but by the look on his face Cissy thought he seemed rather disappointed that she was being escorted by Hamilton and not himself.

They were ushered to the booth which Sir Guy had reserved for the duration of the occasion and the evening was filled with entertainment. On a raised stage, reputable actresses were dancing and singing, and there was a full orchestra which was elevated so that they were easily visible to all-comers. The food which was brought by the attendants was superb and the spectacular firework display was breath-taking and except for the company Cissy had a thoroughly enjoyable evening. Although she had to admit that Guy Hamilton was a perfect gentleman the whole time and it made her wonder what had come over the man.

Maybe I really have misinterpreted his actions, she mused to herself, as she watched him conversing easily with her Aunt. Perhaps I caught him on a bad day, she thought, thinking back to Lady Kendrow's soiree, attempting to give him the benefit of the doubt and by the end of the evening after he had duly conducted them home in a most gentlemanly and dignified fashion, she decided that she had definitely misjudged the man.

****

Chapter 10

It is the day of Cissy's come-out ball and at last she is ready. As she is descending the impressive staircase to the extensive hall, Aunt Ellen is standing there at the foot of the stairs to behold her.
Cissy is stunningly resplendent in a satin ball gown in deepest emerald green which compliments her breathtakingly styled titian hair, which is swept up behind her ears and is swirling in curls down her back. The gown itself is fitted neatly from her bust to her waist and plunges softly at the neckline where she wears the stunning diamond necklace her parents have had especially made for this auspicious occasion. Her hair is set with eye-catching feathers in a golden clasp and she wears a pair of diamond-droplet earrings which match the necklace. She is wearing matching emerald coloured elbow length gloves of the finest silk and at her left wrist is a most magnificent diamond bracelet to complete the set. All the pieces of jewellery are reflecting in the candlelight and they accentuate her delightful countenance as she makes her way down to the dimly lit hallway. She has on a pair of beautiful matching velvet slippers and attached to her right wrist is a very pretty colourful posy.
"Cissy you look enchanting!" exclaimed her aunt. The sight of her niece completely taking her breath away. "Your mother and father will be so very proud of you, my dear".
"And it's all thanks to you, dearest Aunt Ellen" Cissy said, as her aunt raised her hand to take her own and lead her across the extensive hall to the drawing room where they,

The Enchanted Glade

especially her mother, were anxiously waiting to escort her to the celebrated Assembly Rooms for what could be the most important night of her life.

As the door opens Annabel catches sight of Cissy and she feels her own eyes brimming with tears as she beholds her beautiful daughter in all her finery. "Oh Cissy, my darling, you look absolutely magnificent" and at that moment she could say no more for fear of completely losing her own composure.

Even her father muttered his approval "You look splendid! Now let's get you out there to get you married off as soon as possible to the highest bidder" he smirked as Cissy frowned at his twisted sense of humour.

He had to try to spoil it, didn't he, thought Cissy as she took his arm to be led out to the carriage already waiting outside on the cobbled thoroughfare. Well I will not let him ruin my evening, she deliberated as she smiled and appeared to accept his comments in good part.

All four of them boarded the carriage and settled in for the short journey along Brock Street to The Circus, and then off The Circus was Bennett Street where the renowned Assembly Rooms were situated.

What Cissy did not see, as she walked to the carriage with her father, was the dark figure waiting in the shadows watching her as she went on her way. Guy Hamilton was leering at her and as her carriage rumbled passed him he hid in the unlit doorway next to Ellen's house. "You seem to think you've seen the last of me, Lady Templeton, but you couldn't be more mistaken" and no-one was in earshot to hear his deranged laughter as he skulked away to continue in his pursuit to bed the most beautiful young woman he had ever come across.

Cissy's party arrived at their destination quite swiftly and although they were not late, others had already assembled. Cissy was thrilled to see Edwin waiting in the foyer looking very debonair in his evening attire. He was escorting his aunt, Lady Kendrow, who looked approvingly at Cissy as she entered. Secretly Cissy knew that Edwin's aunt was hoping for a match between them. As she passed them on her father's arm she mouthed to Edwin "I'll see you in a moment". He nodded with a smile.

Cissy was then escorted into the large ballroom to be formally introduced to everyone, especially all the eligible bachelors who had effectively been 'rounded up' and invited with her betrothal in mind. They had probably been invited to every come-out ball held in the city this season.

As she entered the impressive room she marvelled at the ornate decoration, the awe-inspiring sculptured ceiling and glittering chandeliers. She couldn't even imagine how many candles it took to light the ballroom so effectively. Her aunt had booked the venue months ago but although Cissy had been staying with Aunt Ellen for quite a while she had not been allowed in to view it before because her aunt wanted to see the surprise on Cissy's face when she entered. Ellen was not disappointed.

After procuring the table which had been allotted to them Cissy sat down to await the succession of men who were eager to secure a dance on her card. She was inundated and within ten minutes her dance card was full, Edwin was very disappointed to have only acquired one dance, but at least it was a waltz.

Apart from Edwin, Cissy was uninterested in all of the others, although whilst dancing with them she had enjoyed herself very much. She certainly couldn't imagine being wed to any of them and as she had not felt an affinity towards any one of them she didn't think she was going to secure a match tonight. There were many other lovely young ladies in the room but she was so enjoying being the centre of all the attention she was receiving as the belle of the ball.

Her waltz with Edwin made her feel very special and she really did like him. He held her very close and as she glanced up into his soft grey eyes, looking at her with complete tenderness, she realised that he was the only man in the room she was remotely impressed with but he still wasn't Alex and instead of concentrating on the dance she closed her eyes and her mind wandered back to her waltz with Alex by the lake after Louise's come-out. She knew she must try to forget Alex in that context. He was her best friend and loved her like a sister, and she couldn't imagine that he felt about her in any other way, however much she wished it.

It was later when she was alone for a few moments in the ladies powder room that her mind wandered once again to Alex and she wished so hard that he could be here. He was the only one that she really wanted as a husband but as he wasn't here and there was a slight possibility that he would not make it back… oh! No, she shuddered at the thought of it and then sadly realised that at this very moment he could be fighting for his life in a bloody battle in Spain whilst she was enjoying herself here. She couldn't bear to contemplate it and immediately tried to put the thought out of her head but she could not, and after that it played on her mind all evening and she then couldn't wait for the proceedings to end.

At midnight the ball ended and although she had enjoyed it overall she knew that her first come-out hadn't been a huge success.

When she returned to her aunt's house that night she resigned herself to the fact that Edwin was the only man at her come-out that it would be remotely possible to envisage as a husband and although she didn't love him as she did Alex, maybe it would come in time. She decided there and then that if Edwin approached her father to ask for her hand she would accept his proposal of marriage.

Cissy had arrived home three days ago after a tearful farewell at her Aunt's house. She had so enjoyed her summer with Aunt Ellen and felt she was deeply in her debt, especially in respect of all of the beautiful gowns and outfits that she had so kindly bestowed upon her, which were to be sent back to Monkton Grange within the next few days. When she had mentioned her gratitude to her Aunt, Ellen wouldn't hear of such a thing and had expressed the fact that she had enjoyed it as much herself and wouldn't have missed it for the world, though she added that she would most certainly miss Cissy's company immensely.

Cissy had been upset that Louise couldn't be at her come-out so she decided that today she would write a secret note to her sister and she would also pen a note to Alex to tell them all about it.

Cissy very rarely spoke to her father; in fact she hadn't seen him since her come-out last Saturday. If she ever encountered him it was only when they had company, then she found it was easier to mingle with the other guests and avoid talking to him altogether. At mealtimes she sat as far away from him as possible, so she was very surprised when Kitty knocked on the door and after entering informed her that she was summoned to his study and was asked to attend upon him immediately.

She concealed the note she was writing in the small drawer of her dressing table and put her pen and ink away and it was with tremendous apprehension that she descended the staircase and approached his study. She was intensely curious as to the reason for this unexpected summons and felt slightly nervous as she knocked the door and awaited his command to enter. His tone when he answered was unusually polite and not the gruff bellow she was used to hearing. Knowing that her father acted differently in company she presumed he must have a visitor. She entered when her knock was acknowledged and as she was closing the door the gentleman in question turned to greet her and she was absolutely astounded to see Sir Guy Hamilton stood as bold as brass beside her father's desk. As he bowed to her in

The Enchanted Glade

welcome she noticed that a shadow of a smile touched the corner of his mouth almost mocking her which made her even more nervous.

He approached and took her hand which he immediately brought up to his lips and with an unusually confident look in his eye he purred "It's a pleasure to see you again, my Lady".

Cissy's mouth was agog wondering why he was here.

"Come along, don't dally, let's get this thing sorted" her father sounded his usual impatient self. "Cecilia, you are quite well acquainted with Sir Guy Hamilton, are you not?"

"Well, yes" Cissy answered guardedly, wondering what was to transpire from this conversation. Perhaps Sir Guy had come to ask her father if he could walk out with her. She did like him a little more now that she had come to know him a little better and he had been most accommodating when he had taken Aunt Ellen and herself to the gala night at the Sydney Gardens. As she was thinking this she gradually digested the words her father was uttering now and she was so completely stunned that she asked him to repeat it

"Sir Guy has asked for your hand in marriage, and as you were unsuccessful in procuring a match last week, I have agreed".

"But..." stuttered Cissy

"No buts" her father interrupted "I have already posted an announcement in The Times and the banns are to be read...."
Cissy's heart and soul went into complete panic; she didn't even hear the rest of the declaration coming from her father's mouth. She almost swooned at the shock of it. Granted, Sir Guy had seemed very gentleman-like and they had exchanged pleasantries in the last few weeks but she didn't want to marry him for pities sake.

She vaguely heard her father ending his oration with "the wedding will take place within the next three months and you will have a betrothal party in four weeks time, on the bank holiday weekend, that is, if there is enough time for your mother to organise everything".

"Does Mama know about this?" Cissy spluttered, still unable to comprehend the position she had found herself in.

"She will when I inform her later today" her father said dispassionately.

"Do I have no say in the matter? I have only known Sir Guy a little short of two months and that is hardly enough time to contemplate marriage". They were conversing as if Guy Hamilton was not even in the room.

"You have no say in the matter, I have arranged your dowry, everything is settled and my word is final" and with that he turned his back on her as if dismissing her from his presence. Cissy glanced at Guy Hamilton and as he began to speak he extended his hand to her but she turned and fled from the room, not even requesting leave as was polite to do so.

Tears were running down her cheeks now, but not with pity for herself, only in anger at her father. How dare he treat her like this? The trouble was that Cissy was only seventeen which made her under-age and as such she had no say in her life whatsoever. She had effectively failed to secure a match at her come-out but Edwin was the only other man besides her beloved Alex that she would even contemplate a courtship with, let alone marriage.

She ran upstairs to try to find her mother but her search was fruitless. Surely her mother wouldn't agree to this fiasco when she found out. How very conceited of her father to go ahead with all of this without consulting her mother. Typical of the man, she thought. She actually hated her father at this moment. There had been no love lost between them ever since he had beaten her years ago, she had just tolerated him and had been as polite as a daughter should be to her parent, but now he was placing her in an intolerable situation. She decided to go down to see Emmy and quickly descended the back stairs to the kitchen and as soon as she entered Emily knew something was afoot.

The Enchanted Glade

"What is it, my chick" she said as she raised her arms in welcome. Cissy ran to her, now completely overcome with emotion.

Between sobs Cissy gulped "My father has given my hand in marriage to Sir Guy Hamilton and although I am not averse to the man, he is the last person on earth I would wish to marry".

As Emily relaxed her hold on Cissy her mouth dropped open and she gasped "Oh my gawd! Whatever is the mat'er with 'is lordship? When did all this 'appen?"

Cissy, still shaken to the core, and now frantically pacing up and down the kitchen floor, relayed the events in her father's study. "I can't find my mother, Emmy, do you know where she is? I must talk with her urgently" she was beside herself with anxiety.

"I think she was goin' to one o' those afternoon tea gatherin's with Lady Lavinia at the 'all, and I 'eard that they was talkin' abou' 'avin' some charity event 'ere on the August bank 'oliday Monday, when all the folks from the village was to be invit'd, like a fair or somethin'."

"My father wants to hold my betrothal party on the same weekend so I do hope my mother wins in this, the longer I can put off the betrothal the better".

Emily had made Cissy a drink now and bade her sit down and try to calm herself for a minute. "Per'aps it will all turn out for the bet'er, let's keep our fingers crossed" Emily said sympathetically. Cissy just sighed and wished that she could feel as optimistic as Emmy in this matter.

Later that afternoon Cissy heard the carriage draw up outside and flew downstairs to meet her mother when she came in. Before Annabel had even had time to remove her coat that Ambrose the butler was assisting her with, Cissy blurted out that she must speak to her mother before her father could curtail her.

"Whatever cannot wait until I have taken my coat off, Cissy, what is the matter with you?" Annabel sounded alarmed.

"Please Mother we need to talk about something very important". Although Cissy was very fond of Ambrose Harris as he was like a grandfather figure to her, she couldn't possibly discuss anything with her mother in front of the butler, so after the coat was finally removed, she hurried her mother through to her sitting room.

Cissy then passed on the information she had been given by her father and a horrified Annabel asked Cissy to go to her room whilst she spoke to her father and assured Cissy she would come to her as soon as she could, hopefully with some good news.

Annabel stormed into her husband's study and was not surprised to smell the stench of brandy from the open bottle on the desk. "Celebrating our daughter's betrothal are you?" The sarcasm poured out of her mouth.

He glanced around from his slumped position on the chair and with a smirk he drawled "The chit has told you then?" with that he raised his glass towards Annabel and slurred "Cheers, that's got rid of another one".

She had taken all she could from this man, who was supposed to be a husband and father. He didn't even know the meaning of the words.

"So! You have promised Cissy to Hamilton, have you? That's like leading a lamb to the slaughter. Cissy is an innocent young lady and Hamilton has the reputation of a rake, as if you didn't know, you spend enough time together at that club of yours. You are both tarred with the same brush, gambling, women and drinking are all you ever think about" she was fuming "Well I shall not allow this".

"Too late! I knew you would take the chit's side so I posted it in The Times myself yesterday and I went to the bank to arrange the dowry. Can you bear the threat of another scandal, Annabel? or will all of your so-called friends rally

The Enchanted Glade

round to help" he was being indulgently sarcastic now."You only just endured the last one, you may not survive another, and will your friends still want to know you when that happens. Anyway, you are wrong about Hamilton, splendid chap, knows how to keep a woman in her place. Oh, just go woman and get on with the arrangements".

Annabel was so angry she was tempted to smash the brandy bottle over his head, but she wouldn't stoop that low. Oh, how she wanted to hurt him at this moment, just as he had hurt her and her children for years now. Although, he had hit on a sore point. They had pulled through the scandal of Louise running off with the blacksmith, and it was little short of a miracle that the scandal of the rape had remained a secret. Annabel had fiercely loyal friends who had always stood by her and helped to save her reputation when it was in danger of being damaged. The only satisfying part here was that her husband had no idea that through her friends Lavinia and John Bartholomew she was in regular contact with Louise and her family and now saw her two grandchildren as often as she could. He couldn't know about this or he would not allow it to continue, but then the plans she and her friends had devised were ingenious so she didn't think there was much danger of him ever finding out.

It seemed pointless continuing with this conversation as he never took any notice of anything she said so she turned and left the room. She would consult with Cissy to see how she was feeling and explain the dire situation she had found herself in.

Cissy was sat alone, still fretting, in her room as her mother knocked the door and entered. Cissy's face took on an appearance of expectation.

"Cissy I feel as if I am a failure as a mother" Annabel's face was rife with sadness.

"Oh, please, Mother, never think that of yourself. You have been the most wonderful of mothers".

"Your father has informed me that he has already posted your betrothal in The Times and the only way for us to avoid a scandal is for you to accept the situation and marry Hamilton" Annabel saw the horrified look on Cissy's face.

" I do not want this any more than you do, Cissy, but after the scandal with Louise I doubt that we'd survive another. Cissy…" Her mother said thoughtfully. "Did you not say that you were very taken with Edwin Lichfield, Lady Kendrow's nephew?"

"Yes, Mother I am very fond of Edwin. Why, what do you have in mind?"

"I was wondering if we could persuade your father to admit that he named the wrong person in the announcement. I am quite sure that anyone reading the paper will assume that a mistake has been made anyway. No-one will believe that your father would tie you to a man of Hamilton's reputation so I will ask Aunt Ellen to have a word with him. She may be able to persuade your father to admit he has made a mistake in announcing it. At least you will be marrying someone that you may come to love in the future, Edwin seems a very honest and decent man and I am sure from what I've seen and heard he is very fond of you".

"Goodness, I am so confused" Cissy shrugged her shoulders almost in disbelief at what was going on. "and what if Father refuses. All he can think of is that Sir Guy has a title whereas Edwin does not. He is training to be a humble surgeon; I cannot see Father agreeing to anything else. He has already informed me that he will not be swayed and that I have heard his final word on the matter. Mother, I cannot bear to cause you any more grief and if your reputation is seriously at stake I will take my chances with Sir Guy. I quite like the man but it was the blatant way in which my father handled all of this that has made me so angry".

"Cissy, darling, you know that all I have ever wanted is that my children be happy, happier than I have ever been,

The Enchanted Glade

anyway" Cissy had never seen such sadness in her mother's beautiful eyes.

"Please, Mother, don't fret anymore. Let's hope that Aunt Ellen can change his mind and if not then I must marry Sir Guy however much I loathe the idea. In fact at this moment I really do not want to get married at all".

Annabel gave Cissy an impromptu hug and then left the room to hopefully get a message to Ellen to ask her to call as soon as possible.

Meanwhile Cissy decided to stay in her room so she lay on her bed and closed her eyes before the tears came.

"Alex" she murmured aloud "please, Alex come back to me. I need your help so badly". Alex had always looked out for Cissy, was always there for her whenever she needed him in the past. She needed him now more than ever but she knew that it was almost impossible to hope for a miracle.

****

Chapter 11

Meanwhile in Spain Alex had just returned from a particularly traumatic battle and as he reached his tent he almost collapsed in a heap on his insubstantial bed as he sat for a moment to regain his composure. The endless days marching had been intensely harrowing. All the men had suffered blisters from their ill-fitting boots as they'd marched. They'd had to carry everything on their backs in haversacks, loaded with their blanket roll and a canteen of water, water which was very scarce and not always fresh. Some days their balance was impaired as they wilted in the intense heat, even though they didn't march from mid-day until four in the afternoon some would still be overcome and couldn't continue. Often, during their siesta, as they sat on a hillside in the shade the olive trees Alex would watch them, their faces showing the familiar signs typical of senseless wars. Just like him they didn't really want to be here. At home many of them had been out of work so being here had given them a sense of purpose at first but now nearly all of them were regretting the rash decision to volunteer their services for their country. Many of the young men under his command were on their first mission and were sickened by the stench of death and the bloody corpses. They were also being driven mad by the constant sound emitted from Napoleon's heavy cannon, forever growing nearer.

As he sat thinking back over the events of the day, as a superior officer he felt a tremendous responsibility for the men he had lost in the harrowing battle. And what had they

The Enchanted Glade

gained from it, he thought? A few miles of land advancing towards the enemy, but today the tables were turned and the enemy had advanced on them. He always led from the front, never expecting any of his men to do anything he was not prepared to do himself, but he had been totally taken aback by the feeling of revulsion he had felt as, one by one, over twenty of his loyal men had lost their lives in the affray. The French had overwhelmed them this time but he was determined to analyse the formations and regrouping of his men to ensure that nothing like this happened again. Well not if he could help it.

Alex had arrived in the summer of 1811 and the first few months had been hell. He was a very brave man yet even he had found it hard to acclimatise himself to this barren country, its terrain, the blistering heat and the subsequent events that had occurred ever since he arrived.

In June last year he had been with the allied armies that had successfully taken Salamanca, a battle which had been a damaging defeat to the French but now he was tired of this contest between Napoleon and the allied powers of England, Spain and Portugal. Was all this bloodshed worth it, for control of the Iberian Peninsular?

The war had begun when the French had invaded Portugal in 1807 and although it seemed that they had won the battle today, Alex felt most determined that the French wouldn't win the war. He had heard that the years of fighting in Spain had worn down the French armies and although they were often victorious in battle the British intelligence had reported that their vital supplies and communications were relentlessly tested and their units were frequently harassed by the partisans who were extremely active in this area.

As he unbuttoned his jacket anticipation of the next battle brought a rancid taste to his mouth and throat and as his thoughts came back to the present he reached for his canteen of water to wash the bile away. There was water in a bowl on the small table beside the bed so he began to remove his clothes as he was eager to wash the stench of today's battle from his body.

After he had finished, as he was rubbing the rough towel over his hair, he reached under his pillow and clasped in his hand the little package that he always kept there. As he removed it from its wrapping he turned it over and looked intently at the face of his beloved Cissy in the miniature photo frame she had given to him before he had left England. He brought the frame up to his lips and kissed her beautiful face "I will see you again, princess" he murmured as he felt tears welling up at the back of his eyes "I promise" he really meant it but he hoped that fate would be on his side and deliver him home to his family and Cissy in one piece when this dreadful war eventually ended.

He hadn't even realised the extent of his love for her until he was here in Spain. He had missed her beyond comprehension and during the times he had been alone she was never far from his thoughts. On reflection, he thought back to the night of the Louise's come-out party when he and Cissy had danced together beside the lake and he had realised that he was in love with her. In a way he was glad he wasn't at home right now as the temptation to make love to her would have been too much. But from today he decided that he would carry her with him where-ever he went but for now he placed the picture of Cissy back on the bed.

He continued his ablusions as he had been summoned to join the Duke of Wellington to report on the outcome of the battle today and he wasn't looking forward to the evening at all.

When he was ready he started out to join the other officers in the Duke's tent, but was waylaid by a corporal bringing mail. "A letter for you, Sir" the soldier saluted.

"Thank you, Robbins". Alex conveyed, taking the letter from the man's hand and placing it in his breast pocket, he decided to read it as soon as he returned from his military meeting.

The Enchanted Glade

The evening was rather tedious and after what the men had endured today there was not the usual cheerfulness that normally followed these gatherings. He was rather relieved when the meeting ended and he left the Duke's tent without delay. As he made his way back to his own tent he felt himself swaying a little, perhaps the wine the Duke had provided was a little more potent than Alex was used to.

He entered his tent and immediately reached into his pocket for the letter which he guessed was from Cissy or his mother and he couldn't wait to read it. He removed his jacket and settled down on the bed holding the paper close to the candle on the table so that he could see more clearly and then he carefully opened the envelope.

He recognised her writing immediately and began to read intently.

July 1813

Dear Alex,

    I hope my letter finds you well. Your mother keeps me informed of developments and I truly hope that you are safe and looking after yourself.

    The latest news here is that Louise and Sydney are expecting another baby which is due in the Spring. She is hoping it is not twins again as they may prove to be a handful with William and Mary not yet two years old.

    Aunt Ellen is well and I have been staying with her for the season. She kindly arranged my come-out ball which proceeded satisfactorily, although I missed you immensely and wished you were there.

What Alex read next cut him to the quick and Cissy may as well have thrust a dagger through his heart.

Suddenly there was a commotion outside and Alex carefully folded the letter, blew out the candle and rose from his bed to investigate.

A spy had been caught infiltrating the camp's perimeter and the rest of the night before retiring was spent interrogating the Frenchman. It was in the early hours of the morning before he returned to his tent and he immediately reached under his pillow and took out the little frame and kissed Cissy's beautiful face as he had every night since he arrived. He then reached over and placed her picture in the breast pocket of his jacket, but he couldn't think straight remembering the words she had written in the letter.

Next day he went into battle not caring if he lived or died and misfortune followed him into the affray as he sustained a severe injury to his left arm. He could have been killed but for the miniature picture frame of Cissy in his breast pocket which averted the shot away from his heart.

That night as he lay wounded in the hospital tent he asked the nurse for his jacket and reached inside the pocket to read Cissy's letter again. It had continued:

> My father has arranged my betrothal to Sir Guy Hamilton as he thought it a good match. I didn't agree with it at first but my father announced it before he advised me which was very disconcerting. As my parents, especially my father were so incensed about Louise and the elopement I couldn't taint my family's reputation anymore by declaring that I would go against my father and refuse the proposal. I do not love Sir Guy but maybe that will come in time. He has been very pleasant to me and appears to be a man of honour and integrity.

Alex was completely infuriated; honour and integrity were the last words he would ever use to describe the blackguard that was Guy Hamilton. What was the matter with Templeton, had he taken leave of his senses. Hamilton was a scoundrel and a rake of the highest order. He was a disreputable gambler and a notorious womaniser. Surely Cissy's

The Enchanted Glade

father had heard of Hamilton reputation in town but more to the point maybe he didn't care.

My betrothal party has been arranged...

Alex couldn't read any more of the letter so he folded it and placed it back into his pocket. At this moment in time he had neither the courage nor the fortitude to cope with the situation. He took out the mangled picture frame and peered intently at the damaged portrait "If it wasn't for this I would probably be dead" he smoothed his thumb over Cissy's portrait as he spoke "You said I was always saving you, my darling, but this time it was you saving me"
He thought back over the years to the first day he had met her when she was lost in the glade and he'd taken her home. How her cruel father had beaten her, how a few weeks later she had fallen into the lake and he had saved her. He knew then that he loved her but had never realised how much. He also remembered a time when there had been a family gathering and Cissy had disappeared in the castle and Oliver had sought Alex out to rescue her again. He sighed and turned over in the bed to try to sleep clutching the picture in his hand, but his arm was painful so he almost sat up to make himself more comfortable. He knew that with the thought of Cissy having anything to do with Hamilton on his mind, sleep would be virtually impossible tonight or any night until he returned to England.

His injured arm continued to heal but not to the extent that he was able to join his men in battle again. So it was with a heavy heart that Alex left Spain to return home at the end of August in 1813. The thought of his loyal battalion, which he had left behind, was forever in his thoughts.
Throughout the journey home all he could think about was Cissy and added to the fact that he was seasick whilst on the ship, didn't help. On one of these occasions he smiled to

himself after retching over the side, his father owned shares in a shipping business which he would inherit at some time in the future, and here he was with no stomach to take even the shortest trip across the channel. He sat back down on the deck, thoughts awry and not knowing how he was going to cope knowing his beloved princess was in the arms of another man, especially one like Hamilton. He vowed there and then to do his utmost to protect her come what may.

His parents had promised to send a carriage to Dover to meet his ship. He couldn't face an onward sea voyage from Dover to the port of Bristol, so although he knew he would be very relieved to be on dry land again he really wasn't looking forward to the long carriage journey to Amberley.

Night was closing in so he made his way to his cabin hoping he would eventually be able to succumb to sleep.

As Alex's ship was making its way home, back in England it was the evening of Cissy's betrothal party. Her parents had decided to compromise with the clash of events by holding the betrothal party on the Saturday evening and the fund-raising event all day on the August Bank Holiday Monday.

The ballroom at Monkton Grange had been transformed for the occasion with huge vases of flowers being placed at either side of the entrance and also at each end of the room. Long colourful floral garlands were draped above the french windows which so reminded Cissy of Louise's come-out ball and she thought of how unhappy her sister had been on that night. History is repeating itself, she mused, Louise being in love with another at her party, and here was Cissy in love with another at her own betrothal. She now understood exactly how Louise had felt that night. Cissy was circulating, smiling and making polite conversation with all of the guests and was trying so hard to appear as if she was enjoying herself, but she most definitely was not.

The Enchanted Glade

Dear Emily as always was organising the refreshments in the large room which was adjoining the ballroom and had prepared a succulent feast for all to enjoy.

Tonight Cissy had chosen to wear a gown of peach taffeta and the diamond jewellery that her parents had given to her on her come-out ball. She always looked absolutely stunning in whatever she wore. Her hair was swept up on the top of her head, with some pretty peach flowers entwined through it, and small ringlets of curls were dangling in front of her ears. Although she had tried to make an effort with her appearance, with Kitty's help, of course, she felt an apathy that she couldn't control, engulfing her. She had at last resigned herself to this match but it didn't mean she wanted it.

She danced the first dance with Sir Guy and had felt rather conspicuous as it was in honour of their betrothal and as the dance had ended everyone applauded and, unlike her come-out ball, tonight the last thing she wanted was to be the centre of everyone's attention. Her father then proposed a toast and in full view of everyone Guy Hamilton dramatically placed the betrothal ring on her finger. She had envisaged that her first step to marriage would be an extremely romantic occasion in which her husband-to-be would drop to one knee and propose in private. She was not prepared for this very public show of insincere affection. However, as disappointed as she felt, she radiated a fictitious smile and accepted the ring graciously.

Later as she was returning to the ballroom after a visit to the ladies powder room Sir Guy waylaid her and suggested a walk in the garden. Not wanting to seem as if she wasn't trying, she agreed. It was still light and the early August evening was still quite warm so she didn't take her wrap.

Sir Guy took her arm and they strolled out of the french windows into the garden. They made light conversation as they walked in the direction of the Italian garden. Although he was speaking Cissy's hardly heard a word he was uttering as her mind was wandering elsewhere.

They soon arrived at the ornate garden with its beautifully sculptured flower beds and as they walked leisurely passed the large fish pond Sir Guy noticed the castle ahead and expressed a wish to scrutinise the old ruin. They climbed the old worn steps and as they reached the ramparts the sun was just beginning to drop a little in the sky. "It's such a lovely view from here" Cissy said attempting to point out some places of interest.

"Not as good as the view I have from here" he said with a lurid tone in his voice.

She curiously turned to look at him and didn't like what she saw. The look in his eyes, the shape of his mouth alarmed her. At this precise moment she realised that she had fallen into his trap and she was feeling very vulnerable indeed. She turned away from him so nervous that she couldn't even speak.

Apparently he was not the type for rose-tinted endearments, the trappings of romance and soft words of love meant nothing to him. He was a man driven with passion and he so wanted to hold her in his arms. He wanted to hear her breath catch as he kissed her lips. He wanted to know how she would feel against his naked body. He was imagining what it would be like to cup her pert round bare breasts in his hands and his lips were salivating at the thought of how her nipples would feel in his mouth. He felt as if his loins were on fire. Suddenly he lunged towards her and before she realised what was happening he had grabbed her hair, pulled her head back then she was in his arms and his mouth was ravaging hers. She struggled but he was too strong for her and as she tried to defend herself he wrestled her to the ground.

How foolish she had been to trust the man, she had thought him to be the gallant and chivalrous man her father had made him out to be. How wrong she was!

The Enchanted Glade

By now she was fighting him off, his hands were everywhere. "That's what I like, a woman with a bit of spirit in her" his haunting laugh appalled her.

Although he was not a big man he seemed to have the strength of a lion and escape seemed impossible. Please God help me she prayed as they rolled on the floor of the old ramparts. This was not how she had envisaged losing her virginity and she vowed she would continue to fight tooth and nail to preserve it.

He was kissing her neck now and suddenly she realised that he had one hand in the bodice of her dress. He managed to expose one of her breasts and as he enclosed his mouth over the nipple, which horrified her, she managed to free one of her hands and hit him on the back of his head.

Although he seemed a little dazed he brought his head up and as he leered at her he said "You can be sure I'll not wait until we are wed to take you, so it may as well be now". And he threw his head back and laughed lavaciously.

Although struck with a panic she had never felt before, Cissy managed to bring her hand around the side of his ear and as he was laughing she summoned all of her might and hit him with a force even she hadn't imagined she possessed. His head hit the stone floor of the rampart and this time he seemed more than stunned. She was struggling to remove herself from his inert body when it occurred to her that she might have killed him. She managed to get to her feet and gathering up her skirt she ran down the winding staircase.

He slowly regained his composure, got up and started after her but mysteriously she had completely disappeared. He emerged from the door of the old ruin and looked around but she was nowhere to be seen. How she had gotten out of the castle that quickly completely baffled him. Then he considered that perhaps he had been stunned for a lot longer than he thought so he decided to make his way back to the house alone.

Linda Dowsett

Cissy meanwhile was shaking with shock and disgust and was trying to compose herself after adjusting her bodice. Luckily she had remembered the door to the old secret passage which she and Oliver had found when they had first explored the castle years ago. She had then used all the strength she could muster to open the big old door and then close it behind her as quickly as she could before standing with her back against it. She was absolutely terrified that he would realise where she was.

She stood behind the door as quiet as a mouse as she listened for his footsteps as he passed on the stairs. She stayed very still and silent for a while longer as she couldn't be sure if he was still out there. She then felt for the small hole in the wall, to find the lucifers that she and her brother had discovered years before. The walls of the tunnel were cold and damp and as she removed one of them she prayed that it would light. She picked it up and struck it on the wall and luckily it flared into life. She quickly lit one of the lanterns that were always left there, so that she could see her way down the old passage to the library. Her progress was painstakingly slow and as she had to stoop low to avoid all the horrendous cobwebs, her back felt as if it was breaking. She absolutely hated spiders, ever since Oliver had put some in her bed years ago. But at this moment she would rather have the spiders for company than the snake she had just escaped from. As she proceeded her thoughts went back to Guy Hamilton, and she wondered what depravation he had suffered in his life that had led to his inward hostility.

She was also wondering how she was going to explain this to her mother. She knew her dress would not only be dirty but was probably torn.

All of a sudden relief flooded through her as she became conscious that she had arrived at the other end of the passage and that she had reached the secret door into the library. She listened very intently to discover if there was anyone in

The Enchanted Glade

the room beyond. She was in luck as all was quiet so she pulled the lever to open the secret door and then blew out the lantern and carefully placed it on the floor inside the passage. She was so relieved to be back at the house and she suddenly felt a lot safer. She very quickly closed the passage door from the other side and swiftly made her way to her bed chamber and rang for Kitty, her maid, to assist her.

"I thought you were downstairs with everyone else, my Lady" the maid sounded somewhat concerned.

"No, Kitty, I went for a walk in the garden and I've soiled my dress so I need to put on a fresh one. Could you please fetch some hot water from the kitchen and bring my light green silk from the wardrobe and I will freshen up and change".

"Are you alright, my Lady?" Kitty enquired as she helped her mistress out of her soiled dress "you seem a little breathless and very flustered. Do you think you may be coming down with something?"

"Please, Kitty could you just do as I've asked and as quickly as possible. I have to go back downstairs immediately".

"Very well, my Lady" Kitty really loved Cissy and worried about her constantly and would have been horrified to discover the real reason that her mistress was in such a dishevelled state.

After Kitty had gone to fetch the hot water Cissy's composure left her and she broke down and sobbed quietly. She put her hand to her chest and thought over what had just occurred. The absolute worse thing was that when he had enclosed his mouth over the nub of her breast and suckled it, she had experienced a most unusually intense stirring of passion in the lower part of her body which she didn't understand and the realisation that he had awakened that sensation inside her absolutely appalled her.

Whatever had she let herself in for? When she had first agreed to court Sir Guy, which she had only done to appease her mother, she knew there had been no intense feeling of excitement which she would have expected to feel if love was ever to be remotely possible between them. From the first time she had met him she had felt uneasy. Cissy's heart ached as she realised that true love was never proud, selfish, arrogant or vain and Guy Hamilton was all of these things. A feeling of complete panic engulfed her at the thought of a lifetime of misery with this horrible man.

There was a sudden tap on the door and Cissy's thoughts came back to the present and she quickly composed herself as she realised that Kitty had returned. The maid placed the bowl of water and a towel on the dresser and then as speedily as she could Cissy refreshed herself and put on her green silk gown. Her maid then tidied her hair and was shocked to find a host of cobwebs tangled in the curls but she didn't like to mention it to Cissy as she knew that it was really none of her business. She was just there to do a job and get on with it but it didn't stop her wondering what had happened in the garden tonight. It only took a few minutes to rectify the problem and soon with her hair looking a little more presentable Cissy was ready to go downstairs to face everyone again.

"Thank you so much for your help Kitty. Can you see where I put my evening purse, only I seem to have mislaid it?"

"No, my Lady, I can't recall seeing it since you went downstairs earlier".

"Oh, never mind Kitty, we'll look for it tomorrow. I had better hurry now" and with that Cissy walked towards the door of her room, her heart in her mouth at the thought of going downstairs to face anyone let alone that dreadful man. As she reached the top of the staircase and began to descend she noticed that her mother was at the foot of the stairs.

"Where ever have you been, Cissy, we've missed you, Darling?"

The Enchanted Glade

"I didn't feel well Mother so I went to lie down for a moment".

"You should have told me, oh, I see you've changed your dress!"

"The other one was creased when I laid on it" she lied "I have only come down to bid everyone goodnight, if that is permissible. I have a most terrible headache and would like to retire early, if I may". Although she had pleaded the headache she knew that it was not her head that was hurting, but her heart, it was almost breaking after what she had just endured.

"Has the emotion of the evening become too much for you, my dearest?" her mother asked placing a reassuring hand on her daughter's arm, not knowing how close she had come to the real reason Cissy had wanted to leave the party.

Her mother then led Cissy into the ballroom to apologise for her premature departure. All the guests were very understanding and then there was Guy. He drew her to one side, away from the others and brought one of her hands up to his mouth and ran his lips seductively across it. Provocatively kissing her fingers one at a time, he then placed special emphasis on the third finger of her left hand on which she wore the sapphire and diamond ring he had placed on that finger earlier in the evening. He then brought his face up to hers and placed a kiss on each of her cheeks, she felt her whole body stiffen as he touched her. Then as he drew away he whispered into her ear "I'll have you, you little vixen, you can be sure of it" his eyes were dominating her vision and she saw that they were smouldering with desire and his leering smile made Cissy feel sick at the thought of it. Cissy's body became more rigid as she now realised that his lovemaking would be neither tender nor subtle, but most likely blunt and brutal, and she was already dreading her wedding night. She quickly regained her composure and her voice faltered a little, as she replied quietly "You are under some misapprehension, Sir, if you think that I will ever give myself to you now or at any time before we are wed". She could feel her voice quivering as she spoke.

"And you, my dear, are under some misapprehension if you think that I will wait" As he said this he looked deeply into her eyes once more but this time she quickly averted her gaze and pulling her hand from his she walked towards the others and bid everyone else farewell and hurried upstairs to her room.

That night as she lay in bed with tears streaming onto her pillow, she despaired of ever finding true happiness and everlasting love. She knew she would just have to be content to dream of the one person on her mind, her one true love, Alexander Kingsley. She knew now, that because of her betrothal to Guy Hamilton, the possibility of a life of love with Alex could never be.

After he had returned to his residence that night Guy Hamilton was reflecting on the events of the evening and he placed his hand into his pocket and withdrew the item he had deposited there earlier. He smiled to himself as he smoothed his fingers over the top of the silk purse he held in his hands and was about to open. Cissy hadn't realised that she had dropped it as she was fleeing from the ramparts and he had retrieved it from the steps as he went after her. He removed the silky-smooth handkerchief from inside and he drew it up and touched it to his lips, inhaling the scent of her perfume in the process.

"I will possess you, you brainless little chit and I will have your virginity before the week is out and I will revel in the taking of it, I always get what I want" the conceit spilled out of his mouth like water from a overflowing stream and his piercing blue eyes, as he handled her handkerchief once more, were flaming with wanton desire.

Alex had been back in England for a few days now and felt well enough to venture out. He had requested that Billy

The Enchanted Glade

hitch up a carriage as with his arm still in a sling he was unable to manage Sir Galahad single handed. He was conversing with his father in the foyer as the carriage arrived at the front entrance of Amberley, so taking leave of his father at the door, he boarded and one of his more experienced grooms, Ned, conveyed him to George Street in Bath where the gentleman's club he had previously frequented for a little light gambling, was situated. He alighted from the carriage on arrival and as he walked across the high pavement towards the door he was greeted by several other club members as they entered the building at the same time as himself. Each of them professing it a pleasure to see him safely home again after his time in Spain. News travels fast; he thought as the uniformed doorman greeted him and assisted Alex in removing his coat. He then instructed an usher to advise Alex of a few changes that had occurred at the club whilst he had been away. He was informed that there had been a change of cook and the succulent food lay out on the table before them, to which the usher was referring, appeared much improved. "We have also recently installed some private rooms upstairs, my Lord, should you wish for some female company during your visit" the man was actually whispering behind his hand. Although Alex smiled at this gesture, at this moment he didn't even have an appetite for the food, let alone the women. "I have just come for a quiet game of cards tonight, but I thank you for the information". The usher nodded and then excused himself. Alex made his way up the flight of stairs to the gaming room. He ordered some drinks to be brought to his table and played a few hands of card, winning some, losing some, and then suddenly he became bored with it. The hubbub of noise around him and the stench from others perpetually smoking cigars was reminding him too much of occasions abroad. It seemed pointless to stay here if he wasn't enjoying himself so although he had only been here for approximately an hour he rose to leave. He descended the staircase and was making his way towards the entrance hall and as he approached the foot of the opposite staircase in the club he glanced up and saw none other than Sir Guy Hamilton emerging from the room of a courtesan above. The satisfied smile on the man's face conveyed the fact that he had obviously, very much, been enjoying 'some female company'.

As Hamilton descended the stairs, knowing that Alex had seen him leave the room, he tried to brush the incident aside by changing the subject. "One of them got you then, I see, Kingsley" he was, of course referring to Alex's arm, which was still in a sling.

Alex was completely incensed "How dare you disrespect Lady Cecilia!" he spat, referring to Hamilton's obvious taking of the woman upstairs.

Of course Hamilton knew exactly what he meant so he leaned towards Alex saying, "Jealous, old boy, that I can have her and you cannot" the leering look in the scoundrel's eye was in a manner unbecoming of gentlemen.

"You lay one finger on Cissy to hurt her and I'll kill you with my bare hands, you……….." The bile rose in Alex's throat as he fought to keep his temper under control. He knew it would do Cissy no good if he caused a ruckus here.

"You'll do what" he heard Hamilton's arrogant reply as he retrieved his coat and hurried towards the door not wanting to stay a moment longer in the company of this rogue.

He summoned the carriage and as it returned to Amberley, he sat inside deep in thought. How was he going to free his beloved princess from the clutches of this charlatan? He would have to come up with something. He had always saved her every time she needed rescuing before, but how was he going to save her now.

****

Chapter 12

The first thing Alex noticed was her gorgeous hair. The titian curls were cascading tantalisingly down her back like a waterfall of fire, reaching well below her waist.

He had discreetly entered the ballroom at Amberley and was observing the dancing from a secluded corner. He just couldn't take his eyes off her. He knew that Cissy was beautiful but as she turned to face him he realised that, whilst he had been away, an enchanting butterfly had emerged from the chrysalis and she was quite the most stunning creature he had ever encountered.

The sapphire blue gown she was wearing was clinging seductively to every curve of her voluptuous body. Even from here he could see the sparkle of laughter in her twinkling eyes and he watched as she whirled around, her hands holding those of a dashing partner. Then his heart heaved an intense sigh as he saw that her partner was none other than Guy Hamilton. His chest then tightened with sadness when he realised that the contented smile on Cissy's face seemed to indicate that she was actually enjoying herself with this notorious scoundrel, but that didn't stop him having an uncontrollable urge to protect her from the man. Little did he know that it was all a charade on her part.

How could her father have approved this match, Templeton must have been mad to even consider such a thing? Hamilton was a gambler, a womaniser and a rake of the highest order. Surely her father had heard of the man's reputation in town or maybe it didn't bother him. How cruel could a man be to sacrifice his daughter to a man like Guy Hamilton.

Suddenly his mother's voice invaded his thoughts.

"Alexander, where ever have you been, everyone has been waiting for you, after all this ball is in your honour. Why have you been hiding?" she smiled as she said that, then she suddenly she realised that somehow the noise of the music and the hundreds of voices may be disturbing for him after being on the front line in battle.

"I'm not hiding, Mother" he answered returning her smile "I'm just observing the jollity of the party. After Spain and the war it is heart-warming to see everyone enjoying themselves here". He was grateful to his mother for organising such a tremendous celebration on his return from the Peninsular although quite frankly he would have preferred no fuss.

Just at that moment the dance ended and Alex glanced over his mother's shoulder. Cissy had caught sight of him and was making her way towards him. His mother, distracted for a moment, didn't notice that Alex and Cissy's eyes had met. This was the first time they had seen one another for over two years. Cissy's eyes lit up like sunshine and she could not prevent the sudden flare of excitement that coursed through her on seeing him again, but he discreetly shook his head and she took the hint.

She moved with her partner to sit down. The buffet supper was announced as being served in an adjoining room so she asked Guy to fetch her something as she was quite breathless after the dance. When he left her side she was alone for a moment and Alex quickly took advantage of the opportunity and crossed the room to talk to her. " Meet me on the terrace in five minutes" he whispered in her ear and then he was gone.

When Guy returned she said she needed to use the powder room for a few moments. He nodded and sat down as she rose from her chair and made her way across the dance floor

The Enchanted Glade

towards the ladies room. Unseen she made a slight detour and diverted to the terrace. Alex was waiting in the shadows and she hurried towards him so excited to see him.

Wary of unseen eyes he quickly arranged to meet her in the Glade the next afternoon at 2 o'clock. "Now please go quickly, Cissy, I would not wish to embarrass you should someone see us". To be discovered in such circumstances would be the outside of enough.

As she returned to her seat no-one was any the wiser as to where she had been, other than going to the powder room. On the way back to her table she encountered Lady Kendrow, and she ventured to ask after Edwin.

"Edwin has returned to the south coast to finish his studies. He is a very capable young man and very talented" she sounded proud of her nephew. She couldn't let Cissy know how heart-broken Edwin had been when he'd heard of Cissy's betrothal.

"Please remember me to him, my Lady" she whispered in Lady Kendrow's ear. "I was very fond of him and I did not wish things to end as they did. Will you please tell him that I wish him well?"

Lady Kendrow knew of the circumstances of her betrothal as Aunt Ellen had informed her, so she held no ill will towards Cissy "I will, my dear, and thank you"

After taking her leave of Lady Kendrow's party Cissy made her way back to her own table and sat down beside Hamilton. The food was delicious and Cissy, still feeling rather ravenous after emptying her plate, informed Sir Guy that she was going to fetch some more. She had half expected that he would want to fetch it for her or at least accompany her to the buffet table, but as he was deep in conversation with another gentleman at that moment, he just waved her off so she left the room.

As she walked to the buffet table she heard a familiar voice call to her.

"Cissy, how lovely to see you". She turned her head and saw Imogen, Alex's sister, as she added "How are you?"

"I am well, thank you, Imogen, and how are you? My mother told me you have been to staying with an old friend. Is it nice to be back at home?".

"It's always nice to come home, Cissy. I usually go to stay with Jessica for couple of months each year and catch up with mutual friends. But I hear you have been very busy whilst I've been away, you're going to be married soon, congratulations!" Imogen's beautiful face emitted a beaming smile but Cissy's face was immediately engulfed with a frown and Imogen thought that Cissy' countenance betrayed a definite look of unhappiness. "What is it, Cissy, is everything alright?" Imogen sounded very perturbed.

"It's alright, I just haven't gotten used to the idea yet" the sadness in her voice was evident and Imogen realised that the look on Cissy's face was most certainly not convincing.

"Darling, we'll have to meet up one day next week and have a good chat, catch up on everything. I think my mother is having one of her afternoon get-togethers on Tuesday" at that point Imogen winked at Cissy " you know what I mean?".

"Yes" answered Cissy, totally confused. She didn't really know why Imogen had winked at her when she mentioned the afternoon tea and also didn't know why she had admitted to knowing about something that she didn't. "I was just going to the table to fetch something to eat perhaps you would like to join me?" she thought that changing the subject would give her some time to fathom what Imogen had meant.

Alex was circulating around the ballroom and every few moments during conversations with various guests he found himself scanning the room to see what Cissy was doing. Well actually, he was looking to see what Hamilton was doing. He didn't trust the man as far as he could throw him and he was so worried about Cissy's welfare that he realised he was becoming obsessive about it. He was also trying to

The Enchanted Glade

keep his distance from Cissy because if he got too close to her he may betray his feelings. He realised that Cissy was not sat at the table where Hamilton was engrossed in conversation with another man, probably talking about gambling or other women, he thought.

He wondered where she might be and as he walked into the room which housed the buffet he saw Cissy conversing with his sister. Should he approach them, they had seen him now and surely it would be ill-mannered to just turn and walk away.

"Alex, dearest, come here and talk to us, you have been neglecting me all evening" Imogen complained.

As Alex began to reply he caught Cissy's eye and her lashes immediately brushed her cheeks as she glanced down at her clasped hands, almost as if she couldn't bear to look at him. Where had that smile from earlier disappeared to? "It was remiss of me not to have sought you out before now, please accept my humble apologies". He was directing his words to his sister now.

"Oh, don't sound so serious, Alex, I was only joshing. Have you afforded your felicitation to Cissy and her beau on their forthcoming marriage". After seeing the frown on Cissy's face earlier she wasn't sure that she should be mentioning it, but she knew it wouldn't be long before she found out if there was anything wrong.

" Oh, yes, Cissy, I understand congratulations are in order". He had really wanted to say, commiserations.

"They most certainly are" an arrogant voice sounded from behind him. Hamilton…damn! he couldn't stand the man.

Guy Hamilton walked passed Alex and held out his hand to Cissy. When she didn't reciprocate he put an arm around her shoulder and with a satisfied smile on his face he boasted
"Cecilia, my beautiful bride-to-be……."

As Hamilton was waffling on, Alex realised that he'd said Cecilia, which roused his spirits somewhat. He hadn't called her Cissy, so she may be marrying the man, but he wasn't her friend. Then his sympathy went out to her, my poor little princess is marrying a man who isn't even her friend. He was brought out of his reverie when he heard his sister's voice.

"Alex, are you alright? All this noise isn't too much for you is it?". Imogen was conscious of the fact that her brother was just staring into space as if he wasn't in the same room as everyone else.

He was actually looking at Cissy and it pained him to realise that he had never seen her looking so sad and that her usually bright violet eyes had lost their sparkle. "No, I must be getting back to our other guests or they, like you, will think that I am neglecting them". As he took his leave he bowed slightly and forced a heart-warming smile at Cissy and she was almost undone.

As Imogen turned her attention to Cissy and Guy, she smiled as she asked "So, tell me, when is the wedding to take place?" she spoke to dispel the tension that had been created when her brother had encountered Hamilton. It was quite obvious that the two men despised one another although she had to hand it to Alex; he had held his temper well as the other man had arrogantly bragged about marrying Cissy. Had these two clashed before or did Guy Hamilton know that Cissy and Alex had been bosom pals for years. She also thought Cissy's actions had been unusually reserved.

"We are to wed on the last Saturday morning in October, at 10 o'clock, in the village church" Hamilton piped up. It seemed that when Cissy was in his company she didn't have a lot to say. In fact Imogen realised that Cissy hadn't spoken a single word since Alex had entered the room.

"I will hope to be invited then". Imogen then asked to be excused as she needed to use the ladies room. She hinted very strongly at Cissy accompanying her but Cissy didn't take the bait.

The Enchanted Glade

"Come along, Cecilia, the dance floor awaits" as Hamilton took her arm to lead her back to the ballroom Cissy glanced at Imogen and shrugged her shoulders in resignation.

Imogen went off to the powder room deep in thought.

Because his arm was still causing him pain he had asked his mother to excuse him from any dancing, yet at this very moment as Alex watched Cissy dancing with Hamilton he was not only jealous but he was wishing that it was his arms she was enclosed in not that scoundrel's. He had been in many a tricky situation in Spain and almost always he had found a solution to escape from it. How was he going to find a solution for this dreadful situation Cissy had found herself in. He was convinced that there was something not quite right between her and Hamilton and he had to get to the bottom of it. Well, he was seeing Cissy tomorrow in the Glade and perhaps when he knew more he would be able to help her.

Next day as the old grandfather clock in the hall was chiming 1-45pm, Cissy was making her way to the back of the house and left by the kitchen entrance. She hurried down the winding track towards the woods and her excited heart was pounding loudly in her chest at the thought of seeing her beloved Alex again.

As she ran towards the glade she could see him through the trees standing in the sunlit clearing. He saw her running as fast as her legs would carry her and she came towards him with her arms outstretched. He couldn't wait to see her either and moved forward to catch her as she fell into his arms and his warmth enveloped her as he stooped to take her lips. Cissy could hardly believe that the kiss she had waited for, for so long, had at last materialised and all her senses were alive with the response she felt as she leant against him.

For her it was a dream comes true as being enclosed in his arms was all she had ever wanted and at that moment he gave her hope that there was some substance in the dream she had of them one day being together forever.

As he ended the kiss he began to apologise but she placed her index finger to his lips to silence him and as they looked deeply into each others eyes he realised that Cissy loved him just as much as he loved her.

"Oh, Cissy, I have missed you so very much" he couldn't tear his eyes from her beautiful face.

"And I you, Alex" she frowned as she added "I was so worried when I heard you had been wounded".

"It was nothing, just a scratch. Not half the pain I felt when you wrote to tell me of your betrothal to Hamilton".

"I do not love the man and I do not want the marriage but my father insisted upon it after he had announced it without my knowledge and also after what had happened with Louise my mother begged me not to cause another scandal".

"Cissy, I'm so sorry to have to ask you this, but has he touched you?"

"No, Alex, he has tried but I am determined to be a virgin on my wedding night who ever I marry".

"I was so incensed to see you together last night, I cannot bear the thought of you in his arms but I can see no way out of this. I cannot believe that your father did this to you, does he hate you so?"

"You have probably realised that my father is never sober enough to know what he is doing. He thought that Guy Hamilton was affluent and honourable and he ordered me to marry him. Surely Alex you must know that it was not what I wished, I despise the man"

"Oh my poor darling" and as he gathered her into his arms once again, he held her cheek close to his chest and resting his chin on her shining soft curls, he added " The only way we can see each other now will be here in the Glade. I will send a message as often as I can but we must be very careful so that no-one suspects anything, the last thing I want is to involve you in any scandal".

The Enchanted Glade

"Maybe I could come to Amberley to ride out with Velvet" she moved out of his embrace as she spoke and looked earnestly into his eyes hoping for his agreement.

"I think it would not be 'proper' for you to ride out with me when you are betrothed to another, but we may still meet coincidentally at family gatherings. Now, although I do not wish it, you must be getting back, before you are missed". His hands were now resting on her shoulders as he looked directly into her eyes again and declared "I had always loved you as a sister in the past, Cissy, but now I love you as a man loves a woman and I have done so since that night we danced by the lake and it was only my love for you that kept me going throughout the war in Spain. I only wish I had told you before I went but at the time I was not aware of your feelings for myself".

Cissy was completely overcome to realise that Alex felt the same about her as she did about him and was unable to stem the tears that suddenly stung the back of her eyes. " I know the situation is impossible for us but I need to tell you that I have adored you since the very first day I met you here in the Glade and my love for you will never die, I know I will love you until the end of my days" she could no longer hold back the tears and she buried her head in his chest and sobbed uncontrollably.

"Please don't cry, Princess, I know there will never be a happy ending for us, it is out of our hands, but whatever transpires know that I will always love you forever".

His words were filled with tenderness and Cissy was undone. She just clung tightly to him and let out all the sadness that had enveloped her as he stated the obvious… they would never be together.

Withholding his own emotions Alex held her close to him, never wanting to let her go.

Linda Dowsett

On Monday after a weekend of reliving her rendezvous with Alex over and over again in her mind, Cissy came down to breakfast smiling.

Her mother greeted her warmly "Cissy, you seem in good spirits this morning. I thought you were coming down with something on Saturday evening at the ball, you seemed very subdued towards the end".

"I'm alright, Mother, I expect I was tired after all the dancing. Oh, Imogen said you were going to see her mother tomorrow for afternoon tea; would I be permitted to join you? I'd like to catch up on Imogen's news".

"Oh, um… yes, um… certainly, can you be ready at 1 o'clock" her mother seemed to be stuttering over her reply.

"Are you sure it's convenient for me to accompany you" Cissy frowned, thinking that 1 o'clock seemed very early for afternoon tea. But maybe her mother and Lady Lavinia wished to discuss things before the others arrived. They were both intensely involved in local charity work so Cissy thought that may be the reason.

"Of course it's convenient, why shouldn't it be?" was her mother's almost snappy reply.

Just at that moment there was a knock at the door and after Annabel had acknowledged it the butler entered. "Madam, Sir Guy Hamilton's man is here" he handed Annabel a calling card.

"Thank you, Ambrose, would you wait outside for just a moment". She read the card then handed it to Cissy. Hamilton was requesting that Cissy ride out with him this afternoon. "Would you like to accompany him?"

"Mother, can you please send a note back saying that I am unwell. I have no wish to see him today". Nor ever, Cissy added in her mind.

"But Cissy you are to marry the man, you cannot avoid him forever. Did something untoward occur on Saturday evening that you haven't told me about?"

The Enchanted Glade

"No, Mother, but whatever happens I need a chaperon whenever I see him". Cissy had made sure that every time she and Hamilton had been together, since the evening in the castle ruin when he'd almost raped her, that she was never alone with him.

Annabel left the dining room for a second and proceeded to her study. She quickly scribbled a note to advise Sir Guy that Cissy was unwell and therefore unable to accept his kind invitation today. She then rang for Ambrose and when he arrived she asked him to convey the note to Sir Guy's messenger.

She then went back to finish her breakfast with her daughter.

On Tuesday afternoon at 1 o'clock Cissy and her Mother were boarding the carriage to travel to Amberley. As soon as they were underway her mother spoke. "Cissy, I must confess that there is no afternoon tea arranged for today. I'm so sorry I didn't take you into my confidence before but the least people who know about this the better".

Whatever was her mother insinuating.

Annabel continued "We are going to Amberley but from there we will be going to Dr Bartholomew's".

Cissy guessed immediately. "Oh Mother, are we going to see Louise?"

"We are. This has been going on for quite a while now. It is the only way I can get to see my beautiful grandchildren without your father finding out"

So that was why Imogen had winked at her when she'd mentioned the afternoon tea. Obviously Imogen was in on the secret. Their mothers were pretending to hold these gatherings and it was concealing the real reason for the visit. Cissy was so excited; she hadn't seen Louise and her family since she had been staying with Aunt Ellen. "Oh, Mother, what a fantastic idea, how clever of you all! I can't wait to see them"

"You really don't mind that I didn't let you in on the secret?"

"Of course not".

"Your father may have suspected something was amiss if I had included you before as our gatherings do not usually include children. Well I know you are not a child, Cissy, but you understand my meaning, don't you?"

"Perfectly, Mother, now think no more about it and anyway you are not telling an untruth when you say we are going out for afternoon tea because we are, just to a different location". The wide smile on Cissy's face was the happiest Annabel had seen on her daughter for quite some time "now don't fret about it and let's just look forward to our visit".

Alex saw the carriage coming towards the Hall and he went outside to greet Annabel. He had no idea that Cissy was there and she saw the surprise on his face as he handed both women down from the carriage. He squeezed Cissy's hand tightly before he relinquished it and escorted them both to his mother's sitting room. It seemed that Alex also knew all about the secret trysts but Cissy hadn't minded being kept in the dark, just as long as her mother was seeing Louise and her children, that was all that mattered.

Alex was wildly trying to think of a way to see Cissy alone.

"Would you have time to come to the stable to see Velvet, I'm sure she'd love to see you" then he directed his gaze towards his mother "I could tell Billy at the same time that you'll be ready for the carriage in say, twenty minutes".

"I'm sure half an hour would be better, I have some things to discuss with Annabel. You may as well come up from the stable with the carriage after your visit with Velvet" Lavinia knew that Cissy would want to see the little mare as she hadn't visited for quite a while. Also their two mothers' had no qualms about Cissy and Alex being alone together as they had always thought of their connection as brother and sister and had no idea as to the real circumstances of their current relationship.

The Enchanted Glade

Cissy and Alex left the room and as they were making their way outside they passed the library and Alex caught Cissy's hand and pulled her into the room and locked the door behind them. Immediately Cissy was in his arms enjoying another of his heart-warming kisses. She knew that these secret meetings would not be able to continue after she was married to Hamilton but she was certainly relishing every moment of them now.

"Oh, my love, what an unexpected pleasure" Alex whispered as he ended the kiss "but we must hurry now before anyone sees us"

The kiss had been so surprising and had thrilled Cissy, but she knew that they were playing with fire in seeing one another surreptitiously.

They left the library immediately and rapidly vacated the house and went to see Velvet.

After the visit to the stables one of the stable hands advised Alex that the carriage was prepared and ready to leave so he and Cissy boarded immediately and as they rode through the secluded avenue of trees towards the front entrance of the Hall they stole another kiss, but as Alex alighted and left her in the carriage to await the others she realised that this was no answer to their dilemma. She was still betrothed to Hamilton and could not bear the thought of him touching her after she had been in Alex's arms. This thought was foremost in her mind as she saw her mother, Lady Lavinia and Imogen leave the house and walk across the drive towards the carriage, then one of the many footmen at Amberley assisted them in boarding and when they were all settled in he instructed the driver to commence. Although Imogen and Cissy were seated together Imogen was loathe to mention Cissy's wedding, as if there was a problem, and she suspected there was, she was sure Cissy would not admit to it in front of her mother so she stayed silent and thought that she would try to talk to Cissy if the opportunity arose later.

They arrived at John Bartholomew's home, 'Heathview House' in Monkton St James and Louise and her family were eagerly waiting inside. The doctor now regularly sent his carriage to fetch them from Paradise Street so that Annabel could see her grandchildren. Cissy was so excited to see her sister and the twins again and the contented look on her mother's face was so very comforting. They talked about the impending pregnancy and of Louise and Sydney's joy when they had realised that they were to enlarge their family and the fact that they were so looking forward to filling their little house with more children. Cissy was suddenly filled with envy at her sister's happiness in a loving family atmosphere knowing that she would never feel as Louise did now. The thought of Hamilton imposing himself upon her and actually impregnating her with his seed revolted her and she was feeling positively nauseous as she sat mulling it over in her mind. Louise seemed to notice her sister's dejected look and suggested that maybe Cissy would like to help her to feed Mary or Frederick. Cissy's face brightened a tad as she took the little spoon from her sister and held her tiny niece and began to feed her with the delicious egg custard that the doctor's housekeeper had so kindly prepared for the two toddlers.

After partaking of a most appetising tea, the very pleasing visit, which lasted for approximately two hours ended, and after warmly thanking John for arranging it Annabel bid her daughter's family a fond farewell and they parted once more. Lavinia's carriage travelled back directly to Amberley Hall even though they literally passed Monkton Grange on the way. There was no way Annabel could allow William to find out about the secret visits and if Lavinia had set them down at home he would wonder why they had not come back in their own carriage.

Imogen was itching to tackle Cissy about the proposed marriage but hadn't found the opportunity to do so. Therefore her spirits were raised when her mother invited

The Enchanted Glade

Annabel and Cissy in as she had forgotten to give Annabel some information about another fund-raising event they were organising. From her private sitting room Lavinia rang the bell to summon Fenton her butler. Even though they had already had tea at the doctors Lavinia ordered light refreshments to be brought directly so this gave Imogen the opportunity to talk to Cissy alone. "Let's go out onto the terrace whilst we wait for the tea".

"That would be lovely" answered Cissy, her eyes actively glancing around wondering if Alex was still there "it is such a lovely day".

When they reached the terrace they sat down and Imogen immediately asked "Cissy, is everything alright between you and Sir Guy Hamilton, only I was sure that I detected a feeling of apprehension when we spoke last weekend at Alex's celebration"

"Oh, Imogen" Cissy shoulders drooped in gloomy resignation " I am not in love with him, in fact I don't think I even like the man, and I am honestly dreading everything about the wedding and married life thereafter" Cissy went on to confide the story of the betrothal and the subsequent events, not entering totally into detail about the night on the castle ramparts. She also couldn't mention any elements of her relationship with Alex as that may jeopardise their clandestine meetings and Cissy couldn't bear to forfeit those at present.

"Oh, dearest Cissy" Imogen's sympathy was evident as she reached out and took Cissy's hand in her own. "I wish there was something I could do to assist you but I can think of nothing at present that I could do to help"

Imogen had never felt so sorry for anyone in her life as Cissy continued "It seems that I must resign myself to enduring my daunting fate whether I am partial to it or not". Imogen's mother then interrupted them as she called to her daughter that the tea had arrived so as they rose from the seat in the garden Imogen embraced her friend and was at that moment at a total loss to think of a solution to poor Cissy's dilemma.

Cissy didn't see Alex again that day but as Annabel and Cissy returned to the Grange later in the afternoon Cissy felt, that if nothing else, she was now a little wiser to the real meaning of her mother's afternoon tea sessions

****

Chapter 13

Alex rose before sun up this morning knowing that today would determine his fate for the rest of his life. He dressed in his riding habit and went straight to the stables to fetch his horse. His insides were in such turmoil that he couldn't even face anything to eat before he left.

Last night he had asked Billy to saddle Sir Galahad early and advised that he would meet him at the stables at 5am.

As he arrived he thanked Billy for rising so early to accommodate his needs and asked his loyal servant to keep his silence in this matter and advised that all being well he would probably be back before the household was awake anyway.

All was quiet as Sir Galahad cantered along the Bristol Road towards Bath and as he entered the outskirts of the city, a little after 5.30am, the only sounds he heard were from the activity of the tradesmen scurrying about delivering early morning orders.

He made his way through the vicinity of Widcombe, passing the small miner's cottages standing silently in the dark, everyone seemingly still asleep.

He ascended Widcombe Hill which constituted a very steep rise out of the locality and as he turned the acute bend at the top he looked left to observe the dormant city below.

Reaching the brow of the hill he dismounted and leading Sir Galahad along a rough path they passed through a small opening in the hedge. On his left was Sham Castle, the folly that had been commissioned by Ralph Allen. It was bathed in shadows as the early morning sun rose behind it in the east.

He led his horse through the dense foliage on foot for a few hundred yards; then he stopped under a large old oak tree as the early morning sunshine was now filtering through its leaves and there he tethered Sir Galahad to one of the branches. From here he discovered that he had a good vantage point to observe the proceedings that were about to take place in the clearing approximately one hundred yards in front of him. He had felt compelled to come today to witness the event about to take place as he knew the outcome could have a marked effect on his future.

One carriage had already arrived. He saw an acquaintance of his, Lord Overton who was stood beside his carriage with two other men whom he didn't recognise. Alex concealed himself further behind the tree as another carriage approached. His heart beat began to race faster as he saw Guy Hamilton emerge haughtily from the second carriage with two more men.

A third carriage then appeared and a man with a black bag stepped out and joined the other six men.

They conversed but Alex was too far away to decipher what was being discussed. Then he saw a long box being opened and two pistols were removed from it. The seconds came forward and each one inspected the firearms ensuring that they were loaded correctly. Then one was handed to Lord Overton and the other to Hamilton who were both instructed to stand back to back and on the second's command they began their paces. As the walk proceeded Hamilton suddenly turned prematurely and shot and wounded Lord Overton, who stumbled as the force of the blast hit his right shoulder, however he quickly composed himself and stood upright again. At this point Overton was livid and aimed his pistol directly at Hamilton's chest and with all the passion of a wronged husband he shot him right through the heart.

The Enchanted Glade

As the doctor hurried to attend the wounded men, Alex inched a little closer and he heard every word as the doctor delivered the verdict. Hamilton, lying in a crumpled heap on the grass, had died instantly from his wound.

Unheard by the others, Alex crept stealthily away, his emotions boiling over and as he reached Sir Galahad he struggled to hold back the tears pricking the back of his eyes. He walked the horse back to the main road and mounted to ride back to Amberley, elated beyond comprehension.

Cissy was free, free from her betrothal to Hamilton, free to marry him.

Later that afternoon Cissy was in her room readying herself for one of her mother's afternoon tea gatherings. It was a bona fide meeting this time and Aunt Ellen had arrived earlier to participate. Unexpectedly she heard a knock at the door and as she called "come in" her mother entered looking very perturbed.

"What is it, Mother?"

"Cissy, I have some very bad news".

Cissy's face suddenly appeared gaunt. Alex, oh my God, something has happened to Alex. Panic ravaged through her whole body as she thought the worst.

"Sir Guy Hamilton was killed today. Rumour has it that he was having an affair with Lord Overton's wife. Apparently Overton caught them together" Annabel didn't elaborate with any more details. She had been horrified at what she had heard and to think that she had persuaded her daughter to marry this dreadful man to save her own reputation.

Cissy felt a tear creeping from her eye and tried to stem it.

"Oh! You are upset, darling?" her mother reached out a hand to comfort her.

"No, Mother, I'm definitely not upset. These are tears of relief and happiness at being released from a situation that would have resembled a prison sentence and I was dreading it". She then related to her mother the events at the Sydney

Gardens and her intrepid feelings on the first day she had met Guy Hamilton, then the encounter at Lady Kendrow's music evening when he had man-handled her, the theatre trip and the dreadful occurrence at the castle ruin that explained the circumstances surrounding her change of gown and the feigned headache to get away from him.

Suddenly everything fell into place, Cissy not wanting to go riding with the man and insisting on a chaperon. "Oh, Cissy, my poor Darling, what you must have been suffering these past few months. I am so sorry" her mother came towards her with outstretched arms and hugged her precious daughter to her breast. At the same time she was furious that her errant husband had even contemplated the match if he knew Hamilton so well. "Whatever happened to Hamilton today, we must thank God because you have had a lucky escape".

"Please don't worry, Mother, I'm sure everything will be alright now" she couldn't wait to see Alex to tell him.

But she couldn't wait to tell someone else either, so after her mother had left the room she sped down the back stairs to the kitchen and her dear friend Emily's face was a picture as a beaming Cissy ran into her arms. She began to explain what had transpired but she was so excited that Emily couldn't understand her immediately.

"Oh, me little chick, you 'ave me 'ead in a whirl, whatever are you tryin' to tell me" Emily had never seen Cissy so exhilarated.

Cissy tried to calm down and then she poured it all out, telling Emily the 'good news'.

The two of them then hugged each other as Emily realised that at last it seemed that Cissy's dreams were about to come true.

Alex had sent a note asking her to meet him in the glade this afternoon. Cissy struggled with her luncheon as she was so tensed up inside she couldn't bring herself to eat anything. The time seemed to be dragging but at last she left the house

The Enchanted Glade

to meet him. She had told her mother she was going out to get some fresh air and Annabel had agreed that it would be beneficial for her to take a stroll after the traumatic morning she had endured.

As she approached the glade Cissy was swept away with excitement as she spied him through the trees. The whole glade gleamed in the light of the late afternoon sunshine; there wasn't even the slightest hint of a breeze and the leaves that were still on the trees were glittering in the golden autumn silence. This was the most enchanting place on earth and it was their place, a place where they could talk in private, a place where they could be alone together, a place where they could be in love.

They fell into each other's embrace and the wonder of his kiss surpassed all her expectations. She knew then that he had already heard the news, what she didn't know was that he had witnessed the event first hand.

As their kiss ended he looked directly at her, and immediately he noticed that the previous sadness in her eyes had disappeared and they were now sparkling with happy tears and he was reminded of the joy in her eyes on that night beside the lake.

"So, you've heard?" he asked earnestly.

"I have, and although I would not normally wish ill on anyone, I have never been so completely relieved in my entire life".

They then proceeded to sit down on the lush green grass and Alex enclosed his beloved Cissy in his arms.

"Alex, do you mind if I speak about Hamilton, I need to get one or two things off my chest. I have already explained my feelings about him to my mother after we heard the news today, but I must tell you…." Cissy then told him about the event at Sydney Gardens and then relayed the encounters at Lady Kendrow's, the theatre and her betrothal party.

Alex was completely sickened by all he heard and then apologised profusely to her for not being here to protect her.

"No matter, my darling, you are here now and we are together at last" the smile she afforded him was priceless.

"But it must have been hell for you, yet you didn't mention any of this in your letters".

"Oh, I wouldn't have wanted to worry you as you already had enough to cope with whilst you were away"

His darling princess was more concerned about him than herself. He stood up and offered her his hand and he gently raised Cissy up onto her feet. Then after kissing her again he held both of her hands in his as he knelt down on one knee, looked lovingly up into her beautiful eyes and with all sincerity he asked "Will you marry me, princess?"

Cissy's dreams were all coming true "Oh, Alex my darling, yes, yes". As he rose to a standing position she wrapped her hands around his neck and he pulled her towards him once more and as he settled another passionate kiss on her lips she felt as if she was in heaven.

Before they parted Cissy said she was concerned at the scandal that may ensue if they were to announce their betrothal so soon after Hamilton's death. But Alex answered that he would wait as long as he had to, knowing that she was to be his at last. Cissy decided that it was best to talk to her mother or Aunt Ellen about it and they could take whatever advice they gave.

Alex promised her a ring as soon as it was possible to announce their betrothal and eventually they decided to leave the wedding until the spring.

March 1814.

It is the morning of Cissy and Alex's wedding. The ceremony is to be held in the village church at noon and the whole of Monkton Grange is a flurry of activity. Emily has worked very hard with the new cook and her kitchen maids over the last two days to prepare all the succulent food for the wedding breakfast, which Lady Annabel has decided will be

The Enchanted Glade

held in the ballroom as they are expecting over one hundred guests. Some of the guests had arrived the day before and were either staying at the Grange or at the local coaching inn, The Axe and Compass, which is situated almost adjacent to the main gates on the perimeter of the estate.

The servants have been up since before dawn, lighting the stoves for the hot water and scrubbing, sweeping and polishing the rooms which are to be used today. They have positioned the wedding party's table at one end and across the width of the ballroom. All other tables have been placed lengthways so that each guest will be able to enjoy all the proceedings normally afforded at weddings. All the tables are covered with pristine white table cloths and the servants have been instructed to lay out the best china and silver cutlery. Colourful flower arrangements adorn the centre of each table and many candelabras have been placed around the room should the celebrations go on after dark, as is expected.

In the stables behind the house the lads have prepared the coach and horses to take Cissy and her father to the village church at Monkton St James. The inside seats in the coach have been re-upholstered with the finest burgundy velvet and the outside completely repainted and the Templeton family crest has been painstakingly etched on either side. The horses have been groomed to perfection and are to have white ostrich plumes attached to their heads. It seems that nothing is too much trouble for her father to arrange for this wedding, although Cissy knows that he is only going to all this trouble to try to impress her future in-laws.

Cissy was now remembering how furious her father had been when he had first heard of Hamilton's demise, as all of his well laid plans for her marriage had been thrown into disarray. But of course he changed his attitude completely when Alex had asked for Cissy's hand in marriage at Christmas, as his daughter was now going to marry a man of much higher standing in the community than Hamilton. How fickle her father was, she mused.

Cissy and Alex had decided, on the advice of Aunt Ellen, to announce their betrothal at Christmas as it seemed that sufficient time would have then lapsed since Hamilton's death to announce it without causing any undue gossip in the community. Aunt Ellen, of course, had been thrilled for them both, especially when Cissy explained all the circumstances.

Cissy's thoughts came back to the present as she heard a tap at her bed-chamber door and her maid Kitty entered bringing in her breakfast.

Cissy was still in bed and she asked Kitty "Could you please tell me what time it is?"

Kitty informed her that it was just after 8.30am and advised Cissy to eat her breakfast as soon as possible before it got cold, but Cissy wasn't sure if she could eat anything as she was so excited.

As she sat up in bed with the breakfast tray on her lap she gushed "Oh, Kitty, I really never believed that this wonderful day would ever arrive. I am so lucky that things have turned out as they have".

"You deserve it, my Lady and so does Lord Kingsley. Never were two people more suited than you two. I am so very thrilled for you both" her maid was emitting a beaming smile as she spoke.

"Thank you Kitty. As soon as I have finished my breakfast I will need to bathe, has the hot water been ordered from the kitchen?"

"Don't you worry, my Lady, everything is in hand, as soon as I ring for it, it will be brought up" Kitty couldn't help smiling at her mistress' obvious pre-wedding nerves.

After she had eaten what little breakfast she could manage Cissy was ready for her bath. So she stepped out of her bed and walked over to the window to peer out at the glorious sunny day that was unfolding before her. Then breathing in

The Enchanted Glade

the scent of the lavender oil from the bath water she removed her night shift as she crossed the room towards it and stepping into the soothing water she felt exhilarated. She then exhaled a huge sigh of relief as she sank down into it to try to relax for a while before this exciting day began. With Kitty's help she washed her hair with rosemary essence and at last she felt thoroughly invigorated as she dried herself before putting on her chemise.

Cissy then sat in front of the mirror of her dressing table as her maid rubbed her hair dry with a towel then began styling it. Kitty swept her mistress's beautiful titian hair back behind her ears and fashioned it into tumbling curls flowing luxuriantly down her back. Alex had asked Cissy to wear it in the same style that she worn it on the night of his welcome home party as when he had seen her for the first time in over two years her looks had taken his breath away. The curls at the top of her head were to be held in place with a diamond tiara which was a family heirloom and had been handed down from her Great Grand-mother. When Cissy's hair was finished Kitty then applied a little chalk powder to her cheeks and carmine to her lips to enhance their appearance. Soon it was time for her to change into her wedding apparel for the most important day of her entire life so far.

Her white bridal gown was exquisite and she once again felt like the proverbial princess as her maid helped her to dress. The bodice was of the finest muslin, with a square neckline which exemplified her ample cleavage. It was completely covered in small sequins which had been delicately hand sewn onto it by the wonderfully talented modiste, Madam Bouviere, whom Aunt Ellen had recommended. Around the neckline she had trimmed it with layer upon layer of exquisite lace which Cissy's aunt had ordered and imported from Italy from some previous aqaintances of her first husband, Barnaby. As the weather was still a little chilly this early in the year, Cissy was relieved that she had chosen long sleeves that reached down to her wrists, where they were edged with more lace and tied with satin ribbons. The gown was tapered into her tiny waist where it flowed out into a full skirt made of the most shimmering satin imaginable. At the waist was a wide sash tied in an ornate bow at the centre of the back. She wore an attractive five row pearl choker set with diamonds at her neck which Alex had presented to her as a wedding gift and as she surveyed her countenance in the looking glass she was near to tears thinking suddenly that this day could so easily not have come about and she thanked God from the bottom of her heart for bringing this day of joy to both herself and Alex.

Suddenly the door of her room opened and her mother entered, full of exuberance. "Oh, Cissy, my darling, you look stunning. I have never before seen you look so beautiful".

Kitty had just finished placing the diamond tiara and veil onto Cissy's head as she spoke.

"Thank you, Mother, you look lovely yourself"

Annabel wore a full length dress in cream silk with a matching heavy brocade bolero and a floral creation in her hair which was swept up behind her head. Her rich brown curls enhanced her beauty and as Cissy glanced at her mother she thought what a fine figure she still had at nine and thirty years.

"Are you nearly ready? It's almost 11.30am and I'm sure you don't want to be late" her mother sounded a little fretful.

"I have only to put on my slippers, Mother and I believe my flowers are downstairs, so I can pick them up on my way to the carriage".

"The carriage is now waiting at the front door and your father is in his study" God forbid he isn't at the bottle, thought Annabel suddenly as she continued "everything is ready when you are. I will be leaving myself, with Oliver and Imogen in a moment but I wanted to see you before I left for the church to wish you 'good luck'" A dejected expression suddenly appeared to replace the earlier smile.

The Enchanted Glade

My dear Cissy, how I envy you just starting a new life with a man you adore and having a husband who adores you, Annabel pondered, as her heart sank for herself but was elated for her beloved daughter.

"Thank you for your good wishes, Mother" Cissy rose to her feet to embrace her mother and added "I'll see you at the church in a little while". Cissy could see that her dear mama's eyes were now glazed with unshed tears as she bade her farewell for the moment and left Cissy and Kitty to go downstairs.

Alex turned around to admire his gorgeous bride as she walked towards him on her father's arm. He felt himself emit a huge sigh of contentment as he took her hand from her father. Ever since the night by the lake at Monkton Grange he had dreamt of this moment. All those long days and nights in Spain when he'd thought of nothing else but his beloved Cissy and here she was, standing beside him about to become his wife. How very fortunate he felt at this moment.

As she reached Alex's side Cissy turned and handed her flowers to Imogen who was standing dutifully behind her as her attendant today.

Meanwhile melancholy had overwhelmed Annabel as she had watched Cissy walking on her father's arm, down the aisle towards Alex at the front of the church. Her thoughts were now with her dear Louise, as not only had she, Annabel, missed her daughter's wedding but now because of her beast of a husband, Louise and her lovely family were missing this one.

Louise and Sydney had been thrilled in January with the arrival of another pair of delightful twins, two sweet little girls called Catherine and Anna. Annabel couldn't have been happier for them and had, with the help of her two dearest friends, Lavinia and John, been able to see them soon after their birth. They were now two months old and were very healthy and well, due to the constant care afforded by her dear friend Doctor John Bartholomew.

Annabel suddenly realised that whilst she had been woolgathering, Cissy and Alex had made their vows and had pledged themselves to one another. She felt tears of joy falling as she watched the happy couple gaze lovingly into each others eyes and she wished she had known herself even a minute part of the love they were obviously sharing at this moment.

"I now pronounce you husband and wife" the parson glanced at Alex as he spoke "you may now kiss your bride". Alex turned Cissy towards him and gently enfolding her in his arms and kissing her with featherlike tenderness he whispered "I love you, princess" as they looked lovingly into each other's eyes and their joy was evident for all in the congregation to see.

The marriage was recorded in the register at the church and after signing that and their marriage document the happy couple then emerged from the church into the spring sunshine.

They boarded the carriage that had brought Cissy and her father to the church earlier and waving vigorously to all of the other guests they began the journey back to Monkton Grange for the wedding breakfast.

Alex smiled as the carriage left the church gates behind them and he placed a protective arm around Cissy's shoulders and drew her towards him in the carriage "My very own darling wife" he murmured and he then proceeded to carry on where they had left off in church. Cissy wallowed in the kisses that her dearest husband, she liked the sound of that, was bestowing on her as the carriage moved on towards her home.

"My darling husband" she replied as they ended the kiss.

"I can hardly believe we are wed".

"Well believe it; because it's true and very soon we will be in our very own house"

The Enchanted Glade

Alex had bought the impressive Lyndhurst Manor as their marital home which was situated on the outskirts of the village of Weston, near Bath. It afforded six bedrooms and at the end of the upstairs corridor Alex had installed a recently invented indoor water closet which was so much more convenient than chamber pots. Downstairs they had three reception rooms, plus a large study for Alex, which accommodated a small library, and a small private sitting room for Cissy and an amply sized kitchen which had a scullery, a stillroom and a laundry room leading from it. There was a considerable sized garden and the stables were located near the rear entrance. It was much smaller than either of them was used to, but Cissy was thrilled with it and couldn't wait to move in.

They had now arrived back at the hall and Cissy spied Ambrose Harris, the butler, at the top of the steps. As he descended and walked towards the halting carriage she could see that he had on his smartest livery and he was smiling copiously.

He proceeded to open the carriage door and Alex was the first to alight. Alex then held Cissy's hand to assist his new bride in all her finery, as she stepped down from the carriage.

"May I offer my sincere congratulations to you both, Lord and Lady Kingsley" Ambrose bowed as he spoke and Cissy felt elation well up in her breast as she heard herself addressed as Lady Kingsley for the first time.

"Thank you, Harris" Alex replied first, smiling as he did so. Then Cissy added her own acknowledgement "Thank you, Ambrose. We are enjoying such a happy day"

The butler noticed the shine on Cissy's countenance as she was talking to him. She had been a favourite of his ever since she had first moved here eight years ago and it pleased him immensely to see her so happy.

As they reached the front door Emily came running out of the house to greet them. "Oh, my chick, you look ever so bootiful" Emily hadn't asked to see Cissy before she had left for the church as she knew her father would have forbidden it.

Cissy held her arms out to embrace her dear friend. "Emmy, I am so very fortunate" she glanced at her beloved Alex as she spoke.

"As I am" he whispered in her ear as he took her arm to lead her to the front door. "We had best make our way inside and prepare to meet our guests Cissy, they will be arriving soon". Emily fussed over Cissy as they made their way to the ballroom. As they entered Cissy noticed that the sun was shimmering across the crystal chandeliers and her mind wandered back to the very first day that she had entered this room in the first week they had moved into the house and she remembered how she had twirled around pretending to dance with an imaginary partner. Well today she will be dancing with her beloved Alex, her best friend and now her new husband. She thought about the host of events that had occurred in her life since then, to bring her to this day and although she had a few regrets her feelings were exhilarated beyond comprehension when she realised that all her dreams were becoming a reality.

Cissy and Alex stood at the entrance to the ballroom and very soon everyone had been greeted, then seated and the delicious meal was served to their esteemed guests. When all of the formalities were over it was time to clear the room for the dancing.

The first dance was reserved for the happy couple and as they danced Alex whispered in her ear "I wish I could spirit you away from here and take you to our new bed and prove how much I love you".

Suddenly Cissy was horrified. She hadn't thought about that side of her marriage, as her mind had been taken up with all the arrangements. She realised she was absolutely dreading it and set about thinking of any way she could to resist the occurrence. As they were dancing with their heads close together Alex didn't see the look of panic on his beloved

The Enchanted Glade

Cissy's face. As their dance came to an end everyone applauded the newly weds and the party commenced.

At the end of the afternoon Cissy and Alex were scheduled to leave to go to their new home before departing on their honeymoon to Alex's family's residence, Kingsley House, in London. Alex's family normally stayed there when in the capital on business or when the season was in full swing during the summer months. So after going upstairs to her own bed-chamber to change into a day dress suitable for travelling they bid everyone farewell and left in Alex's carriage for Lyndhurst Manor.

As they travelled along the Bristol Road towards Bath he noticed that Cissy seemed rather subdued. "Is everything well with you? You seem upset, no regrets I hope" he grinned nervously as he said it.

"I was just so very sad that my sister was not allowed to attend our wedding today. I have no notion as to why my father cannot forgive indiscretions especially as he has committed so many himself"

"I'm so sorry; Cissy, but there was nothing any of us could do to appease that situation".

Very soon they had arrived at Lyndhurst Manor and as they alighted from the carriage and approached the front steps, Walters, their new butler opened the door to welcome them. Alex then smiled seductively at Cissy before picking her up. With one hand behind her back and the other under her knees he lifted her and carried her over the threshold of their new home. How positively romantic, Cissy thought and as she hugged him and buried her head into his chest she was reminded of the first time Alex had carried her down to the garden all those years ago. Goodness me, she thought this is certainly a day for reminiscing.

As he tenderly placed her feet upon the floor she reminded him of the conversation they had begun in the carriage and she then pleaded with Alex to go along with a scheme that she had been harbouring in her mind for weeks now but hadn't any idea how she was going to put it into practise. Alex listened intently as she explained her plan, then he readily agreed to help her.

So on that Saturday afternoon, directly after they had arrived at the Manor, a messenger was sent to Paradise Street.

So it was, that on the morning of the Sunday, the day after their wedding, when everyone thought that they had already embarked on their honeymoon, a carriage was sent to Paradise Street to fetch Cissy's sister Louise, her husband Sydney and their four children, Frederick and Mary and the new twin baby girls, Catherine and Anna.

The footman alighted and proceeded up the slope to No 10 and as he knocked on the door it opened immediately and as the family were ready he escorted them directly to the carriage. The two older children were so excited as they loved to ride in a carriage because it usually meant that they would be seeing their wonderful grandmother. But this time it was not their usual trip to Doctor Bartholomew's house, today they were going to see their Aunt Cissy and meet their new uncle, Alex.

The whole family were well turned-out in their Sunday best attire and Louise felt as proud as she ever had as Sydney holding one of the babies and she carrying the other, boarded the carriage and after settling the two older twins on the seat either side of their father, it set off to the newlywed's new home. This was the first time that they had been invited to any family gathering since Louise had eloped with Sydney almost three years before.

The children took great pleasure in the entire journey and they soon reached Lyndhurst Manor which was located deep in the countryside, on the outskirts of the city.

Cissy was overjoyed to welcome Louise and her family and ran outside to greet them on their arrival. She had only seen them once at Dr Bartholomew's since she had stayed at Aunt Ellen's before her come-out.

The Enchanted Glade

"Oh Lulu" she was almost in tears as she encircled her sister in her arms. "How wonderful to see you, dearest, this has made my perfect wedding complete".

"Thank you for inviting us to your new home, Cissy dear, you cannot imagine how much this means to us both. I was so overwrought yesterday at the thought of you being married and I couldn't be there". Louise was almost crying too. Cissy then dropped to her knees to embrace her niece and nephew, who at just over two years old were a little confused as to what was taking place. She got up and turned to face Sydney who was still holding Catherine in his arms and as he was waiting in the background Cissy extended her hand towards his and said "How nice to see you again, Sydney, are you well?" From the first time she had met him at the doctor's house just after Frederick and Mary were born, Cissy had taken to Sydney instantly.

"Please can I hold this dear little mite" Cissy was overawed as it was the first time she had set eyes on Louise's second set of twins since they had been born at the beginning of February and as she took the baby Sydney answered her question.

"I am very well, thank you, my Lady and I am beholden to you for arranging this visit, especially for Louise" he smiled at Cissy with such sincerity that at that moment she knew exactly why her sister loved him so much.

"My name is Cissy, Sydney" she said with a smile "Come, we must introduce your family to Alex" Cissy was addressing her sister and as she handed Catherine back to Sydney she went to Louise and kissed little baby Anna on her cheek, at the same time she held out her hands to the two little ones and they made their way towards the house. "I have a surprise for you, Lulu".

They entered the house just as Alex, who had been upstairs changing, walked across the spacious hall towards them.

"Oh Alex, here they are at last" an excited Cissy brought the children forward and introduced them to their new uncle. After a warm hug Alex turned to Louise whom he had known for years and as he embraced her he exclaimed

"How wonderful to see you again Louise, I hope you are well after having the little ones".

"We are all very well, thank you, Alex" then turning to Sydney she held out her hand towards him but spoke to Alex "this is my husband, Sydney". Louise sounded very nervous and looked extremely apprehensive as she glanced towards her spouse. Alex moved forward and firmly shook Sydney by the hand and smiled "Welcome to our home, it is so good to see you all".

Cissy looked on with pride to witness that her wonderful new husband was being so affable. "Come along we have lots to do" Alex and Cissy's eyes met and Louise seemed puzzled at the mischievous look that passed between them.

"Now Louise and I must go upstairs so if you and the children could please follow Alex" she then directed her words towards Sydney "he will take you into the drawing room to wait".

The two sisters eagerly went upstairs after Alex had clumsily taken Anna from Louise and escorting them all into the drawing room he then rang for Kitty to help with the children.

Sydney surveyed the room and wondered why there were two rows of chairs facing an ornate table and was also mystified to see a parson standing beside it, and a violinist next to him.

There was a knock at the door and Kitty, who now worked for Cissy and Alex, was instructed to enter.

"Could you please sit here and help us to take care of the children, Kitty" and as Cissy's maid nodded she relieved her master of his little bundle. Alex turned to Sydney and quietly explained what Cissy had planned and Louise's husband was elated.

Meanwhile a perplexed Louise had followed Cissy to her bed-chamber where she marvelled at the beautiful wedding

The Enchanted Glade

dress which was laid out before them. Next to that was an elegant gown in a deep pink silk and a floral headdress matching the one beside her sister's dress? There were also two attractive floral bouquets of daffodils on the table.

"This is for you, Lulu" Cissy picked up the pink gown and held it out to her sister. "Would you like to be my matron of honour?"

Louise looked even more bewildered.

"I so wanted you to attend my wedding but father forbade it so I asked Alex if we could perform the ceremony again for you and your family today" Cissy then began to explain the rest of her plan which she had been arranging for quite a few weeks now. The tears began flowing profusely down Louise's cheeks before Cissy had finished speaking and then her sister just crumpled into a heap on the floor. Cissy quickly came to her sister's aid and helped her to her feet then Louise just fell into her arms unable to comprehend what her sister was insinuating for a moment. Then it sank in as Cissy revealed all and through tears and laughter the two of them hugged each other and danced around with delight. Then they hurriedly helped each other into their gowns and as soon as they were ready they made their way downstairs. Cissy had ensured that Louise's gown was especially made to allow for the fact that her sister had not long given birth to the second set of twins.

As the two sisters walked into the room the violinist played and Alex peered around at Cissy and smiled broadly which took her mind back to the day before when she had entered the little church in the village and he had done the very same thing.

The staff were all seated to one side, including Emily, who hadn't been allowed to attend the wedding the previous day because Sir William had banned all the staff from the ceremony, just because he himself hated to be in the company of any servants. On the other side Sydney sat beside Kitty and his children in the front row and he felt a satisfaction that he hadn't felt for a long time as he watched his beloved Louise fulfil her role as her sister's attendant, a role which only the day before he would have thought impossible.

Cissy reached Alex and as he took her hand she turned to pass her flowers back to her sister.

Cissy and Alex then proceeded to re-enact their wedding, including their vows and the parson who had officiated at their wedding the previous day was only too happy to oblige especially after Alex had pledged a hefty sum towards his parish funds.

Emily was crying as soon as the parson said "Dearly beloved we are gathered here……. She had loved Cissy ever since the first day they had met and had always treated her as the daughter she had never had.

After the ceremony which was almost as emotional as the one the day before, Cissy embraced everyone thanking them for joining herself and Alex on this special day.

When she reached Emily she could see that she had been overcome with emotion. "Dearest Emmy, please don't cry" Cissy hugged her friend close to her.

"Oh me little chick, you look as wonderful today as you looked yesterday, I can 'ardly believe you're all grow'd up and looking so bootiful and married to the man you've loved for so long" there was a little twinkle in her eye as she smiled at Cissy and added "and I must say don't the master look fine'n'dandy 'imself today".

"Thank you Emmy". Cissy knew that above everyone Emily had been the one to guess her feelings for Alex from the very beginning.

"Now I must be off to see to the refreshments, it's all laid out for you, I hope it will be alright"

"Of course it will all be alright, Emmy, everything you make is wonderful, why on earth do you think his lordship has employed you, he thinks there is no other cook like you.

The Enchanted Glade

Now do stop worrying and ask Walters to announce the luncheon when you are ready".

Emily smiled gratefully at her much-loved mistress. She was now employed at Lyndhurst Manor in charge of the kitchen and staff. Cissy and Alex had approached her before their wedding and asked her to come to work for them and as she knew she would be much happier working for them she had accepted immediately. She didn't want to leave Lady Annabel in the lurch so she had found them a reliable replacement cook, Maggie Wilmer, whom she had known for years since before she had started working for the late earl. They had always kept in touch and her old friend who was in need of work and a live-in position was now grateful to be installed in the kitchen at Monkton Grange.

Louise in the meantime was talking to Alex and enquiring after his sister Imogen whom she had been very friendly with before she had eloped with Sydney. "How is Imogen? I haven't seen her for a few months now". Alex knew that his sister had visited Dr Bartholomew's with his mother and Annabel to see Louise as often as she could.

"She is very well"

"Is she walking out with anyone or betrothed".

"Not yet, but I have high hopes that she will not be left on the shelf" Alex was smiling broadly. "She seemed to be getting on very well with your cousin Miles yesterday".

At that moment Walters announced that the refreshments were available so all of the guests then proceeded to the dining room and partook of the superb feast that Emily had laid out for everyone.

At the end of the celebrations and knowing that the happy couple had to set off early in the morning Louise suggested

"I think the little ones are getting tired so we had better be on our way".

"All right, dearest" and Cissy beckoned to Alex who came right away. She asked him to arrange for the carriage to be brought around to the front door and she went to her sitting room to fetch the little gifts that she had purchased for her sister and her family, as mementos of the day.

Louise was overjoyed and couldn't thank her sister enough for the most enjoyable day since their own wedding. Cissy promised to try to call on Louise and her family as soon as she and Alex returned from their honeymoon. Now that she was living nearer to her sister it would be much easier to arrange future visits and she would look forward so much to seeing her little nieces and nephew more frequently.

After they had left Cissy thanked Alex profusely for arranging the events of this wonderful day.

Then she went upstairs to spend some time with Kitty to finalise which garments should be packed for the trip. She thought it might be a good idea to have an early night as they would be setting off to London just after dawn the next morning. She was fast asleep when Alex retired to their bed-chamber just as she had been the night before on their wedding night. He was beginning to despair of ever enjoying a customary wedding night with his new bride.

****

Chapter 14

Next morning the carriage drew up outside the front door of Lyndhurst Manor and after the trunks were loaded onto the back Alex and Cissy set off on their journey to London. As it was March it was not exactly the time of year to have the carriage windows down so the carriage seemed rather stuffy. Cissy and Kitty were sat on one side of the carriage and Alex and his valet, Albert Brandon, sat opposite them. Not a great deal of conversation was forth-coming and the atmosphere within was a little tense. Here and there either Cissy or Kitty would look out of the window and comment on something that they had just passed or that was appearing up ahead.

Alex had informed Cissy that the journey would take two days but added that he had arranged an overnight stop at a reputable coaching house in Marlborough in Wiltshire. He had sent one of his men on ahead, two days before with specific instructions for the inn keeper.

They arrived at the inn as it was getting dark and their carriage driver called for an ostler who quickly hurried from the stables to tend to their horses. Cissy, Alex and their servants alighted from the carriage and made their way to the entrance. The owner of the inn cordially welcomed them "Greetings, my Lord and Lady, everything is ready for you, as instructed" he bowed to Alex as he uttered other salutations, and then ushered them through to an old desk inside the door. Whilst Alex sorted the finances Cissy waited near the bottom of the staircase to be shown up to their room.

When all fundamentals had been dealt with the inn keeper's wife, who was nearly as round as she was tall and of a very cheery disposition, then escorted Cissy and her maid to the bed-chamber and seemed very attentive as she showed them around. "This is the best room in the house, your ladyship" she swept her arm out widely in a movement that encompassed the whole room. "And the bedding is the finest you'll ever find round these parts".

The reason they had been given the best room was most probably because Alex had paid her husband well over the odds for their accommodation thought Cissy as she smiled at her, wondering why the poor woman felt the need to justify herself. "It will be fine thank you, Mrs…?"

"Fanny's me name, milady, just call me Fanny"

"Thank you, Fanny. What time will our meal be ready?"

"Oh, come down as soon as yourself and his lordship pleases"

"And the room for my maid" Kitty was to sleep in a smaller room down the hall but she had decided to stay a while to help her mistress unpack the things she would need for this short overnight stay.

"The one next door, your ladyship" she was positively fawning all over Cissy "was there anything else?"

"No thank you, Fanny. We will be down to eat shortly"

"Well as there's nothing else I can get you I'll be off then" and curtseying, she turned and left the room.

After she had closed the door behind her Cissy and Kitty just looked at one another and giggled.

As they continued to unpack the items that were needed for tonight there was a knock at the door "Come in" Cissy called. Her husband peeped around the door smiling "Is everything to your liking, Lady Kingsley".

Cissy smiled back at him. Alex's smile never failed to move her "Thank you, yes".

As her master came into the room Kitty excused herself and left advising her mistress that she only had to summon her if she needed any assistance later on that night.

The Enchanted Glade

After the maid had departed Alex took Cissy into his arms uttering seductively "I have reserved a private dining room to enjoy dinner alone with my wife. We have not spent much time alone together since our wedding"

Was he being facetious or was she imagining it. Cissy grimaced a little.

"Maybe afterwards we can retire here to enjoy the rest of the evening" and with that he bent his head towards her lips and kissed her tenderly.

She absolutely adored Alex's kisses and she longed to stay within the safety of his arms forever but she knew that one thing would lead to another so she quickly ended the kiss and told Alex that she needed to ready herself for the meal as she was ravenously hungry.

Not as ravenous as I am for your beautiful body, he mused to himself, as Cissy went behind the screen to remove the clothes she had travelled in and to freshen up before putting on a clean gown.

Alex was freshening up himself in the room and changing his clothes at the same time. He had told his valet that he wouldn't need him any more tonight, as he was desperate to be alone with his beautiful wife.

As Kitty wasn't there either, Cissy asked Alex to unfasten the buttons at the back of her gown and he was delighted to help her. His fingers were caressing her skin through the thin chemise under the gown as his hands moved up from her waist. By the time they reached her neck her insides were tingling uncontrollably and she was certain Alex knew what he was doing to her. When he had finished unfastening the buttons he pushed the bodice of the gown forward and as it fell away he pulled her closer towards him and enclosed his arms around her until his hands were fully encompassing her pert breasts which were veiled under the thin material of her chemise. Then he lowered his lips to gently caress the back of her neck.

Cissy didn't know what to do. Oh dear God the feelings were unbelievable but she still couldn't bring herself to go any further and was so relieved when a knock sounded at the door. Alex, cursing as she had never heard before, was most displeased that they had been disturbed.

It was the landlord of the inn advising that their evening meal was ready and enquiring as to whether everything was to their liking. Alex very irritably answered that it was and that they would be down directly then he closed the door with a thud in the man's face.

He then continued to assist Cissy in fastening her clean gown and thought he might take up where he left off later.

When Cissy was ready they made their way downstairs together. Kitty and Albert were to eat in the public bar and Alex had Cissy all to himself for the entire evening. The landlord's wife waited upon them, bringing thick vegetable broth, freshly cooked steak and ale pie with potatoes, vegetables and homemade bread. As she brought the milk and newly churned butter to the table she advised them that it was from their own cows which were housed in a byre at the rear of the inn. She then cheerily enquired as to what they would like to drink. Cissy asked for fresh water, but Alex ordered himself a pitcher of ale and as he was feeling rather perplexed with reference to the non-events of the last two nights and the rude interruption earlier, he downed the entire contents of the jug during the satisfying repast. This resulted in Alex, himself falling asleep as soon as his head hit the pillow, when they retired to their bed-chamber later that evening. This secretly gave Cissy an immense feeling of relief as tonight she didn't have to think of yet another excuse to avoid her marital obligations.

Cissy was up bright and early the following morning and was dressed and ready to depart before Alex had even stirred in his bed. As she drew back the drapes at the window the early morning sunshine beamed into the room and she heard a drawn out groan from her husband as he

The Enchanted Glade

pulled the bed covers over his head. She left him there and descended the stairs to eat her breakfast in the private dining area, after which she and Kitty took a stroll outside for some exhilarating fresh air before they entered the stuffiness of the carriage for the rest of the journey.

Within a couple of hours they were all packed up and on the road again. The tension inside the carriage since their last stop continued to be palpable as it trundled on towards London. Although Cissy had to smile to herself every time the carriage rumbled over a bump as Alex's face was a picture. She had never seen him intoxicated before last night and wondered if he made a habit of it. She doubted that very much, Alex's behaviour was always exemplary so she knew that it must be their present situation that was causing him such anguish, which made her feel rather guilty. They politely talked about the weather and such like but beneath it all Cissy knew that their situation could not continue like this indefinitely.

It was late in the afternoon as they arrived at their destination. The Kingsley's home, built in the fashionable Grosvenor Square in London, was superb and as they arrived at the house Cissy was rather wide eyed as with Alex's assistance she stepped down from the carriage. The mansion house had a large front door which was considerably wider than any she had seen before and the front façade of the house was at least seven bay windows wide across each floor. It consisted of a basement below, three main storeys and an attic for the servants. It was almost as big as the main part of her own home, Monkton Grange. Oh, she quickly corrected herself….her previous home at Monkton Grange. She really must get used to the fact that she didn't live there anymore now that she was married to Alex.

The front door opened immediately on their approach and Alex greeted the butler warmly.

"Hello Duncan, is everything prepared for Lady Kingsley and myself" he didn't doubt for one moment that it was, as the butler, taking his master's coat, nodded in assent.

Alex turned to assist Cissy in removing her cloak and handed it to Duncan "Lady Kingsley" he loved how that sound rolled off his tongue, his dearest Cissy was now his Lady Kingsley "may I introduce Duncan Proctor, our butler here at Kingsley House".

"I am delighted to meet you, your ladyship. May I welcome you and offer my heart-felt congratulations on your marriage to our esteemed Lord Kingsley" he bowed deeply to Cissy who smiled sweetly and answered in return.

"Thank you, I am delighted to be here".

"Shall I show you to your rooms now, my Lord?"

"Don't worry Duncan I will show her ladyship later. You did make sure the special suite was ready"

"Yes, Sir"

"Could we please have some light refreshments in the small dining-room?"

"Certainly I will attend to that immediately, my Lord" and he left to make his way to the kitchens.

Alex had asked that Kitty and Albert unpack and stow their clothes away as soon as possible. So one of the maids had directed the servants to their mistress and master's quarters and they were also shown to the rooms they would be occupying for the duration of their stay.

The small dining-room here was almost as big as the family one at Monkton Grange but apart from a subdued atmosphere which she felt that she herself was creating she was very happy with what she had seen so far.

She sat on the chaise and Alex sat opposite in one of the exquisite armchairs.

"Are you feeling well Cissy after such a long journey?" she thought he was just making polite conversation.

"Yes thank you, Alex. And you, how are you feeling?"

The Enchanted Glade

If only you knew, he thought to himself. He just wanted the rest of the world to disappear so that he could be alone with his beloved Cissy.

"I am tired and hungry" he sighed with a smile "but I am thrilled to be here and I am looking forward to spending the next two weeks with you, very much indeed"

She smiled back at him as she contemplated what he had said. Oh, my, how could she or even he, as a matter of fact, stand the next two weeks? She was quickly running out of any other excuses she could think of to avoid the marriage bed. How long would he put up with her refusal. Well she hadn't refused him exactly but she had been in no way forthcoming to his advances. What if he were to seek pleasure elsewhere. Oh, she couldn't bear to even consider that avenue of thought. There was no way she felt she could face what was expected of her but she knew that this predicament in which she now found herself could not continue, well, not without confrontation.

As she looked at her husband he seemed to be anticipating a comment on his last statement. "I am also looking forward to our visit. I have never been to London before so I suspect there is much to see"

Oh my goodness, Alex thought, she's come hoping for a honeymoon seeing the sights! Although then something suddenly occurred to him, as Cissy had never been married before or been on a honeymoon, perhaps she was very naïve and didn't know what was expected of her. Surely not? On the other hand his mind went back to their meeting in the Glade when he'd asked her if Hamilton had laid his hands on her and she had seemed to comprehend what he was talking about then.

There was a knock at the door and at Alex's invitation to enter Duncan brought the refreshment that his master had requested and all thoughts of marital relations by either party were deferred for the moment.

After they had finished their tea Alex summoned their butler and asked him to clear away the china and ensure that their evening meal was ready at seven o'clock to which the butler nodded. Alex then held his hand out to Cissy, she took it and they made their way towards the exquisite central staircase to ascend to their bed-chamber.

Alex was behaving so affable, was it to impress the staff, she wondered. No, she assumed Alex was always like this, she had known him for eight years now and he had never acted any differently in all that time. He was always politeness and kindness itself, and he was so loving, any woman would be glad to be in her position. How different her life would have been if she had married Guy Hamilton. When she had thought about being bedded by him she had resigned herself to the fact that it was her duty to give herself to her husband after they were married and she was dreading it then. Now she was married to Alex, the one man she had always loved, why, oh why was she behaving in this way. Hamilton would have forced himself upon her whether she agreed or not but she knew that Alex would never take her against her will, but how long could she hold out.

They had reached the top of the stairs now and still holding her hand Alex walked towards and opened the door of the master bed-chamber. It was huge, with rich burgundy coloured drapes, bed covers and furnishings and there was a roaring fire burning in the hearth. In fact it looked like a young lover's paradise.

Alex indicated the dressing room at one end of the room and then pointed out the adjoining door at the other end, explaining that this door led to a separate bed-chamber. He walked over and unlocked the door and invited Cissy to inspect it. She knew that it was for her if she required it.

He showed her the dressing room which led from the other end of this room and then enquired as to whether she would like to lie down before readying herself for dinner.

The Enchanted Glade

Panic ensued, did he mean to take her now. Think quickly Cissy, she prompted herself.

"That's so very thoughtful of you, darling, but I think I had better write a note to my mother to advise her that we have arrived safely, she does fret so".

"But surely you can do that tomorrow! We've only just arrived and after such a long journey I felt sure you would need to lie down for a while before we dress for dinner. I have some things I need to take care of, but I would not wish to neglect you…."

Cissy interrupted "Oh, please Alex, don't let me stop you. Perhaps you are right and it would be sensible for me to rest for a little while, then I won't be so tired later".

Oh goodness, what had she just insinuated. I do hope he doesn't get his hopes up for later, she thought as Alex came towards her smiling and he kissed her so very tenderly before taking his leave.

Cissy lay down on the bed her thoughts in disarray. She was becoming obsessed with this problem but she still had no notion as to what she was going to do about it or how to handle it. Alex was such a wonderful man and he did not deserve to be treated so. He was so kind and considerate that she was almost sure he would not broach the subject with her directly.

The next morning Kitty crept quietly into the room and woke Cissy, then she opened the drapes to reveal a beautiful sunny morning. After a fitful night Cissy was feeling dreadful and it must have been quite obvious to her maid that she had not slept in her husband's bed, which made Cissy feel even worse. She was on unfamiliar ground here and this made her feel a little uncomfortable. In this enormous house she only knew Alex, his valet and Kitty. Thank goodness she had Kitty with her, but there was no way she could confide in her maid. She hated the thought of the servants talking behind their hands about them, but as far as Alex's servants were concerned, she didn't think that they knew anything was amiss. She thought she should die of shame if they found out. She knew that Kitty was loyal but what about all the rest.

She rose from the bed and walked towards the window. The house overlooked an enormous central garden which she presumed was for residence only and she wondered if a brisk walk in the park would help her. Perhaps she would suggest it to Alex later at breakfast. So with Kitty's help she began to ready herself for the day.

As he emerged from the master bed-chamber Alex spied Cissy almost creeping along the corridor. "Good Morning, Lady Kingsley, and how is the headache this morning?" and although a devastating smile shone from his countenance he was suppressing a feeling of intense regret that on the previous evening when he had expected, at last, to make passionate love to his beautiful new bride, he had spent the night twiddling his thumbs, as he had every night since they were wed.

Was he mocking her? Cissy wondered. She felt terrible, she hadn't slept a wink and she knew by his tone that he was extremely disappointed in her. What sort of wife denied her husband his conjugal rights on his wedding night and every night since. Well she had and although she felt bad about it she just hadn't been able to face it.

"I am much better today thank you, Alex" she answered him but didn't look at him.

She looked ghastly and he guessed that like him she had probably had very little sleep last night. But why was she acting like this.

Last night dinner had been very amicable and they had seemed just like any other newly married couple. Laughing happily together and chatting about many different things and then the time came for them to retire for the night. They reached the master bed-chamber and then Alex's hopes

The Enchanted Glade

were dashed as Cissy proclaimed that she must have drunk too much wine as she suddenly had a most terrible headache. Alex just shrugged in resignation, kissed Cissy goodnight and watched her walk through the adjoining door to the next room. He had then quietly closed the door as he retired to his own room once again seemingly very disenchanted with his new wife.

He offered her his arm and she took it. "Shall we go down to breakfast together?"

"Yes" she spoke in a whisper.

"Where would you like to go today?"

Home, she wanted to shout, but she knew that was out of the question right now. So she took a deep breath to calm herself and answered "I have never been to London before so I have no idea what goes on here".

"Well it's too early in the season for many outside activities" Alex had actually hoped that they wouldn't be venturing far from the bed-chamber this first week

"Perhaps we can walk in the park today. The one outside which I saw from the window this morning"

"I was actually thinking of venturing further-a-field. We could ride to Rotten Row or Green Park. I imagine that the people of the ton have already heard that I am here with my new bride so I suspect that when we meet up with them we will receive many invitations to call. Are you up for that, my darling?"

"I'm not quite sure, Alex, I think the travelling has also caught up with me a little, but I will try not to be a disappointment to you in front of your friends".

"Cissy, you could never be a disappointment to me and many of them are not my friends anyway. Now let's have some breakfast and we'll see how you feel later".

The dining room overlooked the rear garden behind the house, it was charming and spring flowers were blooming in abundance. There were daffodils and primroses and apart from the fact that there were fewer trees, it reminded Cissy of the first time she had entered the Glade. The first day they had met. Such a lot had transpired since that day. She loved Alex with all her being, but that did not afford a solution to her dilemma. She had only ever loved him, no-one else and she suddenly wondered how many lovers Alex had laid with before he realised that he loved her, or how long it would be before he took another if she was unable to go to his bed. Once again dread coursed through her at the very thought of it.

An exhausted Cissy returned from the ride out that morning feeling rather confused with the names of all the different people they had happened upon in Green Park. After a light luncheon she excused herself and went to bed and slept for the whole afternoon. She was still feeling very lethargic when they dined together that evening and later, on retiring to bed, she quietly whispered to Alex that her courses had started so they went their separate ways once more.
Alex was really becoming quite distraught now that he would have to wait another week before he could make love with his new wife.

The following Wednesday of the second week, the day before they were due to start their return journey home, Cissy decided that she really must make a concerted effort to fulfil her marital duties so before dinner that evening she bade Kitty arrange for a hot bath in her dressing room. She bathed in lavender scented water and after washing her hair she felt completely revitalised. She dressed in her most provocative gown and went down to the dining room. Alex rose from his seat as she entered and complimented her on how very beautiful she looked and she felt herself blushing like the new bride she was as he embraced her and held out the chair for her to sit down. She and Alex then enjoyed a delicious meal and although he made no mention of it she

The Enchanted Glade

indicated to Alex in an indirect way that she would come to his bed tonight.

Alex acted as if he had not comprehended what she had insinuated and excused himself after he had finished his meal and left the room.

Was he playing her at her own game? She pondered. She thought he would jump at the chance to bed her, perhaps she was wrong. Perhaps she had left it too long and his patience had run out.

Cissy retired to her bed-chamber but couldn't hear any movement from the other room so after an hour or so she peeked through the door and found no-one there.

She then put on her slippers and made her way downstairs thinking that Alex may be in the study or the library. Soon she was lost so she found a room and pulled the bell then waited by the door for a response. Duncan appeared and bowed to her, at the same time looking rather puzzled.

"Sorry, Duncan, but I am looking for his lordship and I seem to have lost my way"

"Lord Kingsley left the house earlier, Madam, and informed me not to wait up. I do believe he has gone to White's for the evening"

Cissy's heart sank "Could you please show me back to the main staircase please. I want to go to bed"

"Certainly, my Lady, please follow me" and with that Duncan escorted her to the bottom of the stairs, after which he offered to escort her to her room but she assured him that she knew her way from here.

Once inside her bed chamber she broke down in tears. Why are you surprised or upset that he has gone out? It's your own fault, she chided herself. White's, White's of all places, she cried. She had heard after Hamilton had died that he had a bad reputation for visiting gentleman's clubs especially White's. These clubs were apparently full of gamblers and courtesans and that a man could get anything or anyone he wanted. She felt so wretched. She had driven him away. She cried herself to sleep that night and realised that perhaps married life was not as promising as she had expected.

Alex had gone to White's that night but not for what Cissy had imagined. He had arranged to meet a business associate of his fathers, who had been unable to see him during the day and he had enjoyed a few drinks and concluded the business and had then come home. He had looked in on Cissy when he retired to his own room, but she was fast asleep so he didn't like to wake her.

The next day was very strained and then it was time to go home. As they were travelling back they were both sat silently thinking what a disaster their honeymoon had been. Cissy was blaming herself and Alex wondering where he had gone wrong. The atmosphere in the carriage was once again very tense and the carriage stop at the inn at Marlborough seemed even worse than the last time. Cissy was relieved to arrive at Lyndhurst Manor and before they retired she asked Alex if they could visit her mother the next day. He, of course, agreed thinking that perhaps Cissy needed to talk to her mother about married life in general.

It was mid-morning and they were travelling to Monkton Grange to visit Cissy's parents for luncheon the day after they had returned from their honeymoon in London.
The conversation in the carriage still seemed a little formal and after a considerable bout of silence Cissy glanced over at her husband and saw that he was peering out of the carriage window seemingly deep in thought. After what had transpired over the last two weeks she was loathe to speak in case he gave her a negative response. She knew it was her fault but she was unsure how to deal with the situation in hand.
Alex was actually feeling very anxious. They had been on their honeymoon and what should have been the most

The Enchanted Glade

wonderful time of their lives had in fact seemed like a nightmare. Each night for the entire two weeks since their marriage Cissy had either made futile excuses or refused to lay with him as he had expected any wife would do. He loved her above all else and he knew he had to get to the bottom of it.

They arrived at the house and Alex alighted from the carriage first, then holding out his hand to Cissy he turned to help her down the steps, Cissy thanked him but he noticed that she didn't make eye contact with him when she said it. He had the distinct feeling that she felt guilty. As they crossed the path to the front door Ambrose was there to meet them and then bowing as they entered he said

"Welcome home, my Lady, and you too my Lord, I do hope you have had a wonderful time"

"Yes, thank you, Ambrose, I'm glad to be back" Cissy answered.

I'll bet you are, thought Alex; you certainly didn't seem to be enjoying yourself whilst we were away. His heart sank to a new low.

Ambrose escorted them to the family sitting room and announced them and then left as they were greeted by her mother. "My darling I've missed you" Annabel rose to embrace her daughter.

"I've missed you too, Mother". Cissy sounded almost gloomy.

Annabel frowned this wasn't like the Cissy she knew. She had expected a starry-eyed, smiling, bubbly Cissy not the sad eyed little puppy she beheld before her. In fact Annabel was sure she detected a note of disenchantment.

"Was London agreeable, the weather was alright?"

"Yes, thank you" whatever has the weather got to do with it, thought Cissy.

As her mother gave Alex a welcoming embrace, her father entered the room and immediately rang for Ambrose. He acknowledge the two newly-weds with a loose embrace for

Cissy, which she didn't care for, and a handshake for Alex. She had never really bonded with her father especially since the family had moved to Monkton Grange and she still felt uncomfortable being in the same room as him. When the butler returned Sir William ordered luncheon to be served immediately and asked Ambrose to bring a bottle of their best vintage champagne from the wine cellar to toast the newly-weds. Annabel raised an eyebrow when she heard her husband's request presuming that it was probably masking the real reason which was, that he couldn't last too long without having an alcoholic drink himself.

When Ambrose announced that the luncheon was ready they made their way through to the dining room and sat at the table. Cissy was seated beside her mother and Alex, who was seated next to her father, was in deep conversation with him for almost the whole time. They all enjoyed the meal immensely and when the maid came to clear the table Alex asked her to convey his compliments to the new cook.

Immediately after the meal had ended Alex requested that he and Cissy be excused for a while as he wanted to take some air and he suggested a walk in the garden.

Annabel realising that, although they had only just returned from their honeymoon, the young lovers would probably like some time on their own, agreed. Alex held out his hand to his wife and as she reached out he enclosed his hand over hers. They proceeded from the dining room to the garden, through the French windows and began their stroll across the lawn at the rear of the house. Cissy commented on how improved the gardens looked as they ambled towards the side of the house and started down the track which led to the woods. They were suddenly aware that they had reached the Glade and Alex told Cissy that he desperately needed to talk to her.

She turned around to face him and placing one hand on each of her shoulders and looking lovingly into her eyes he asked

The Enchanted Glade

"Please Cissy, tell me the truth. Why do you not want to lie with me" he could feel himself welling up inside and his voice was full of emotion.

Tears began to roll down Cissy's cheeks as she reveals "I can't". She tried to turn her gaze away from his but he put his index finger under her chin and turned her face back towards his and tilted her chin so that she was looking directly at him.

Alex, not being able to bear seeing his beloved weeping then took her into his arms, drew her closer and looking deeply into her beautiful eyes he asks earnestly "Cissy, do you still love me?"

"Of course I do" she sobbed "I love you more than anyone else in the whole world".

"Then tell me why won't you come to my bed?"

Cissy felt her heart begin to beat furiously in her chest as she confessed "Because I'm frightened".

He pulled away from her and he astonishingly proclaimed "You're frightened of me?"

"Oh, no Alex I could never be frightened of you"

"Then whatever are you frightened of?"

"The sexual act"

He saw that she had the expression of a frightened child on her face "But why?"

Cissy is sobbing profusely now and blurts out all the details about Minnie and seeing all the blood and being so sorry at the hurt that the little scullery maid had suffered after being raped at the hands of her father. She also revealed how her mother had told her that her father was brutal in the bedroom and he had always hurt her so much that she hated the sex act. "I'm just so frightened that you will hurt me".

"Cissy, please listen to me" Alex pulled her once again into his arms and held her head close to his chest so that his chin was resting on the top of her head, then very gently stroking her beautiful titian curls he declared "I would never intentionally hurt one hair on your head, my darling Princess". He continued to tenderly run his fingers through her flowing locks, then turning her head towards him as he looked directly into her teary, yet beautiful violet eyes he added softly "It's true that the first time you lie with a man it can be a little painful but I will be as gentle as I can. Oh, Cissy, please trust me, I love you, I need you and I want you so very much".

Cissy had stopped crying now and returning his gaze she nodded agreement. So he released his hold on her then cupping her cheeks in both hands he pulled her face towards his and as she leant back to receive his kiss he took her mouth completely.

When the kiss ended he buried his face into her hair and then his lips began initiating a path from her forehead downwards. He continued down to her cheeks where he leisurely kissed away her tears as he went. When he reached her mouth he brushed his lips lightly and sensually over hers, sending an uncontrollable quiver vibrating through her entire body. At first he was very gentle, then pressing firmly yet tenderly he deepened the kiss and very soon he and Cissy were frantically making love.

He eased her slowly down onto the grass and gradually began to undress her, kissing her all the while. Cissy knew that undressing in front of Alex would be a far more intimate act than she had ever experienced before but as he continued unfastening her buttons she suddenly began to feel more comfortable with it. After lovingly kissing her neck he continued his descent and as he unbuttoned it, the front of her bodice fell open and he lowered his head further as once more he sought an erotic path downwards. As he tenderly kissed her breasts she felt frissons of heat searing through her body to the very core of her femininity. He then unhurriedly removed the rest of her clothes until she lay naked in front of him and he marvelled at the stunning magnificence of her body, that was soon to be all his.

The Enchanted Glade

He resumed delighting her with his kisses and gradually working his way lower, he was determined to make sure that Cissy enjoyed every moment. She had never experienced anything like this before, she was delirious with desire for her beloved husband and suddenly she felt the stirrings of passion growing within her. She was completely startled by the feelings that were engulfing her. Suddenly she reached the pinnacle of her pleasure and she felt wave after wave of the most exquisite sensations of desire coursing through her entire body and she was whimpering with elation as Alex softly asked if she was ready for him. Cissy was feeling extremely emotional and could feel the tears of joy flowing down her face, after experiencing the most wonderfully stimulation of her life. She nodded and after removing his own clothes he drew her towards him and she felt the erratic beating of his heart against hers as their naked bodies touched for the very first time. He then entered her as gently as he could and felt euphoric himself as she surrendered her womanhood to him.

She winced a little but as he slowly and tenderly moved within her she became more comfortable and she realised at last that they were one.

For Alex all the waiting was worthwhile as he took himself to the limit. All of the frustration and tension spilled out of him as he shuddered in release and as they climaxed together both he and Cissy felt as if they were in heaven.

As they came back down to earth, all of her senses were on fire and she lay in his arms feeling suddenly warm and cherished then she murmured "Oh, Alex that was incredible! It was the most beautiful experience of my whole life"

"Did I hurt you, sweetheart?"

"Not really" she smiled and then added "I'm sorry, my darling, so very sorry".

"Whatever for".

"I'm sorry I made you wait".

"Now I know why, I can fully understand your reasons".

"Well I won't keep you waiting any longer, in fact…." she smiled seductively at him with a twinkle in her eye, as they lay on the grass entwined in each others arms.

Alex laughed aloud as he drew her towards him and lowered his face to hers until their noses were almost touching.

"I want to take you home now to our lovely new bed and make passionate love to you all night long"

At last he'd had Cissy completely just as he'd dreamed of for months and he knew that now they had passed this first challenge from this day forth their life would be much sweeter.

****

Epilogue

Nine months later.

Alex heard the sound he had been longing for… his baby's first cry and he bounded up the stairs as fast as the wind. Reaching the door of Cissy's bed-chamber he gasped out breathlessly, as he knocked "Please can I come in?"

"Please wait a while until I call you, Master Alex" Dotty called in reply.

Dotty Cropwell had been Alex's nanny when he was born and he had always had a soft spot for her in his heart. She had willingly returned to work for Alex and Cissy as soon as they had discovered that Cissy was pregnant.

He resumed the pacing up and down he had thought to leave behind him downstairs. Dear God, please let Cissy be alright, he prayed as the minutes ticked by and he began to worry that something was amiss. So many women died in childbirth now-a-days, he deliberated, and he couldn't bear the thought of his beloved Cissy suffering.

Suddenly the door opened "You can come in for a few moments" Dotty was stood on the thresh-hold and Alex entered immediately and hastily crossed the room into Cissy's open arms. "Oh, Alex, we have a fine-looking baby son. Thank you so very much".

"My Darling, Darling Cissy, why are you thanking me! It is I who should be thanking you" he whispered as he enveloped her in his arms. "I took great pleasure in making him and you have had all the pain and discomfort of bringing him into this world. I will be forever in your debt". He brought his lips to hers and kissed her with all the loving tenderness he could muster. As he ended the kiss and looked longingly into her beautiful face he saw that all the love in the world was shining from her sparkling violet eyes and as they glistened with tears he knew no greater love than that which they shared at this moment.

The tender moment was then broken "Come along you lovebirds, I have work to do" Nanny was walking across the room towards them. "You may come back later when I send for you".

"Please may I hold my son before I am banished from the room, Dotty?" he afforded her a dazzling smile.

"Of course, Master Alex" she could never resist that look even now after all these years. So she crossed the room and lifted the little mite from the crib and brought him to his father.

He gently took the babe into his arms and Cissy's tears of joy were falling as she watched her beloved Alex cradle his first born in his arms.

"My son, my son" he uttered, looking lovingly at the baby as silently a stray tears escaped from the corner of one of his adoring eyes. "What shall we call him, Cissy" he said as he moved across to the bed to sit beside her.

"Could we decide later…I'm a little tired…do you really mind if I rest now?"

"Oh, how thoughtless of me, Darling. Here, Dotty" he moved towards their nanny "will you take him so that Cissy can sleep now. I'll go downstairs to my study and write some letters advising of his birth". Alex then kissed Cissy fleetingly on the lips, mouthed "I love you" and left her to rest.

His feet didn't seem to be making contact with the ground as he made his way down to an excited group waiting at the foot of the stairs.

"Is Mistress Cissy alright, Your Lordship" it was dear Emily. She loved Cissy like a daughter and as usual she was

The Enchanted Glade

worried about her little friend. Poor thing, he noticed she was wringing her hands as she spoke and she was so anxious to see Cissy and the baby and make sure that they were both well.

"Emily, she is fine and so is our new son" he sounded so proud as he spoke.

The hall erupted to the sound of cheering as all the servants came forward to congratulate their master. Then as Emily approached to shake his hand he whispered quietly to her

"I will let you know when you can go up to see her"

She smiled broadly as she stepped away and she asked if he needed anything directly. He assured her that he couldn't eat a thing as he was so excited, but he would advise her if the situation changed. Alex had the greatest respect for Emily, as she did for him, and as he watched her walk back towards the kitchen he was grateful for the genuine loyalty of his servants.

He made his way to his study as the first task he had to undertake was to send a messenger to Amberley Hall and Monkton Grange with the news to their parents and then he would spend a couple of hours writing letters to all of their other relatives and friends advising of their son's birth whilst Cissy rested for a while.

He sighed with elation as he sat writing the correspondence and he had to stop himself from thinking that he was dreaming. At last his life seemed complete. He had his beloved Cissy and now they had a cherished child…his son and heir… how fortunate he felt right now. All the while he was still trying to think of a first name. They had already chosen Nicholas as a third name, but Cissy didn't particularly want William after her father so they had chosen Edward for the fourth name, after her paternal grandfather.

The hours soon passed and he had now finished the letters and decided to go upstairs again. But first he went to the kitchen and bid Emily come with him to see Cissy and the baby. Emily was overjoyed and gushing with excitement as they climbed the stairs.

"Thank you so very much, milord, I have been frettin' so about the pair o' them and I am so thrilled for you both".

"That's very kind of you, Emily, I feel so blessed that I have Cissy and I am relieved that she is satisfactory after the birth and that now we have a son. I can hardly believe it myself". They had reached the bed-chamber and Alex raised his hand to tap the door.

Cissy was awake now and she heard the knock as Nanny went to the door to scrutinise the visitors. Cissy and the baby were her main concern at the moment and she wasn't about to allow just anyone to disturb them. As it was Alex, Dotty let them in and as her husband and her best friend entered the room Cissy's beaming face was a picture to behold. Emily ran to Cissy and embraced her warmly.

"Oh, Emmy, I have a little baby boy" her beautiful eyes were shining as she spoke

"I know, my chick" she still called Cissy 'her chick' after all this time "'is Lordship 'as told me, and I'm so very proud of you. Are you alright, pet; I was so worried about you during the birth?"

"I'm just fine, thank you Emmy, and now I'm so hungry I could eat a horse" the three of them laughed as Emily answered.

"Well I'll go straight down an' prepare a feast for you. But could I please see the little master before I go" her face brightened with delight as Cissy asked Nanny Cropwell to bring their newborn son to Emily.

As Dotty brought the little babe over and handed him to her, Cissy observed just the tiniest tear falling from her dear Emily's cheek and as she spoke she gazed lovingly into the tiny babes eyes and marvelled.

"Ain't 'e 'andsome, just like 'is father, and I'm sure 'e 'as your eyes, Mistress Cissy" and after cuddling the babe she enquired "what be you goin' to call the littl' man".

The Enchanted Glade

"We haven't decided yet" answered Alex, "but we'll let you know as soon as we do".

"Thank you, milord" and looking kindly at the tiny babe once more, she added "now I must go downstairs and prepare your dear mother somethin' to eat to keep her strength up, so she can feed you up an' you can grow into a big strong lad"

Alex was sat on the bed beside Cissy as Emily spoke and they smiled at each other lovingly, then Alex rose to relieve Emily of the baby so that she could attend to the meal.

"I'll bring your meal up as soon as it's ready, my chick" and she held her hands out to Cissy who clasped them tenderly in her own.

"Oh, Emmy I am so happy and so lucky to be surrounded by so many wonderful friends".

"We are lucky to 'ave you too" Emily answered with assurance.

After their loyal cook had left the room Alex and Cissy sat together with the babe and discussed names. They finally decided on Barnaby Charles Nicholas Edward Kingsley. Barnaby after dear Aunt Ellen's first husband and they both loved the name anyway, Charles was Alex's second name as he had been named after his paternal grandfather. Then Nicholas after his father and as they'd previously decided Edward would be his last name, after William's father.

Cissy, beaming from one side of her face to the other, looked lovingly at Alex and said "We must take him one day to our special place, the Glade. Did you realise that we met in the Glade, we enjoyed our first kiss in the Glade" Alex was nodding in agreement as she spoke "you proposed to me in the Glade and it was the place we first made love and in doing so, this" she indicated Barnaby "is the most pleasing result".

Alex smiled and taking his most cherished wife and babe into his arms he replied "Well we must certainly go back each time we wish to increase our family. It seems that will at least ensure success".

"Oh, Alex, I really do believe it is a magical place" Cissy said with all sincerity "it's very special and it's our very own Enchanted Glade.

****